1

JANUARY 1937

Thelma Dawson dashed from room to room of the house she shared with her daughters at number twelve, Coronation Close, a cul-de-sac of red-brick council houses on the Knowle West estate to the south of the city of Bristol.

Her daughters Mary and Alice, trotted along behind her with indignant expressions and frequent exclamations.

'Ma, you're going to be late for work. We can make sure everything's ready for our George.'

'I can't help it. I so want everything to be perfect. My boy is coming home. I can barely believe it.'

For the third, or maybe even the fourth time, she flicked a duster at the spotlessly clean top of the pine chest of drawers. The item of furniture was newly acquired, sourced for her by neighbour and friend Jenny Crawford. Jenny in turn had found it at Robin Hubert's second-hand furniture shop in Filwood Broadway. Robin was sweet on Jenny so she'd got it for a bargain price.

Thelma had made new curtains, laundered the bedding and bought a brand-new eiderdown from a shop in East Street,

Bedminster, where a variety of shops nestled close to the dominating presence of the W. D. & H. O. Wills tobacco factory. It wasn't often she could afford new, but it was for her boy, her eldest child, and she deemed him worth it.

George was the only one of her children to be born in wedlock, his father having died during the Great War. The fathers of her two daughters had passed like ships in the night, though she had hoped for more at the time. In the past, she'd fallen for men who had excited her, made her feel alive. Her current man friend Cuthbert Throgmorton – Bert as she called him – wasn't exciting. He was safe and almost predictable and in a way she loved him. Even so, she couldn't see marriage ever being on the cards, certainly not whilst his mother was still around. Still, Thelma lived in hope.

She continued to fizz with excitement. 'I want it all nice, comfortable and clean for when our George comes.'

Mary exchanged a long-suffering glance with Alice, who promptly snatched the duster from her mother's hands and tucked it behind her back when she attempted to snatch it back.

'Ma, you could eat a pork chop off the floor in yer,' Mary piped up.

In the absence of the duster, Thelma flicked at things with her bare hand.

Finally she stood in the doorway and surveyed the small but neat box room that her son, coming home from the sea and his profession as a Merchant seaman, would presently occupy.

Excitement at the prospect made her anxious. 'Does it really look good? I mean everything. The curtains, the wallpaper, the furniture...'

The two sisters, totally unlike each other in colouring on account of having different fathers, exchanged a long-suffering look, shrugging their narrow shoulders and shaking their heads.

SHAMEFUL SECRETS ON
CORONATION CLOSE

LIZZIE LANE

Boldwood

First published in Great Britain in 2023 by Boldwood Books Ltd.

Copyright © Lizzie Lane, 2023

Cover Design by Colin Thomas

Cover Photography: Colin Thomas and Alamy

Every effort has been made to obtain the necessary permissions with reference to copyright material, both illustrative and quoted. We apologise for any omissions in this respect and will be pleased to make the appropriate acknowledgements in any future edition.

A CIP catalogue record for this book is available from the British Library.

Paperback ISBN 978-1-80483-405-3

Large Print ISBN 978-1-80483-404-6

Hardback ISBN 978-1-80483-406-0

Ebook ISBN 978-1-80483-402-2

Kindle ISBN 978-1-80483-403-9

Audio CD ISBN 978-1-80483-411-4

MP3 CD ISBN 978-1-80483-410-7

Digital audio download ISBN 978-1-80483-408-4

Boldwood Books Ltd
23 Bowerdean Street
London SW6 3TN
www.boldwoodbooks.com

Alice breathed an exasperated sigh. 'Everything's lovely, Mum. There ain't any dust. Me and Alice checked and so did you – about a dozen times.' The two of them were used to cleaning and cooking. Thelma worked full-time at Bertrams, an up-market ladies' dress shop doing a job that she loved. Little girls they might be – Mary eleven, Alice ten – but they liked taking responsibility for domestic chores. Other girls only played at being a housewife; Mary and Alice did it for real.

Thelma resisted any more fussing, but it was hard. 'I want everything perfect for my boy.'

Her eyes glistened at the thought of him coming home. Only a few days now. He'd been away for almost a year – one in which so many changes had occurred. The country had lost a king and gained another and her new friend, Jenny Crawford, had moved into number two, Coronation Close next door to Mrs Partridge at number one. Her other friend, Cath Lockhart, lived at the far end of the cul-de-sac at number eight. Her house was number twelve from where she could glare across with undisguised dislike at Dorothy Partridge immediately opposite at number one.

Overall, they were a diverse lot. Some of her neighbours kept chickens. One of them kept goats who were sustained by kitchen scraps donated by anyone who had some to give. It saved bothering to put it in the pig bin – the small receptacle the council provided.

The residents of the council houses of Coronation Close were a good bunch – apart from Mrs Partridge at number one, the house right opposite her own at number twelve. That's the way the numbers were in a cul-de-sac.

She had to admit that Dorothy's sister, Harriet, seemed all right, but Dorothy Partridge herself was a troublemaker, the sort who wrote to the council if any of her neighbours put a foot wrong. Thelma was a frequent subject of her letters. So far,

Dorothy had failed to bring Thelma down, but she kept trying. She couldn't seem to help herself.

If the mantel clock downstairs hadn't struck the hour, Thelma might have found another duster or got the carpet sweeper back out and pursued perfection for a bit longer. 'Oh my God. Look at the time. Why didn't you tell me?'

'We did tell you.'

The three of them, mother and daughters, thudded off down the stairs.

Unlike most of her neighbours, Thelma made a point of looking smart no matter what time of day. Most of her clothes were handmade, cut down from decent-quality second-hand stuff she bought from Saturday-afternoon jumble sales. Never would she dream of leaving the house without lipstick, face powder or mascara. Never did she slop around in an old cardigan and slippers, hair in curlers like her friend Cath. The over-mantel mirror proclaimed that her hair was perfect, her lipstick unsmeared and her eyelashes were suitably slick with mascara, while the face powder gave her face a peachy glow.

She was bubbling with excitement. George was coming home. It had been almost a year since she'd last seen him and although she loved her daughters to distraction, George was her firstborn, her only son and the apple of her eye. In the meantime her job at Bertrams Modes awaited her.

'Work,' she murmured grabbing her handbag and checking its contents. 'I must get to work.'

She shouted out to the kitchen, where her daughters were now preparing fried bread and tea for herself and for them.

'Here you are, Ma,' said Alice. She almost tripped over the hem of the adult-size apron she was wearing as she handed her mother a slice of fried bread and a cup of tea. 'It's cold out there. I reckon it's going to snow, if not today, then very soon. You need something inside you,' she pronounced in a manner belying her years. 'Eat your fried bread.'

'What would I do without you two,' she said as she bit into the bread.

'You'd be late for work all the time,' said Mary in her matter-of-fact manner.

'Get that down you and get going. You ain't got all day,' added Alice.

Thelma resisted rolling her eyes and laughing. Sometimes it seemed as though they were mothering her, not the other way round.

'Right. I'm off.'

Goodbyes were said and then her heels were clattering up the garden path.

She bent her head into the bitter wind. The sky was grey and people standing at the bus stop were hunkered into their mufflers, slapping their gloved hands together to keep out the cold.

The bus was on time, but Thelma's mind was so preoccupied imagining the homecoming that she almost forgot to get off at her stop.

'Excuse me. Excuse me.'

After squeezing down the aisle between the seats, she made the rear platform of the bus and jumped off just as it began to move off. Her leap was slightly mistimed. She staggered between kerb and pavement; her fall was impeded by a steady pair of hands.

'Steady on, love.'

She thanked whoever it was. The strong hands continued to grip as she mounted the pavement.

'Thank you,' she said again. 'I can manage now.'

'Do I get a kiss?'

She slapped him away. Cheeky bugger.

'No you don't. Let me go. I'll be late for work.'

Once the grip was relinquished, she hurried off for Bertrams, the dress shop where she had risen from general sales assistant to leading sales assistant in a very short time. Right from the start, they'd recognised she had a flair for fashion, dressed well and flattered dithering customers into making a purchase. She had the gift of the gab and it went a long way to persuading people to buy what they didn't think they needed.

Thelma tottered along on black suede court shoes. She'd never been late for work yet, but today she might be and Mr Bertram hated lateness. A shilling was docked from wages for each five minutes late. A shilling was a lot. She could buy a pair of stockings with that or two pounds of tea.

'Serves me right for being distracted,' she said to herself.

By the skin of her teeth, she made it outside the heavy mahogany doors of the shop, grabbed one of the pair of brass handles and pushed it open.

The smell of the interior of Bertrams Modes never failed to excite her. Silks, satins, wool, cotton and linen all had a smell of their own and she loved every one of them. She also loved the smell of kid gloves that Bertrams sold in several colours, though black, tan or cream were the bestsellers.

Women were Bertrams' lifeblood and as such the place also smelled of them. Face powder and the lingering hint of expensive perfumes mixed with that of the sumptuous materials. Providing a firm and solid background to those smells was the beeswax polish used on the honey-coloured wooden walls, the counters and the chestnut brown lino.

Stiff, unseeing mannequins posed on round raised plinths,

their fingers long and cold. Cashmere dresses, only affordable to wealthy women, clung to narrow hips on some, whilst others wore smart jackets with padded shoulders, pleated skirts, hats with broad brims, small brims, feathers and veils.

Each morning, Thelma acknowledged them as though they were human. 'Good morning, girls.'

They never answered, of course. They were made of plaster, painted and posed to look lifelike.

Thelma loved this place, loved her work and had learned to tolerate those customers who considered that working girls should be slavish rather than of service.

Normally, she was the height of efficiency and good at holding back what she really wanted to say, but today she couldn't concentrate as well as she usually did. It would have suited her if there were no customers today. Suited her too if she could have directed them to a work colleague, but the fact was some customers asked for her by name.

'I said I wanted cream-coloured gloves,' said the aloof and elegantly dressed woman she was currently serving.

Quite tall and of course very elegant, as most of their customers were, she wore a fur coat that looked like mink. The shoulders were square and the coat was knee-length. A net veil trimmed the dark red hat she wore. A pair of overly long feathers sprouted like a peacock tail at one side.

'Oh. So sorry, madam.' Thelma was distracted.

'So you should be. Are you new here?'

Thelma resisted snatching the gloves back. The truth was she just didn't have her usual patience this morning. This evening and George were everything.

'No, madam.'

'Have you a supervisor, a senior sales assistant who knows what they're doing?'

The tone was imperious, the plucked eyebrows arched and the deep-set eyes viewed her with contempt.

'I am a senior sales assistant, madam,' returned Thelma, smiling through gritted teeth. She wanted to slap the woman across her heavily rouged cheek – both cheeks in fact, but her wages were made up with commission. Though it was far from easy, she forced herself to be polite. 'These are the only cream gloves we have,' she said, bringing out a pair from the drawer and setting them out on the counter.

To Thelma's surprise, the woman scrunched one up into a ball in her fist. 'Hmm. It doesn't feel very soft. Are you sure this is really a kid glove? I won't wear ordinary leather. Much too coarse. I have very soft and sensitive skin, you see.'

Thelma glanced at the clock ticking away the minutes and hours on the wall, the time slowly passing before George arrived. Nothing was as important in her life as her children. It made her want to shout and scream at this woman. But awkward customers were nothing new. Instead she decided to lie.

'You're quite right, madam. They're not kid at all. They're chamois and much more expensive than kid gloves. In fact, I think they're the last pair we have and goodness knows when we'll get any more. They're rare, you see. Quite rare. And expensive. Though these are slightly cheaper, seeing as they're the last pair that we have – but still too expensive for most of our customers.'

The woman's red lips parted and Thelma was sure she heard an intake of breath. The covetous look on her face was evidence enough that she was going to buy them. No matter how muc[h] they were, she had to have them, if only to prove that she had t[he] money to do so and to stop anyone else having them.

'Wrap them up.' She gathered her crocodile handbag fro[m] the counter and ordered that the price of the gloves should

onto her account. 'My name's Mrs Justin-Cooper. My husband is the judge, the honourable Mr Justin-Cooper.'

Thelma nodded politely as though her name and status were familiar to her.

'I'll put them in a decent-size bag. Such gloves should be carried in splendour,' said Thelma with a forced smile that didn't reach her eyes. Not that this particular customer would notice that.

Mrs Justin-Cooper swept out past Miss Apsley, the supervisor who mainly oversaw the millinery department and had been partially responsible for taking Thelma on.

Miss Apsley reached for one of the brass door handles, a ready and slightly subservient smile on her face. 'Let me get the door for you, madam.'

With slow deliberation, the door closed softly once Mrs Justin-Cooper had sailed through it.

'Mrs Justin-Cooper,' Thelma whispered into Miss Apsley's ear. 'Her husband's a judge.'

'What did you sell her?' she asked, her hands clasped in front of her.

'A pair of cream kid gloves. The pair that's been hanging around in the drawer ever since I started here.'

'Really?' Now it was Miss Apsley's eyebrows that rose. 'I hope you told her that they're the last pair.'

'I did in a manner of speaking. I just tweaked the description a bit.'

Miss Apsley pulled in her chin, a question in her eyes.

'Don't worry,' said Thelma, already looking to serve the next customer who was presently dipping over the glass-topped counter, eyes on the drawer containing camiknickers. 'She thinks she's got a bargain. A pair of chamois gloves as opposed to common kid.'

'Chamois is kid.'

'That's what I thought, so I wasn't lying. I just elaborated a bit, after all they're both goats, aren't they?'

Miss Apsley smiled and her eyes sparkled. 'Very commendable, Mrs Dawson. Very commendable indeed.'

2

Cath Lockhart's metal curlers jingled like sleighbells as she hurried along at Jenny's side, head bent against the cold easterly wind. They were both on their way to Stan Harding, the butcher in Filwood Broadway.

All the way there, Cath had been expressing her annoyance that Thelma had invited Bert Throgmorton to her son's celebratory homecoming.

'Never invited me though. I thought she would 'ave. I do like a party.'

'Everyone does,' said Jenny. 'But this is a coming home party for her son. It's a family thing. I suspect she wants him to herself for a while.'

Cath wasn't impressed. Her lips were tightly pursed. 'Bert Throgmorton ain't family. He's the rent man.'

'You know as well as I do that Bert and Thelma are close. You could almost call them engaged.'

'Engaged?' Cath sounded dumbfounded. Even her curlers jangled with indignation as she shook her head violently. It was enough to dislodge one that had been dangling on her forehead and send it with a pinging sound onto the pavement. She stopped to pick it up. 'She ain't never said anything to me about them being engaged and I'm 'er best friend. Unless you know different.' She sniffed and tightened the knot on her headscarf.

Cath's tone was resentful and the insinuating barb easy to understand. She'd been Thelma's closest friend until Jenny had moved into number two. Cath lived at the far end of the close. Jenny was under no doubt that she would prefer to be closer to Thelma so she could better see what was going on and be even more inextricably linked in her life than she presently was. The closer they lived, the easier it was for Cath to pop in and out at will. As it was, being at the end of the close she missed things and did resent that newcomer Jenny lived closer..

'All I know,' said Jenny, determined to be as friendly with Cath as she was with Thelma and not to come between them, 'is that he won't leave his mother, so marriage is out of the question for now.'

'Unless she kicks the bucket,' Cath said in a resolute manner. She shook her head, yet again sending her curlers rattling. 'I don't think he'll marry her even then, do you?'

'I've no idea.'

Jenny clenched the handles of her shopping bags, glad of her gloves in the bitter weather. Cath was nice enough, but possessive, jealously guarding her friendship with Thelma. During the week and Saturday morning when Thelma was at work, she popped in to see Jenny. When Thelma was home, it was a different matter and Jenny saw nothing of Cath. Not that Jenny minded being second best. She understood that the friendship between the two other women had existed before she'd arrived and felt awkward at times, though not regretful.

The fact was she'd got on with Thelma from the very first. She had the energy of ten women, was as brave as a lion and her exuberance was infectious. Coronation Close was a far cry from the grim rooms of Blue Bowl Alley in the city centre and Thelma was a breath of fresh air, just like the close itself.

Cath's old fur boots looked two sizes too big for her feet. The tops of a pair of thick men's socks covered half the space between her feet and her shins. The astrakhan fur of her collar was pulled tightly up around her face and she was speaking through the knot of her headscarf. Seeing as it was winter, the headscarf that covered her curlers was of thick woollen check. In summer, it was mostly cotton, or what she called silk but was obviously not. Nobody in Coronation Close could afford silk – not real silk.

They skirted two mothers chatting over the tops of prams and headed for the butchers, where skeins of sawdust formed a lacy pattern over the floor of black and white tiles in front of the door.

'Heard anything from your old man?' Cath asked.

'He's in Palestine,' Jenny answered and tried not to sound casual about it.

She wasn't sure whether that was where Roy had ended up, but knew he was abroad. The slip that accompanied the money the army sent to her said so. It did not disclose a specific location. As long as she received her housekeeping, it didn't really matter.

'Is it hot there?'

'I believe so.' She really did not want to talk about it.

'Is he close to the sea? Nice if he is. He can cool off when he gets too hot.'

Jenny couldn't help the smile that came to her lips. Cath wasn't so much gullible as lacking in education. She didn't read and signed her name laboriously, taking trouble with each letter.

Jenny thought carefully before replying to the simple question.

'I think he's stationed in Jerusalem. Policing operations, so I understand.'

She was only guessing but had read as such in the newspapers.

'Will he get any leave?'

'Not yet.' She couldn't help being curt. Roy was far away and she didn't want to think about him. He would not be home for a long time. He had joined the army because he had been as unhappy with their marriage as she had been. Being in uniform and in the company of other men suited him far better. The only times he'd promised to come home was to see his daughters. She had hoped he might have been home for this last Christmas but he hadn't. Not that she wanted to see him. It was all about saving face, appearing totally normal for her daughters. Being seen to come home would also silence any wagging tongues or any rumours that he might not be just an ordinary married man. The fact that he preferred the company of men was neither here nor there. Freedom had come at a price, but she was fine that he wasn't there. They were happier apart than together.

As usual, there was a queue at the butchers on account of the meat being a bit cheaper than the Co-op in Melvin Square. Stan knew his customers didn't have much money and gave away bits and pieces they could make use of. A marrowbone to make a good stew or a couple of squashed sausages found their way into the shopping bag of someone on their uppers.

Jenny and Cath were next to be served. Jenny stayed upright; Cath bent low, squinting at the pile of pigs' tails, lambs' hearts and pigs' livers. Offal and bony bits were always cheaper than everything else and were presented in huge trays on the counter. Bones anyone could have for free were at one end.

Jenny had her eyes on a breast of lamb. After taking the bones out and cutting off most of the fat, she intended rolling it around a stuffing of breadcrumbs, onions and sage. The sage and mint she'd planted in the back garden had run riot. The onions hadn't done quite so well, but there was still enough to make stuffing for the breast of lamb.

Cheeks as red and glossy as ripe apples, Stan turned his attention to Jenny and Cath. 'Right, me loves. What can I do for you two beauties?'

'Two pound of your best steak but only if it doesn't cost me any more than half a crown.'

Stan's belly, round as a beer barrel, wobbled in time with his laughter. 'My but you're a cheeky one.'

Dimples dented Jenny's cheeks as she shared his amusement. 'I suppose that's a no.'

In the past she'd never have dared banter with any male shopkeeper. Number one she'd never had the time. Roy had insisted she only strayed outside their old home in Blue Bowl Alley if it was strictly necessary and then no fraternising with anyone, especially the opposite sex. Occasionally, she'd chanced her luck and tasted freedom, knowing full well that if she were found out, there'd be hell to play. Thanks to Roy's overbearing manner, she'd just never had the confidence to make idle talk with another man. Things had changed a great deal since moving to Coronation Close and him joining the army.

'I'm off to the greengrocers,' she said to Cath once her order for pork cuttings and a breast of lamb were wrapped and inside her shopping bag.

Cath said she'd catch up with her later. She shielded her mouth and whispered as though it were a huge secret, 'I'm off to Melvin Square. I need to call in at the chemist.'

Woman's things, thought Jenny, smiling as she headed across the broad expanse of grass to the greengrocers on the other side of the Broadway. Anything to do with procreation or feminine bodily functions was spoken about in a low whisper. It included sex, sanitary towels and contraceptive sheaths. Even pregnancy.

None of these very personal things were ever mentioned in front of a man.

Needing to go to the greengrocer meant she had to pass her old friend Robin Hubert's second-hand furniture shop. She hadn't meant to look in to say hello; hadn't meant to even look in the window. As it happened, she didn't need to. There he was, standing in the doorway propped up at shoulder height with one shirt-sleeved arm and smoking a cigarette. The sight of his bare arm in this cold made her shiver.

'Aren't you cold?' she asked him.

'Mrs Crawford. I always warm up when I see you.'

'Mr Hubert. You're too saucy for your own good.' She suppressed a smile, telling herself that she shouldn't encourage him. Still, Robin had always been incorrigible to the extent of being downright cheeky. Not so much of late though, not since he'd split up with his wife. Sadness had depressed his natural exuberance.

Sporting the vestige of a smile, he flicked his finished cigarette into a clump of weeds growing around a drain. 'Out shopping then?'

'I am.' She held up her shopping bag. 'How's business?'

He nodded once, twice, three, then four times as though mentally accounting every recent transaction. 'Not too bad. Not too bad at all.'

'I see you offer instalments.' She nodded at the sign that had been stuck in the window from when he'd first opened.

He folded his arms and grimaced. 'You know me. A sucker for a sob story. Too soft for me own good. Most of them paying on tick pay me a few bob when they can, but some do a runner. Oh well. That's life.'

She shook her head and smiled. 'As long as you're still earning a living.'

'I am,' he said, somewhat more brightly. 'I'd hang on to more of it if Doreen didn't come telling me she can't manage. She'd 'ave the shirt off me back if she could. Bloody cow,' he muttered, flinging the finished cigarette into the road.

Jenny eyed the range of items displayed in the window. A hall-stand, a bamboo table and a standard lamp jostled for space beside a second standard lamp with a tasselled shade. 'How about your lad that was helping? Is he still around?'

'No. He lives in Brigstocke Road. It was a bit too far. Old Fred Fuller comes in to give me a 'and when I need to deliver furniture or move things about. He can drive too, drove a tank back in the Great War.'

'That's good. He sounds capable.'

Robin shook his head and laughed. 'He is for the most part, though I'm not so sure about 'is driving. I keep reminding 'im that it's a van not a bloody tank and we're delivering furniture not shootin' at Germans.'

Their laughter invoked the warmth of a shared past, a time when they'd been close, before Roy had entered her life and Doreen had entered his. They'd been so much younger then.

Once their laughter had died, an awkward silence descended as thoughts returned to the past. Robin gazed across the green expanse in the middle of the Broadway. Jenny continued to scrutinise the items on show in the window.

As she gazed, mostly unseeing of real detail, she found herself wondering how things would have been if she hadn't fallen for Roy, if she and Robin's close friendship had continued.

'Do you remember when we went up the Downs that day in June when we were about ten years old? We took a couple of jam sandwiches and a bottle of ginger ale?'

His recalling of a long-ago day in a distant summer jerked her from where she'd been.

'Yes. It was sunny – well, it was for most of the time.'

'All summers are sunny when you're young.'

'You're right. Every day seemed to be sunny back then – even when it wasn't summertime.' She could have added that it vanished when she'd fallen for Roy, the cloud that had taken the sunshine.

'I hear yer old man's joined the army.'

Immediately feeling uncomfortable, she started, stuttered a little. 'Who told you?'

Robin shrugged. 'I don't recall. You know how it is. Word gets around.'

What word? she wondered. Was anyone privy to the true reason for Roy joining the army? For the rift in their marriage?

The look he gave her was difficult to interpret, but she sensed longing more than curiosity.

'I'd better be going.' She began to step away.

'If you ever want to pop in and have a chat, I'm always here. If you fancy that is.'

She smiled. 'I'll bear it in mind,' then rushed away. Thelma would remain her sounding board, though for the most part Jenny preferred to keep things to herself.

* * *

It felt as though her face was on fire when she left the Broadway. Although Cath must be some way ahead of her by now, Jenny made the sudden decision to follow her to Melvin Square. It would at least cool her face. There was nothing she wanted at the chemist but knew instinctively that Cath would be lingering in there, waiting until there were no other customers so she could ask for what she wanted without anyone overhearing.

Necessities, she thought, but we keep them a secret.

Just as she'd guessed, Cath had waited until the shop was empty of customers. Jenny got there just in time to hear her ask for very strong laxatives.

'Penny Royal. And anything else good for getting things moving – if you know what I mean.'

Jenny realised Cath hadn't heard her come in or her voice would have been quieter – or she wouldn't have asked for what she'd asked for at all.

She'd assumed Cath merely wanted sanitary products. This was more serious.

Cath only looked slightly surprised when she turned round and saw her.

The chemist, however, who'd firstly looked at Cath without batting an eyelid, suddenly seemed nervous, deep hollows appearing beneath sharp cheekbones. A slight cough, and then, 'I'm sure I don't know what you mean.'

Jenny gave the chemist a knowing look. 'We both know that you do. Don't worry. We're friends and neighbours. A trouble shared...'

Cath had an open face. If she felt any guilt at what she was asking for, it didn't show in her expression. Jenny knew very well the reason she was asking for strong laxatives. Sometimes taken along with strong liquor such as gin or whisky, it was a well-known method of ending an unwanted pregnancy.

Jenny patted her neighbour's arm. 'You all right, Cath?'

The shape of Cath's lips was something between a smile and a wince. She shrugged nonchalantly. 'Well. You know how it is. A little problem, but no need to worry. There's ways and means, ain't there?'

A look of feminine understanding flashed from one woman to the other.

Jenny didn't need Cath to spell out what it was she needed to get moving. Cath, mother of six, was expecting again and it was one mouth too many.

'Fancy a cuppa when we get back to the close?' Jenny asked her.

'Love to. Got any biscuits?'

'I think so.'

'Bloody cold today,' said Cath, shrugging her shoulders and blowing between pinched lips. 'Could do with a cuppa. Unless you've got some cocoa that is.'

'I have.'

So it was that they hurried back to Coronation Close, up the path to number two and shut the door firmly behind them.

Cath's coat and scarf stayed in place. She made herself comfortable. Jenny poked the fire before taking her coat off. A few spindly flames flickered then turned to a glow.

It wasn't often Cath came into Jenny's house for a cuppa without Thelma being there. This was one occasion when Jenny felt obliged to have her in for a little chat.

Cocoa was made – ideal for a cold day like today, although Jenny was careful to make it from one half milk to one half water.

After dunking a biscuit then taking a sip, Cath was into her stride.

'Once I reached forty, I thought that was it. No more babies. No more of the other either,' she added, a pale pink flush colouring her cheeks. 'I don't know where my Bill gets 'is energy from, really I don't.'

There was a sparkle in her eyes and her blush deepened before being partially hidden behind her teacup.

'Some women would love such attention,' Jenny remarked. She was curious to know whether Cath wore her curlers to bed but thought it unlikely. The whole point being that she only wore them during the day so her hair was a mass of bouncing waves by the time Bill came home. Thelma had told her that once the clock struck six she let down her hair and changed into a fresh dress and pinny. The thought made her smile.

'Lovely cocoa,' said Cath.

Jenny thought about the contents of the plain brown paper bag. 'Would you like a glass of water now? To wash the pills down.'

Cath looked a bit vacant at first before coming to a decision. 'No thanks. I can wash it down with this cocoa.'

Out came the bottle, off came the top. To Jenny's surprise, she tipped two, then three of the round black pills into her hand.

'Isn't one enough? Two at the most?'

Cath shook her head and tipped all three into her mouth. After a swig of cocoa and a swallow, she managed to say, 'I've always found three work best.'

'You've taken them before?'

She nodded. 'A couple of times.'

A couple meant quite a few, Jenny decided and it struck her that Cath was purposely vague when it suited her. It came as no great surprise when she changed the subject.

'I wonder how much George 'as changed after being all over the world like 'e 'as. Being away from 'ome do change blokes, don't it. Changed my Bill even though 'e was only in the medical corps. Conscientious objector, you see. Didn't 'old with marching off to war in a foreign country. Right too.' She shook her head dolefully. 'All them young men dead and buried miles from 'ome. Don't seem fair do it.'

Jenny agreed with her that it certainly didn't seem fair. Her own husband had only served in the last year of the war, but even so it had affected him. Not so much in a physical sense, but in the sense that he'd believed things would be better once peace had been won. The sad fact was that it hadn't been better and he'd grown bitter about it.

'I never met George. He was already at sea by the time I arrived.'

'Lovely chap 'e is. A dead spit for 'is old man, from what Thelma's said. Mind you, I've never seen a photo of 'is dad. Thelma reckons she does 'ave a photo somewhere.'

Cath took a noisy glug of tea. 'Can't blame 'im going to sea. Young chaps like a bit of adventure in their lives before they settle down.'

'I suppose so,' said Jenny.

She felt Cath eyeing her quizzically. Her guess was that she was leading up to asking questions about Roy, why had he joined up, wasn't he a bit old for that? After all, he was not a young bachelor but married with a family.

Every so often, someone asked her how he was, had she heard from him, when he was likely to come home on leave. She answered cagily.

George, a young man, was one thing. Going off on an adventure at Roy's time of life was bound to have aroused curiosity. As agreed with Roy, the truth of his going would remain a shared secret.

'Goodness, look at the time. It's getting on for four o'clock. I'd better think about getting the girls' tea ready.' Jenny took Cath's empty cup and saucer, piling it on top of her own with an air of finality and hoping that Cath wouldn't notice that it was not long after three thirty.

Cath followed her out to the kitchen. Jenny sensed she had more to say. She only hoped it didn't include questions about Roy. Cath picked up the tea towel as Jenny began rinsing the cups beneath the tap.

'I was wondering whether Thelma might invite us over once

George 'as got comfortable.'

'I've no idea.' Jenny passed her a cup.

'She ain't invited you then?' She sounded surprised.

'No. Why should she?'

Cath shook her way in a so-so manner. 'I just wondered.'

The first cup wiped, Cath ignored the second and poked at the curlers that bundled onto her forehead. 'I'd better get on 'ome and smarten meself up – just in case she does think of inviting me. I do like a party.'

'So you said. But there, Bill must love to see you with your hair down.'

'He does. Even after all these years, he still tells me I'm the best-looking girl he ever went out with.'

Gaps showed in her teeth when she smiled. Her cheekbones were high, and although her complexion was sallow, her appearance hinted at the lovely-looking girl she'd once been.

Thinking of Cath and Bill in a clinch brought the visit to the chemist to Jenny's mind. 'Will you be taking any more of those laxatives tonight?'

'Hmm. I might do. Depends how I feel. Depends on if we've got any gin in the 'ouse either. Might 'ave whisky. Bill likes whisky but ain't so keen on gin. Might 'ave a hot bath too. I usually take a bath on a Saturday night, but I might 'ave one tonight. Just to get things moving, if you know what I mean. As long as Bill lights the boiler for me. Yes. Laxatives, gin and a nice 'ot bath.'

* * *

Three quarters of an hour later, Jenny's daughters, Tilly and Gloria, who were more or less the same age as Thelma's daughters, came in as ravenous as ever, faces pink with cold. Once their coats were off, they swiftly devoured the bread and jam she'd put out, a necessary filler before their main evening meal.

'It's going to snow,' said Tilly.

'No it isn't,' Gloria retorted.

'I felt the first flakes when we came out of school.'

Gloria ignored her and instead asked, 'What are we having tonight?'

'Cold meat with bubble and squeak.'

'We had that in sandwiches at dinner time.'

'You had that at lunchtime,' Jenny corrected. The piece of brisket they'd had at the weekend had served them well. Stewed with onions and carrots and served with boiled potatoes, forced through the mincer to make shepherd's pie and today the last slices to be eaten cold. Having enough for the sandwiches she'd given them at midday had been a bonus.

School began at nine in the morning. Lunchtime was from twelve to one and everyone took sandwiches. Some of the pupils brought in a single slice of bread and dripping for their midday meal. Those who had nothing were given a sandwich by kind-hearted teachers used to working in deprived areas, frequently bringing in and distributing whatever they could.

The morning and afternoon breaks were spent playing in the schoolyard, running off the energy fed into them at breakfast, then at lunchtime. The school afternoon ended at four o'clock. No wonder they were always hungry.

'Did you know that Mary and Alice's brother is coming home today,' Gloria piped up whilst Tilly buried herself in a book.

'I did.'

'They can't come out to play because they're putting on a spread. Do you think they'll invite us? They've got jelly and blancmange.'

'And cake,' said Tilly, without looking up from her book.

Gloria continued with the details. 'Fruit cake. And jam tarts. They made all of it themselves.'

'It's a family affair,' Jenny explained for the second time that day. 'Mrs Dawson wants her son to herself.'

Gloria pouted. 'That's not fair.'

'It is to Mrs Dawson. He's her son. She hasn't seen him for ages.'

After throwing a quick scowl in the direction of her sister, Tilly went back to her book, muttering, 'I told you so.'

Gloria asked if she could go out to play.

'Not for long. It's already dark and if it gets much colder, we'll have snow. And wrap up.'

'She's got a boyfriend,' Tilly whispered. 'She's going out to meet him.'

'She's too young.'

Tilly perched her head sideways. 'Am I too young?'

'Yes. Wait until you leave school.'

'That's two years' time when I'm fourteen.'

'Soon enough,' Jenny said, suddenly feeling a great sadness land heavily on her shoulders. Two years wasn't that far away. Facing her girls growing up in such a short time was disconcerting. To her, they were still children and would be for some time.

Deep in thought, she sliced the last of the cold meat from the bone, placed a plate over it and proceeded to mix leftover vegetables into bubble and squeak. The big frying pan was already on the gas stove, a big lump of lard ready to melt once the gas was turned on.

Being busy helped her blot out the obvious fact that her girls were not children any longer. One daughter out to play and one reading and both growing up fast. *How different my daughters are*, she thought as she turned on the wireless.

Picking up a sewing needle, Jenny prepared to do some mending. As she pushed the needle in and out, a variety of thoughts drifted through her mind, some less welcome than others.

Her world had become a calm oasis since the end of last year when Roy had signed up, though not without concern or incident. She ran through all the good things in her life. The rent was paid – Roy saw to that. Thanks also to him, she had enough money for food and clothes – nothing extravagant or luxurious, but they were fed and dressed. Not everyone could say that.

On top of that, she'd ended up living in a red-brick council house with a garden front and rear, such a contrast to the tumble-down tenement in Blue Bowl Alley. The rooms in the house they'd lived in there had dated from the Middle Ages, was in the centre of old Bristol and had been shared with other families. Water had been drawn from an outside pump and for them had been accessed down flights of winding stairs. In summer, the smell of the drains had wafted through the open windows. In winter, the cold was intense, the only form of heating provided by a small fire grate on which they'd done most of their cooking.

Gaining a house in Coronation Close had seemed like heaven, providing her with everything she wanted, including friends and neighbours. Mrs Partridge next door was the only fly in the ointment. A sour-faced, black-eyed woman who gave the impression of hating the whole world. Jenny had done her best to show friendliness, but her action had not been reciprocated.

Thinking of Thelma, however, brought a smile to her face. She was so bold, so forthright it seemed to her that nothing in the whole wide world could get her down.

Then there was Cath who made no secret of the fact that she and Bill were as in love as they were when they were young. *But there are consequences*, she thought to herself. For her sake, she hoped the pills Cath had taken would do what she wanted them to do. Still, at least she had Bill and he loved her. *Lucky her*, she thought...

At present, she was too busy to think about what she might be missing. There were times, though, when she wondered how long it might be until she felt lonely, but she put the thought from her mind. It wasn't as though she had far to look for someone who had kind thoughts of her. Robin was keen. She knew that but was certain she didn't love him. Charlie Talbot, a shadowy figure in politics, did not hover so strongly in her dreams as he once had. She hadn't seen him for quite a time and perhaps might never again. They were from different walks of life. She could tell that by his cut-glass accent, the well-fed shine to his face, the good cut of his clothes.

The sewing needle paused as she waded through what had been and what was. *No matter, she thought. My life is full. I have my family. I have my friends, and if that wasn't enough we have a street party and coronation to look forward to on May the twelfth.*

After grim years of job shortages and hunger strikes, the coronation would go a long way to lifting everyone's spirits and give them hope for the future. The street party would give the residents of Coronation Close an excuse to forget their troubles, the unending routine of working to survive, and give them cause to celebrate.

Thelma was taking charge of organising the party and had contacted everyone in the street to say so. Everyone had agreed she should run things – except for Mrs Partridge, who thought celebrating should be run by reputable authorities – people of standing who knew what they were doing.

Thelma had reminded her that the people of standing didn't live in Coronation Close and were likely to only get involved with grander, more official events.

Mrs Partridge had slammed the door in her face.

Unperturbed, Thelma had taken the reins regardless – early days yet, but she was most definitely in charge for the residents of Coronation Close.

Good old Thelma, Jenny thought to herself. Her energy was endless, her enthusiasm boundless. Never could Jenny ever imagine her being anything except courageous and loyal. No man would ever bend the redoubtable woman to his will or squash her indomitable spirit.. Nobody would dare.

3

Thelma thought she had the best job in the world selling smart and expensive clothes to wealthy women. She'd never been one for leaving Bertrams on the stroke of six, but this evening was an exception. She almost raced out of the door, swiftly enough to make surprised-looking Philip Bertram comment to Mrs Apsley.

'I've never known her rush off like that before. Have the bus times changed?'

Mrs Apsley, who despite her middle-class veneer and high standards had taken a shine to Thelma, told him about Thelma's son George coming home on leave from the sea.

'She hasn't seen him for ages. I do hope she gets a bus home on time. They're sometimes so crowded at this time of night and it's snowing.'

Mrs Apsley was certainly right about that. The bus queue was long and the weather was getting worse. Collars were turned up against the thickening snow and feet were stamping to contend with the cold.

Flurries of snow showed in the glow of amber street lights,

faster and faster as the blizzard intensified. Lights in shop windows began to go out and darkness reigned supreme.

Like everyone else, Thelma pulled her coat collar up around her face. Her breath steamed on the arctic air. As if the icy pelting of snow wasn't enough to make her shiver, a draught blew up beneath her coat, a flared affair of pleats falling from padded shoulders.

Fat flakes of wind-blown snow intensified from the size of gnats to that of bumblebees.

A bus finally loomed out of the darkness, carefully lumbering forward through mist and maelstrom.

Murmurs of appreciation replaced the grumbles of those waiting for it as they shuffled forward until becoming an ungainly rush of humanity struggling on board, glad to get out of the weather even if many of them had to stand.

The later bus she usually caught tended to be less crowded and she always managed to get a seat. This earlier bus was jam-packed, but at least she got on, though found herself standing in the closely cramped space downstairs. She wrinkled her nose at the mix of humidity and unwashed bodies. Condensation misting the windows turned to trickles.

The bus trundled away. Thick flakes hindered the headlamps and the tyres were beginning to slither on the snow-covered roads.

'Hope we get there,' she heard someone say.

Then someone else: 'I need to get 'ome. I can't walk. Not with my legs.'

Whatever their fears, the bus unhurriedly carried on, not at a great pace, but at a safe one.

She guessed the journey would take longer than usual but contented herself with the knowledge that George had been adamant that he'd be home by midday and before the snow had begun.

Pools of darkness occurred where street lights had gone out. Along the flat main road that was St John's Lane, lights from living-room windows fought an on-going battle against darkness and snowstorm. Coughs and sneezes inside the bus competed with the sound of crunching tyres and grinding gears.

The bus lurched from side to side as it rounded the corner by the health clinic into Wedmore Vale. On their left, barely discernible now out of the misted windows, was Clancy's Farm. Little could be seen of the farm buildings, the whole area a great pool of blackness. For now at least, it remained farmland, though slowly being eroded, new houses creeping ever closer.

As with St John's Lane, Wedmore Vale presented a flat even surface. Everything changed once they'd turned into Glyn Vale, a hill that became Donegal Road, both part of the long climb up to the council estate that had stolen the farmland that had once surrounded the city. Because of its increasing steepness, their progress slowed.

'Blimey. I could walk faster than this,' somebody said.

A few others echoed the sentiment. Grumbles erupted, but riding the bus was always preferable to walking.

The hill became increasingly steep and the outside air became colder, blowing onto the platform at the rear of the bus, helping to dispel the rancid air inside. The higher they climbed, the more intense the snow, a blizzard now, whirling around the bus and obliterating the houses on either side. Their progress became a snail's pace, even slower than before.

Halfway up the very steepest part of the hill, the tyres at the rear of the bus lost their grip. The bus swayed. The rear began to slide from side to side on the cushion of ice and snow.

Cries of alarm went up.

'Oh my God. We're all going to die.'

A man swore. A woman began reciting The Lord's Prayer.

'Bloody 'ell,' somebody else muttered.

One woman screamed.

Another made the comment that at least they weren't going downhill. 'Or we'd slide all the way down past the fish and chip shop.'

A few of the men unlucky enough to be standing on the rear platform which was totally open to the elements exchanged expletives.

The crunch of gears trying to engage sent shivers of vibration through the length of the lumbering vehicle.

The bus slowed even more. The snow faltered long enough to see the lights from council houses. Like soldiers standing to attention, they lined the hill on both sides. Squares of amber light blinked through the blizzard from behind privet hedges. The bus slewed from side to side.

Heart in her mouth, Thelma thought about getting off then and there and walking up the hill, but they were still some way from the top. Her shoes, especially her heels, wouldn't cope with ice. Why hadn't she got out her winter boots? The answer was obvious; she'd been so wrapped up in getting ready for George coming home, nothing else had mattered. Everything about today revolved around her son. He'd promised to be home for a few months – perhaps even long enough to take part in the celebrations for the new king.

The bus continued its sluggish passage. The gears of the bus gave one last wrenching grind before it came to a shuddering halt, sliding slightly backwards until a back wheel lodged against the kerb.

A bigger shout drowned the others: 'Let me through. Move along now. Let me through.'

Nudging the square bulk of his ticket machine into the ribs of those standing, the bus conductor pushed forward. He made his way from the rear platform of the bus to the very front, where he spoke with the driver through a sliding hatch.

Whatever was said, the two men could be seen shaking their heads in abject despair. Even before he'd turned round to make an announcement, people were up from their seats, pushing their way through to the rear platform. Those up top were spilling down the stairs and out onto the platform, swinging on the chromium bar better to support them as they alighted into the snow.

The bus conductor, speaking to a smaller audience now, only confirmed what they already knew. 'Sorry, everybody. But the gearbox 'as gone. It strained its 'eart out getting up this 'ill. This bus ain't going anywhere. You'll 'ave to get off and walk.'

'But we've paid for our tickets,' cried one indignant woman in a tweed coat, her headscarf clamped to her head with wetness.

'Nothin' I can do about that, love. It's the weather.'

Thelma sighed. Like everyone else, she made her way to the rear of the bus, peeved, angry and worried. From the moment she'd got George's letter before Christmas, she'd planned how she would greet her son. And now this. The bloody weather! This should have been such a perfect day. Now it was ruined. She'd be late home.

People peeled off, disappearing into the darkness. The bus that had been full at the beginning of her journey was now empty.

Being careful not to slip, she stepped gingerly down from the bus.

'Take me 'and, my love.'

She took the hand that was offered, felt the softness of a worn leather glove. He had a slight Welsh accent and smelled of tobacco – not fresh tobacco but a dusty febrile smell that permeated his clothes. As she stepped down, the twelve inches between the sloping bus platform icy flakes hit her in the face.

She would have slipped if she hadn't still been holding the helping hand.

'Ta,' she said.

'Glad to 'ave been of service, my love. Far to go, my love?'

My love. Not me love as a native Bristolian would say.

'Yes. Too bloody far,' she muttered through clenched teeth.

'Hold on to me. I'm going as far as the top of the hill.'

The brim of a dark-coloured trilby hat hid his face and Thelma had only time for a quick glance. Her own face was bent into the wind, her steps cautious through the deepening snow. She had no option but to cling to his arm.

Together, her slipping and sliding and leaning on him, they staggered up the hill. Lights still shining from its downstairs windows, the bus was soon behind them. Those that had alighted had dispersed in the direction of their homes, where a warm fire and hot meal awaited them.

Glyn Vale was left behind, but the hill continued up Donegal Road. It wouldn't flatten until they got to the top.

Street lights still working did little to illuminate the hazardous ground beneath her feet. At one point, there were none. She presumed the storm had put them out.

His arm, linked with hers, gripped her more tightly. A hand clenched hers. 'No need to worry. We're nearly there.'

She didn't know what he meant by nearly there. They hadn't yet reached the end of Donegal Road, though the hill had flattened. She recalled a piece of green grass and trees where a small cul-de-sac broached the unending row of brick semi-detached houses.

'Nearly there, my love,' he said again.

Was it the wind or had his voice changed to something less kind; more guttural?

Because of the snow and the darkness of this patch, the distance between them and the houses of the cul-de-sac, it wasn't possible to discern any lights falling from behind curtained windows.

She sensed his steps slowing, his arm clenching hers more tightly to his side.

By rights, they should have been walking straight on by, past the green and the lights of houses blinking through the trees. That's if he was going in the same direction as she was.

His steps veered and, unable to escape his grasp, her feet went with him. Panic suddenly gripped her.

'We're going off course.'

'We're going where I want to go, my love. It's a chilly night and we could both do with warming up, couldn't we now.'

Swiftly, without him giving her time to protest, she found herself being swung round, then bundled towards the trees.

'Slut. Tart.' His voice was a growl now, his grip as hard as iron.

Her scream was lost on the wind and her struggling was futile. He pulled her onto the green, her feet dragging through mulched leaves, sodden snow and frozen mud.

She had no doubt what was about to happen – though by God she would do everything in her power to prevent it. She had to. George was waiting for her. Her boy was home.

'My son's waiting for me. Let me go.'

A heavy slap sent her head bending sideways. She cried out, begged him to stop, shouted at him to stop, but refrained from pleading.

The full force of his superior strength came into play, knocking her backwards. One shoe flew from her foot as he dragged her backwards until finally he slammed her against the trunk of a tree. Bang went the back of her head against it, the roughness of the bark scratching through her hair. The world, already blurred with swirling flakes, turned darker, like looking through the bottom of a glass.

Reeling from the blow, she saw neither his face nor the details of his clothes as he fumbled with his trousers, ripped aside the crotch of her knickers and forced himself into her.

When she found her fists released, she pummelled at his chest. Another slap sent her head reeling.

Her legs were wide and her insides felt as though they were being torn in half. His chest slammed against hers so heavily that she could barely breathe, the smell of him, the weight of him smothering her. His body flexed as he thrust determinedly into her, giving her no choice, merely intent on satisfying his own base pleasure.

'There,' he said. 'Warmer now, ain't we.'

She didn't know how she did it, but from somewhere she had the guts and energy to spit into his face.

'Bitch!'

His hands encircled her neck. At first, she was choking, then everything went black.

* * *

Flakes of snow falling on her face brought Thelma round. Gasping for air, she tasted them in her mouth, gulped and swallowed them down.

Her first thought was for her girls and whether they'd been able to make George welcome and lay the table without her. Of course they had: the sandwiches, the high tea, the blancmange, the cake.

She turned over and got onto her knees. With the help of the rough bark of the tree trunk, she managed to rise slowly but surely to her feet.

Her throat was sore. Her neck was sore, but nothing compared to the pain she felt between her legs and in her stomach.

You mustn't cry. You mustn't cry. Nothing must ruin George's homecoming. She had endured a woman's worse nightmare, but it was over. She refused to be intimidated or let it ruin the rest of the evening.

For a few minutes, she leaned her back against the tree until her head had stopped spinning.

Once her heartbeat had settled and her vision was less blurred, she adjusted her underwear as best she could. Once satisfied that she was halfway respectable, she hunted for her missing shoe, grubbing in the snow with ice-cold fingers.

No matter how much she rummaged around in snow and damp ground, her shoe was lost and she was desperate to get home. George would be waiting, a fact of far more importance than finding a shoe.

The night was dark, but the snow was beginning to ease off. She knew where she was – that half-circle of grass and trees at the top of Donegal Road.

Limping badly due to her missing shoe, she swallowed her disgust and set off for home. Although her head ached and she felt sick inside, she resolved that she wouldn't let it ruin the evening she'd planned.

Her darling George would be waiting for her and she'd let nothing ruin that.

But how would she explain her missing shoe, the mark on her face, her laddered stockings?

'I slipped.'

She said it to the wind, the snow and the deep black night.

'I slipped.'

It was all she could say, not much of an excuse, but believable enough. The truth would lie with her, buried in a dark recess of her mind, never to resurface.

4

The snow of early January had melted away. The hedges dripped with water, but by the end of February, the air was warmer. It was too early in the year for blue skies and the sun was a watery presence behind banks of silver-grey clouds.

The big event of mid-February had been a pancake race around the entire length of Coronation Close. The kids of the close had taken part and, despite a few tossed pancakes landing in the dirt, picked them up and ate them anyway.

The milkman and baker called every day. The coalman less frequently but enough to keep the living-room fire grates topped up. Norman Grimsby, the knife grinder, came around periodically on his tricycle, an intriguing contraption designed for the work he did. His grindstone was perched between the handlebars and the front wheel. The sound of it going round was enough to put everyone's teeth on edge. All the same, keen for the chance to chat, the women stayed there whilst the wheel turned and sharpened their kitchen knives, scissors and household tools.

Carrying a carving knife and three pairs of his mother's dressmaking and kitchen scissors, George Dawson, Thelma's son joined them.

'Good morning, ladies. Bit nippy, ain't it.'

George had a cheeky-chappie expression, an amiable manner and was the husband most would choose for their daughter – once he was in settling-down mode that was.

Since his return home in January, he appeared to be making up for lost time, catching up with old pals and burning the midnight oil when he could. It was known that he spent a good deal of his time round at the Venture Inn with his mates or out at a dance hall.

'Enjoying bein' 'ome with yer mother then,' quipped Maude from number seven, winking at the other women.

'There's no woman like me mother.' George's response was accompanied with a salacious wink of his own.

The women cackled.

Maude chewed her gums before saying, 'Plenty to compare 'er with from what I've 'eard.'

More chuckles ensued, along with a knowing nudging of elbows.

'I bet your mother is spoiling you rotten,' remarked Jenny.

'She is,' he replied with a cheeky grin. 'I daren't shove off too quickly. She might tie me to a chair if it looked likely. Got to fatten me up first before I leave for the seven seas, that's what she reckons anyway.'

'Be nice if you were here for the street party in May. She'll be disappointed if you ain't,' said Maude as she handed over sixpence to the knife grinder and took ownership of her carving knife, a chisel and a pair of garden shears.

George shook his head. 'I doubt I'll be here for that, though I am thinking of leaving the Merchant Navy and joining the Royal Navy when I comes back on me next leave.'

'What about yer mother?' asked Cath. 'What did she think of that?'

'Me joining the Royal Navy? The minute I said it she was dusting off the picture of the king and queen and telling them all about it. Dead excited she was.'

Remarks were made about how Thelma was a fervent royalist. They all agreed that she'd be pleased if he did.

'I would 'ave thought one boat was no different than another,' Cath remarked.

George chortled as he gathered up the newly sharpened items. 'There's only so many banana boats a bloke can stand.'

The women laughed before all eyes went back to Norman Grimsby, pedalling for all he was worth and setting the grindstone spinning again.

Once all his sharpening was done, George bid a cheery goodbye.

'He's a nice lad,' said Maude.

'The apple of Thelma's eyes,' agreed Jenny.

'Shame she's neglecting 'er friends,' said a petulant Cath.

Jenny thought the comment unfair and said so.

'It's understandable whilst George is home. She hasn't seen him for ages. He's her only son. We'll see more of her once he's gone back to sea.'

* * *

'Are you all right, Mrs Dawson?'

Mrs Apsley had come upon Thelma quietly. She had a soft way of walking, the tips of her heels barely making a sound. Because of that she was like a wraith appearing without warning. Not exactly creeping up, but soft-footed, gliding around the store like a ship on a calm and sun-kissed sea.

Taken by surprise, Thelma started but recovered swiftly. She beamed at her. 'I'm quite fine. It's just been a bit of a strain with George being at home, though I'm loving it.'

Mrs Apsley persisted. Thelma was her best sales assistant, always engaged with her job and the customers she served so well. 'You were just looking a bit distracted. Not that I have any criticism of your work ethic. You're an ideal sales assistant – senior sales assistant.' She smiled reassuringly, though a slight furrow remained on her forehead.

Referring to her as a senior sales assistant was indeed an accolade to the esteem in which Mrs Apsley held her. Thelma was glad of that. Her job meant a lot to her, almost as much, though not quite, as did George and her children.

'I've had a phone call from a Lady Grovesner. She intends calling in to look at some peignoirs, silk and cotton. Apparently she's off on the *Queen Mary* to New York and needs some extra items for the voyage.'

Thelma smiled and said she would do all she could to help her ladyship choose.

Mrs Apsley peered through the glass top of the counter to where silky underwear was displayed in shallow wooden drawers. 'Perhaps you might also prepare our very best camiknickers for her consideration. Perhaps rearrange the drawers so the most expensive are at the top.'

Thelma said she would do so.

After Mrs Apsley had moved away, Thelma took out the drawer beneath the glass-topped counter that contained silk camiknickers. Cream, white, salmon pink and the softest shade of mint green. How beautiful they were and she wished she could afford them. She could do with some new ones herself, but the price of these was way beyond her means. Looking smart for work was imperative, but sometimes, just sometimes, she wished she could afford what Bertrams customers could afford.

A pang of remorse hit her as she thought about the torn pair she'd thrown into the rag bag. Normally, she would have mended them, embroidered pretty flowers over holes or sewn on new buttons or threaded elastic into the waistband if needed. The pair she'd thrown into the bin had been those she'd been wearing on the night of the snowstorm. The connection between them and that terrible night was too painful. Lovely as they'd been – made from an old silk shawl – she'd confined them to the bin. Once the bruise on her face had vanished, she'd put the memory behind her. She didn't know his name, just his smell, so going to the police was out of the question. They'd laugh in her face, even insinuate she must have led him on, taking the arm of a complete stranger.

Thelma had never been a willing victim and she refused to be now. She'd explained to George that being late for his home-coming and the bruising on her face was because she'd slipped on a patch of ice.

'Nearly knocked me out it did.'

To her ears it sounded a poor excuse. What had happened could not be undone, so all she could do was get on with life. As for her missing shoe that George had offered to look for, she didn't want that back either. The odd one she'd had left was also consigned to the dustbin. It turned out that locking it from her mind would not be enough. By the end of January, she knew that it wasn't only a shoe missing. Her monthly periods had always been on time. This month they were absent. A few days late perhaps? What to do about it? Should she wait until the next one – just to make sure? Or set the wheels in motion to do something?

At least her job kept her mind off things. She looked around the store, smiled at Mr Bertram as he strolled past, hands behind his back as he inspected his domain. He stopped to have a word with Mrs Apsley.

Pretending to tidy the drawer of pretty underwear, she dipped down slightly to return the drawer to its rightful place. She often paid great attention to the clothes Bertrams sold. Nobody queried why she examined them in such minute detail. They could not guess that she copied them, cut them into the same shapes, sewed them by hand late at night.

The details of those pretty silks was imprinted in her mind. Scraps of silk cut from other garments were stored in an ottoman at the foot of her bed. She'd make herself some more underwear, make some for the girls too, make anything and everything, occupy herself so she wouldn't think of that terrible night that might have changed her life forever. If she let it. If she didn't do something about it.

* * *

It was another icy day. To Thelma's surprise, Bert was outside Bertrams waiting for her in his little Ford car, a boxy shape on wheels.

'Bert. What are you doing here?'

'It's a bit icy. I didn't want you slipping and hurting yourself again.'

Touched by his consideration and verging on tearful, she slid into the front seat. 'What a lovely surprise. And you coming out in this cold.' She leaned across and kissed his cheek.

A glow of appreciation suffused his face. 'Worth it just for that.'

She thought the same. He wasn't to know that he'd lifted her spirits, and never ever would he know what had happened.

Sometimes she loved him for his innocence. Sometimes she just loved him.

She could have done without Cath calling in the minute she saw she was home.

'I saw you get out of Bert's car. Bill's doing some overtime, so I thought I'd pop in. Did he pick you up straight from work?'

There was an edge to the way she said it, but Thelma was in no mood to investigate.

'Yes. He did. And if you don't mind I'm a bit tired...'

'Bill thought he saw 'im the other night after he left 'ere.'

'On his way home. He always likes to leave by ten.'

There was something shifty about Cath's look, and even though she was doing her best to shepherd her to the door, Thelma couldn't help noticing.

'Bill saw 'im round at them old barns at Inns Court that's been turned into workshops and garages. Or thought he did...'

'It couldn't have been him. His mother likes him home.'

'A grown man like 'im!'

Too tired and annoyed to argue, Thelma grabbed her arm and hustled her out of the door. 'Leave Bert be, Cath, and get on home. I'm away to my supper and my bed.'

Once she'd gone, Thelma leaned her head against the closed door and shut her eyes. She couldn't quite believe that Bill had been hanging around at the garages. It just didn't seem like him, but Cath being Cath it might very well be a fib. Over time, she'd got used to Cath's possessive jealousy. This was what this was, she told herself. Just another example of how mischievous she could be.

5

March was blustery and sent daffodils dancing in the wind.

Saturday afternoon was the time when the women involved in the arrangements for the coronation gathered around Thelma Dawson's dining table.

Red, white and blue ribbons were draped over the wall-mounted photograph of the new king, his wife and the little princesses. It was a bit premature, but Thelma liked to think ahead. Even if the coronation wasn't until May, she stressed to anyone that would listen that they should be well prepared so everything ran smoothly.

Standing at opposite ends of the room, Jenny and Cath were winding up lengths of bunting made from scraps of red, white and blue cloth. Bill had brought the string home from work, where it had been used to tie up great bundles of wood for making into pulp and thus for cardboard.

So far they'd wound up eight bundles and there were still lots to come.

'I should think we've got enough to stretch across Melvin

Square and Filwood Broadway, let alone Coronation Close,' Jenny remarked.

'Here's another,' said Cath, pulling out another skein of string.

'Put that down for now. Tea and biscuits first.'

Over tea, Jenny asked Thelma when George was off back to sea.

The corners of Thelma's lips turned downwards. 'I'm trying not to think about it.'

Jenny expressed her sympathy. 'You'll miss him.'

'That I will. Where would we be without our family? Mind you, I certainly wouldn't want any more, though thankfully my days of giving birth are long over. Still,' she said with a nervous laugh, 'you can never tell can you?'

'I thought I was in the family way,' Cath suddenly chipped in. 'But I ain't no more. Wonderful what a drop of gin and some laxatives can do.'

Thelma thudded her teacup down into the saucer. The latter broke in two.

There was a gasp of inhaled breath, followed by silence.

There was purpose in the way she avoided looking at anyone as she gathered up the two halves and, along with her cup, took them swiftly out into the kitchen.

Cath looked surprised. 'I was only saying...'

Maude chipped in. 'Nothing to do with you, Cath. She hates the thought of George going back, especially with all this talk of war.'

Jenny accepted that Thelma wasn't looking forward to George going back to sea but couldn't help thinking that something else was troubling her. She couldn't put her finger on what it might be. In time, Thelma might return to her old self, but something was throwing her off kilter.

Talk resumed around the sewing table. Maude was intent on

making a fancy dress costume. 'Queen of Hearts. A red, white and blue dress covered in playing cards.'

Nobody reminded her that the original plan was for them all to come as dukes and duchesses. Things had changed. Everyone was doing their own thing with the materials they had available.

Thelma came in from the kitchen with a fresh pot of tea.

'What are you coming as?' Jenny asked her.

'A witch. Complete with a broomstick.'

The comment provoked laughter, which helped them forget the incident with the teacup.

'With a big pointed 'at?' asked Cath.

'I can get cardboard from Bertrams to make one, plus a bit of felt and some feathers. Bert can get me a broom from the Parks Department. They sometimes use them for sweeping up leaves.'

She threw Jenny a wink.

Not seeing the wink and finding out that she was only joking, Cath was persistent. 'Why a witch? What brought that on?'

'I could do with a bit of magic,' Thelma replied somewhat glumly. With grim determination, she stabbed her needle into a stubborn hem and drew blood. 'Sod it.'

Her eyes met those of Jenny as she sucked the blood between lips just for once devoid of lipstick.

Rarely had Jenny seen her very good neighbour without make-up and certainly not without lipstick. Even her clothes of late looked ill-considered. With Cath, untidiness was normal, along with the perennial curlers tucked beneath a shabby scarf. With Thelma, it was not.

There was something in the look Thelma had thrown her that Jenny couldn't quite fathom. Just for once, it hinted at helplessness. Just as quickly as it had come, however, the look vanished from her eyes. *Perhaps I was just imagining it*, thought Jenny as the old Thelma returned, laughing as though nothing had changed.

Jenny was instantly reassured, though having a quick word before she went home wouldn't go amiss.

In an effort to get Thelma alone, she determined to grab the crockery and offer to help Thelma with the washing up. As it was, Cath got there before her, grabbing the cups and saucers and heading for the kitchen.

Jenny gathered up her sewing basket and put on her coat. Whatever was troubling Thelma would have to wait for another day when she could get her alone.

On her way to the front door she did manage to ask what she thought quite a searching question. 'Have you run out of lipstick?'

At first, it seemed Thelma was taken aback, but it was short-lived.

'I'm thinking of using another colour. Pink rather than red. Trouble is, I couldn't find a tube anywhere. I'll get one next week.'

Thelma's brazen smile should have been reassuring. Jenny was not convinced and perhaps might have said more, but the clattering of dishes from the kitchen drew Thelma's attention.

'Better go and see what Cath's doing in my kitchen. She's a clumsy cow at times.'

She was gone before Jenny could question Thelma's curtness.

* * *

'*January brings the snow, makes our feet and fingers glow. February brings the rain, thaws the frozen lake again. March brings breezes loud and shrill, stirs the dancing daffodil.*'

Jenny's daughters reeled off the lines of the poem they'd learned at school.

Satchel straps crossed their shoulders and their hats were tugged firmly over their heads.

After waving the girls off to school, she shut the door against the blustery blow. It was Monday and there was laundry to be done. It should dry well in the wind, though there was the prospect of rain, if the BBC was to be believed.

First things first was to light the boiler. She hated that boiler, the way the gas jets popped if the match didn't light the clouds of steam it sent up into the air, the condensation pouring down the windows.

On her first attempt, the match she set to the boiler went out. She heard the hissing of the unlit jet, lit another match and tried again. The gas made its frightening popping sound before igniting into a blue flame tinged with yellow. When she'd first moved in, the flame had been all blue. Jenny hadn't noticed when a change had occurred but decided it was nothing to worry about. She wrinkled her nose at the stink of unspent gas that resembled but was stronger than rotten eggs.

Once the water in the zinc drum was boiling, she added soapflakes and turned the heat down, leaving it gently bubbling.

By mid-morning, the wind was subdued and a slight drizzle was falling. She muttered a few choice words under her breath. There was little chance of bedding drying, so underwear went in first, along with pillowcases. Until the weather improved she would turn the sheets so that the fresher end on which feet had rested would be tucked beneath the pillows.

The weather got worse. Wind and rain intensified. The windows, already streaming with condensation, were thrashed with sleeting rain.

Despite the weather, Jenny opened the kitchen casement to let out the last vestige of evil-smelling fumes.

The laundry would be left to stew. Goodness knows how she was going to dry it. She glanced at the pile of sewing on the dining table, bits of material of every type and colour. First she had to make the beds.

She was just on her way upstairs, her foot only on the second stair when someone knocked at the door.

The milkman! She could see the shape of his cap through the dimpled glass of the front door.

The rain whipped in as she handed him what was due and took two bottles from him. No matter that sterilised milk was cheaper and kept longer, she much preferred pasteurised. The girls could drink pasteurised, but grimaced if forced to drink the other.

She was just about to close the door when she saw another figure coming up the garden path, tipping his hat in acknowledgement at the milkman as they passed each other.

The milk bottles almost slid from her grip when he tipped his hat at her and she saw his smile. The world around her spun so fast it made her feel dizzy.

'Charlie.' She was delighted, until a more worrying thought occurred. Her brow furrowed that he might be bringing unwelcome news. 'Is it Ruth? Isaac? Are they…?'

Isaac and Ruth Jacobs had been good neighbours and friends in the days when she'd lived at Blue Bowl Alley in the centre of Bristol. The moment she saw Charlie Talbot, her go-between with Isaac and Ruth besides being a mutual friend, she feared the worst.

He shook his head. His hair gleamed. His chiselled features stirred her very soul. 'Bad enough, but they're still this side of heaven. Ruth's in hospital. They asked if I could let you know.'

Whatever words she could have said seemed to stick in her throat. The news was bad, but the sight of him was good. Here, living on the outskirts of the city where her life had become safe but somewhat humdrum at times, he only visited in her dreams. She'd never expected to see him again.

His hat was in one hand. With the other, he smoothed back a

Brilliantined lock of hair that had fallen over his forehead. If he hadn't done so, she would have smoothed it back for him. After pushing the inclination aside, she at last found her voice.

'That's terrible.'

Resetting his hat on his head, he stood there, smiling through the droplets of rainwater falling from its brim. He was waiting patiently, smiling at her expectantly, but what for? And then it came to her.

'Oh I'm sorry. You'd better come in. I'll make you a cup of tea.'

'Coffee,' he said, raindrops flicking from his hat as he took it from his head. 'I prefer coffee. Remember?'

'Oh yes. Yes. I do remember.' She wasn't sure that she did and wasn't even sure she had any coffee. There might be a little at the bottom of a bottle of Camp that had been in the larder for ages. 'I'll just take these into the kitchen. Make yourself comfortable.' She guided him into the living room and indicated an armchair with a toss of her head. 'I'll put the kettle on.'

Without needing to look into a mirror, she knew her face was flushed.

She saw him glance at the table, which was piled with a variety of fabrics. Most of it was in bits. She explained that she needed to make a few new blouses for the girls to wear to school.

'You're a clever woman. Seems you can turn your hands to most things.'

She wasn't sure that she could and him saying so made her blush.

After setting the milk bottles on the cold slab in the larder, she filled a kettle and placed it on the gas.

When she got back in the living room, he was still standing, his hat held in front of him with both hands. His eyes, that chill bright blue she saw in her dream, met hers. Heat flared on her cheeks and coursed with her blood through her veins. He was here! Her heart raced but she forced self control and reminded herself he was here because of Ruth.

'It's been a long time since I've seen you, but there, you're a busy man,' she said as she took cups and saucers from the dresser and carried them out into the kitchen.

'I'm committed to changing society. It's a busy time.'

His comment brought Roy to mind. Like Charlie, he had burned with a desire to change things, though not, in the same way as Charlie. They were opposites as far as their politics went but both were heavily involved, though Charlie, who came from a well-off background, was a professional.

'I can understand that.' It was all she could think of to say.

She managed to control her shaking hands as she moved the fireguard, picked up the poker and churned the mixture of ash and coal to make it glow.

'Please sit down.' She indicated the same chair as she had before. 'Would you like to take your coat off? It's soaking wet. So's your hat.'

He pulled his arms from the sleeves whilst she pulled a dining chair from beneath the table and invited him to drape his coat over it.

'The coffee won't be long. Would you like a biscuit?'

'No thank you. Just the coffee.'

Out in the kitchen, she took deep breaths. It had been quite a while since the incident when Charlie had come to rescue her friends, Isaac and Ruth Jacobs from three Blackshirts, one of whom was her husband. The old man, Isaac, had been attacked back in Blue Bowl Alley simply for being Jewish. Jenny had been horrified and had not admitted to either Charlie or her friend that Roy had been part of it and she wouldn't admit it now. She only hoped he wouldn't ask about Roy, where he was and what he was doing. She wouldn't know quite what to say, and anyway there wasn't much she could say.

'Sugar and milk,' she asked through the open door.

'Just black, thank you.'

Just as she'd guessed, there was very little coffee at the bottom of the bottle, only enough to fill a teaspoon. Wanting to please him, she poured water into what remained in the bottle after extracting the final teaspoonful. It seemed a decent amount once it was in the cup.

No amount of taking deep breaths could quell the apprehension in her stomach, the racing of her heart. She was here alone with a man she had often dreamed of. Roy had joined up and she didn't miss him, but now and again felt alone in the world. She loved her girls, but there were times when she wanted a man in her life. Not that she should. The marriage vows held her fast. She couldn't have acted the way Thelma had following the death of her husband. She couldn't easily throw herself into another relationship. People would talk. Of course they would, but deep down, despite all that, she didn't care.

'Sorry about the smell of soap suds. Monday is laundry day,' she explained.

'And I'm interrupting.'

She laughed. 'My family laundry isn't that important. You can interrupt it at any time and I'm always glad to hear about Isaac and Ruth. Now, please tell me, how is dear Ruth? What's wrong with her?'

He took a sip of the coffee and smiled at her before adopting a look of serious intent. 'It seems a bit crass of me not to have sought you out before. I should have done.' He shrugged his broad shoulders. His smile tugged at her heartstrings. 'I did think of turning up on your doorstep. After all, I knew where you lived

– thanks to Isaac and Ruth. I hear you wrote to them telling them that your husband had joined up.'

She nodded. 'Yes.' Here it was. The fact that Roy was away. Her letter to the Jacobs had not disclosed the circumstances of his leaving. She'd left it that he had a yearning to serve his country.

'So basically I've – we've – got Ruth to thank for giving me a suitable excuse. Isaac's legs are no better – even getting onto a bus is something of an ordeal and walking is right out of the question.' His eyes clouded. 'Isaac asked me to seek you out and tell you. I jumped at the chance. I hope you don't mind me saying that, do you?'

Something long buried inside shifted. Her smile was soft and wistful. 'Isaac and Ruth were always very kind to me. I don't know what I would have done without him bringing me fruit and veg from the market. It was a great help. Roy...' She stopped herself from going any further. She had been about to say that Roy's wages had been erratic, but that in turn might have led to more explanation. 'Roy joined the army.'

'I thought he'd be a bit old for joining up.'

'Apparently not, especially abroad. That's where he is at present, so not likely to come home any time soon.'

'Do you miss him?'

Not, you must be missing him. That's what some people had said to her. Now he was asking the question that she felt compelled to answer truthfully and honestly.

'We'd grown apart. We married young. We're different people to what we were back then.'

Had it been her purpose to tell him that she was mostly by herself? It might have been. What if he thought it an invitation to visit more often?

In a bid to cover a comment that could have serious repercussions, she referred to his reason for coming here and asked what was wrong with Ruth and which hospital she was in. 'She's in the General Hospital. It's her lungs, though you've probably already guessed that. TB of course. The conditions they lived in didn't help. They're all right in their new place at Lawford's Gate, but there are a lot of steps to climb. Still.' He shrugged. 'It was the best I could do.'

'It was wonderful,' Jenny enthused. 'Better than that damp old place they moved into next to St James's Church, and miles better than the rooms in Blue Bowl Alley.'

Isaac and Ruth had lived on the first floor in the tenement in Blue Bowl Alley, Jenny and her family in rooms on the top floor. Mice, bugs and cockroaches had also been their neighbours, burrowing into the wormy skirting boards and behind the crumbling plaster.

She looked down into her tea. The light tan-coloured surface was nothing like a crystal ball, but the memories were there, swirling around when she took a spoon and stirred it. It was all so clear and so painful. She blushed, raising her head and meeting his intense gaze. Vestiges of those memories must have shown on her face.

'I must go and visit. As soon as possible. I can get a bus into the centre from Melvin Square.' She said it quickly and kept her head down.

'I've got a car. I can collect you and take you to the hospital whenever you like.'

'Oh, you don't need to do that. The bus stops on Melvin Square and goes all the way to the city centre. I can walk to the General Hospital from there.'

Suddenly he looked towards the kitchen door. His nose twitched. 'What's that terrible smell?'

Jenny sprang up from her chair. 'The boiler. It's probably gone out again – blasted thing!'

Charlie followed her into the kitchen.

When she dipped down to look at the gas ring situated at the bottom of the boiler, she could see it had gone out.

'Oh not again.' She turned the main gas tap off. 'It keeps going out. One day it's going to blow us all to kingdom come.'

'Let me take a look.'

She stood aside.

'Have you got an old brush of some description?'

'Yes...'

She found him an old paintbrush left by the council decorators on which the paint had dried, making it almost impossible to use.

He used it to brush in and around the gas jets, then told her to stand back. Holding a lighted match in one hand, he turned the gas tap with the other. A small pop and a ring of blue flames sprang into life.

'That should do it.'

'I can't thank you enough.'

When his eyes locked with hers, it seemed to her that something strange happened. The painted brick of the kitchen walls, the daisy-patterned curtains, the gas stove and wayward boiler, even the table and chairs she'd been so proud of, were gone. The world around was just a blur of colours. There was nothing else but him.

If he'd kissed her right then and there, she would not have been able to hold back. In that split second, she wanted everything he had to give.

She was disappointed when he didn't kiss her but shook her hand as a friend would do.

'Tomorrow then. Visiting hours are from seven to eight. I'll pick you up at six in the evening and perhaps we can go for a drink afterwards.'

'Yes.'

She said it without thinking, then regretted it.

'I can, but I have to ask my neighbour across the road to keep an eye on my daughters once I've given them their tea. They'll be out to play after that, or if the weather is dire, they'll play board games with her girls.'

After draining his cup, Charlie reached for his overcoat, remarking as he did so how warm it felt. Leaving it gaping open, hat in hand, dark blond hair gleaming, he smiled at her before heading for the door.

'I'll pick you up tomorrow then. Six o'clock.'

'Yes. Six o'clock.'

The sight of a car in the street had drawn a few neighbours out to their front gates. Nods of interest were shared. Jenny guessed a few more pairs of eyes were watching from behind their front windows.

A group of pre-school age children traced sticky fingers along the matt black car, eyes wide with fascination. It wasn't often a car entered the street, so it always attracted curiosity. A van not so much, but a vehicle purely for the use of passengers was a rarity.

Wrapping her cardigan tightly around herself, she watched until it was gone, ignored the questioning looks that fell her way and shut the front door. Once it was shut, she leaned against it, hand on heart, feeling it racing.

It was the first time she'd admitted to herself that she was missing some aspects of a man. As her pulse slowed, she told herself firmly that he had only come here to tell her about Ruth. He hadn't come to see her. Not really. She was far below him on the social scale. Charlie Talbot would never be part of her life. Dreaming of him was one thing. The reality was quite another.

Any thoughts about him were tempered by her concern for dear Ruth. Tomorrow she would find out just how ill she was.

6

Seeing as Coronation Close was a cul-de-sac it was easy for the residents to keep an eye on the comings and goings. Some kept a closer eye than others. Dorothy Partridge was one of those neighbours hiding behind her living-room curtains watching what was going on with narrowed eyes and malicious intent.

'Her next door just had a man visitor. She invited him in.'

Harry, who to the world outside number one Coronation Close was known as Harriet, sighed deeply into the inner pages of his newspaper.

'She has every right to invite him in. He's a visitor. Visitors usually are invited in.'

Dorothy scowled and sniffed. Her face resembled a withered crab apple when she did that, though God knows, Harry wouldn't dare say so. His shoulders tensed as he waited to hear what was coming next.

'He's a good-looking man.'

'But not in there long. It's likely therefore that he's a friend or relative.'

'I don't know that she's got any relatives.'

'How do you know that?'

Dorothy straightened the curtain and turned to face him. 'Her husband told me that they were both orphans, that all they had was each other. Such an upright gentleman and we had so much in common.'

Harry looked up from his newspaper, frowning. 'Like what?'

'He thinks this country is going to the dogs. We agreed that something must be done. Did you see him in his black uniform? He's a friend of that Sir Oswald Mosley.'

Harry shook his head in despair. 'Dorothy, you don't know what you're talking about. That man Mosley and his like are going to lead to trouble. You mark my words. Don't let a smart uniform and military bearing influence your opinions. Anyway, he's not with them any more, not the Blackshirts that is. I hear he's joined the army.'

'And a fine soldier he'll make,' Dorothy declared. 'Fine pair of shoulders and strong views. He'll end up an officer. A commander of men. He won't run.'

Her eyes met his accusingly. Not for the first time, Harry felt diminished by the accusation in her steely gaze.

Dorothy's jaw was set and her thin arms were folded over her narrow chest. Insinuation glittered in her eyes.

'I didn't run,' he said, his voice quivering with emotion.

'No. You fell apart.'

Her manner was scathing. Didn't she realise how much her words hurt? Didn't she realise that he lived with that terrible past and his desertion each and every day?

He got to his feet and headed upstairs.

'If it wasn't for me you'd be in prison, Corporal Harry Partridge.'

Her sharp words carried up the stairs behind him. Closing the bedroom door shut her out, though not the memories. Nothing could ever shut those out.

Tears stinging his eyes, he looked out of the bedroom window. Row after row of gardens stretched along the back of the houses, curving out of sight at the far end of the close. Down in their own garden, clumps of snowdrops were still in flower, though it seemed as though the rain was beating both them and the daffodils back into the mud.

Looking at that mud brought back fragments of memories that still haunted him. Broken men, bits of bodies, flesh and mud churning together. The sky lighting up with flashes of artillery fire, fountains of earth spouting upwards. The air had stunk of cordite and blood. The noise had been deafening. Some got used to it, but he never had and there'd been many more like him.

In the last battle he'd endured, the torso of his best mate had landed on his shoulders. Something inside him had broken.

The night had continued to thunder behind him as he'd headed away, keeping low, winding his way over mud and between craters, making to where the bare branches of denuded trees scratched the sky, his eyes wet with tears, his chest heaving with sobs.

Somehow, ragged in stolen clothes, silent and alone, he'd got away. Somehow, with the help of uncommonly sympathetic fishermen, he'd found himself back in England. Dorothy, the wife he'd married only a year before, had almost fainted at the sight of him. After living like a tramp, sleeping rough, stealing food where he could, he'd arrived in the dead of night, gaunt-faced and scrawny. For the first time in an age, he had slept in a bed, been nursed back to physical health. Not that the experience was entirely behind him. The nightmares robbed him of sleep. There were repercussions, echoes of what he had been through. He started at the sudden banging of a door, the shouts of costermongers in St Nicholas Market.

He was in hiding, had been since that dreadful war and would be, he thought, forever. The unluckier ones, those who'd been caught, had been shot. Some had been imprisoned. Some had committed suicide rather than go back.

Luck had been on his side. Nobody came to find him, a deserter who had fled the trenches, his mind deranged, his whole body shaking as it still did on occasion.

'You're not going back,' Dorothy had proclaimed.

'They'll come for me.'

'You're not going back!'

Claiming mental disorder was no excuse – cowardice, they called it. According to the high command and those who had not been there, every soldier should be willing to die for his country no matter the cost.

Although Dorothy had been one of those handing out white feathers to those who seemed not to have joined up, she made an exception for her husband. It was her idea that he should dress as a woman. 'You're my sister Harriet Osborne.'

He'd been in no fit state to think it over or protest. In meek silence, he had become Harriet Osborne and, as such, had felt safe. The fear of the authorities finding out had never quite gone away. A policeman had once come to the door back in the old place in the city centre. Dorothy had answered the door whilst Harry had lingered in the background. The policeman had handed her a telegram. It was black bordered. Neither of them needed to ask what it was. Harry Partridge was dead. The door was shut on both the policeman and the outside world.

'They must have found my identity tag,' Harry had explained.

'But no body,' said Dorothy in disbelief, the telegram screwed up in her hand.

'No. No body.'

He tried to explain to her that there weren't always bodies, just an identity tag floating in a soup of blood and mud.

Dorothy had listened to him in shocked silence. 'It's unchristian,' she'd said at last.

Following a frank discussion, they had decided that for the foreseeable future Harry would live as Harriet.

Their decision proved a good one. As two sisters, they were given a council house, plus Dorothy had received a war widows pension. It could be said that Dorothy was entitled to one. Harry, as Harriet, enrolled anyway and seeing as there were thousands of widows, mistakes were made. Harriet Osborne had been listed as a widow and also received a pension. They could live their lives free of war – if Harry continued to pass himself off as a woman.

Rods of rain battered the window. His gaze strayed from the muddy garden of number one to next door at number two. Mrs Crawford was dressed in a wet-weather cape of the sort they'd worn on the battlefield and digging up potatoes – the first of the year, no doubt.

He admired her pluck, husband in the army and leaving her to survive as best she could. There was something about her that made him think of Dorothy before she'd been changed by their experiences. She hadn't always been so intolerant of others. He knew what was behind it, of course. The war had spoilt everything and in a way she blamed him for not being brave enough, not being soldierly enough. At the same time, she protected him. Or was it more than protection? Was it a form of control?

The thought disturbed him and it wasn't that easy to push it away, but away it must go. Best think of the simple things of life. He rubbed at the bristles on his face. He needed a shave, a small matter, but enough to help him face another day.

7

Accompanied by a cloud of expensive scent, a woman wearing a mink coat sprinkled with raindrops approached Thelma's counter. A man followed her – a young, well-dressed man at least twenty years her junior.

Thelma recognised the woman who'd bought the kid gloves some weeks ago. Mrs Justin-Cooper had opened a personal account and was here yet again.

She pasted on her welcoming smile. 'Mrs Justin-Cooper. How nice to see you again.' It paid to remember a customer's name. They appreciated it and remembered those staff that did and made a beeline for them when they entered the shop. Sometimes they even asked for a favourite sales assistant by name. Thelma hoped this would happen.

Red lips smiled through a black lace veil. 'Thank you, though, on this occasion, I'm not here to purchase something for myself. My nephew here wishes to buy a present for his fiancée.'

Thelma turned to the handsome young man. 'Good morning, sir. Might I ask if you have anything in particular in mind, or would you like me to suggest something your fiancée can't fail to fall in love with?'

His aristocratic looks almost took her breath away. Although younger, he reminded her of the playboy prince who had denounced the throne. His hair was dark blond, slightly waved and silky and his eyes were a stunning cornflower blue. His smile was enough to take the breath away of the most matronly of women. It certainly took hers away and she was no spinster.

He placed his handsome and very expensive trilby hat on the counter, his hands, nails manicured to perfection, either side of it. Perfect white teeth flashed when he smiled. 'I'm not sure. My ideas don't go far beyond a box of lace handkerchiefs or a silk scarf.' He wrinkled his nose. 'Not very imaginative of me, I know. What would you suggest?'

Ideas flashed through her mind, some of which had to be reined in. Bertrams had some lovely lingerie in stock, but should a fiancé be giving such intimate items before marriage?

She asked if sir knew what size she was?

'Slender but shapely,' he replied.

Was it her imagination or was that a blush on the slender, shapely Mrs Justin-Cooper? Ah, she thought. So that was their game. Too old to be his fiancée of course, but that was their business. Although Thelma surmised this man as a bit of a cad, she had a living to earn and part of her wage was based on commission.

'I think I've got just the thing.' Smiling, she turned behind her to the glass-fronted, beech wood framed shelves where the most expensive silk items were kept. She brought out a mint-green nightdress so pale it shimmered almost silver, and so fine that she could see her hand through it. It was far from being the most revealing in their collection, but at the same time was not matronly. The shoulder straps were formed from wide bands of silk of the same colour as the main body of the garment and banded with lace. More lace trimmed the ankle-length hem.

'So beautiful,' said Mrs Justin-Cooper, her voice barely more than a whisper. The eyes behind the veil eyed the garment with what Thelma could only describe as reverence. 'It's so fine, and the colour...' Another expressive sigh escaped the red lips. She turned to the young man she'd introduced as her nephew, her head held coquettishly to one side. 'What do you think, my darling boy?'

'I'm no expert. I think it's very becoming, but quite frankly I don't feel my opinion would be that reliable.' He looked first at Mrs Justin-Cooper and then at Thelma. 'What do you two ladies think?'

'Absolutely superb, darling. Absolutely superb. So silky. So soft.' Mrs Justin-Cooper ran her fingers over the soft silk. 'No woman could resist it. No man either,' she murmured, the blush returning to her cheeks.

Thelma kept her fixed smile. 'Would the colour match your fiancée's complexion and hair colour?' The nightdress was very expensive – five guineas in fact. A nice commission for her if he bought it.

'Would you wear it?' He directed his question at Thelma.

'I would love it,' returned Thelma without embarrassment. And so would Bert, she thought to herself – if he ever got the chance. But Bert was conservative in his views; nothing unto-ward should happen until the wedding night. That was his view. Whether they ever got round to marrying was another matter entirely and the reluctance was hers. Once her two young daughters were grown, she might consider remarrying. As for George, well, he was a young man now, though goodness knew she wished he wasn't. In her mind he was still her little boy.

The young man smacked the counter, startling her from her musings. 'Then I'll take it.'

'You can put it on my bill,' said Mrs Justin-Cooper, her eyes unusually bright at the prospect of him doing so, a secretive smug smile on her lips.

'No need. Open an account in my name. No doubt I'll be buying more for her trousseau – if she'll allow me to.'

Thelma couldn't be sure, but thought she saw a secretive look flash between Mrs Justin-Cooper and her companion. Dismissing what she was thinking to concentrate on the bill, she asked for the young man's name.

'Charles George Talbot.'

Thelma hesitated making the entry for the briefest of moments. Didn't she know that name? As she scribbled it hastily onto the note for passing to the accounts register, it hit her. Jenny had mentioned meeting up with him, how he was such a straight and upright man who had helped her friends, helped her too. Just recently, he'd fetched her in his motorcar so they could visit those old friends in hospital. She'd also gone for a drink with him afterwards and told Thelma all about it, how he made her feel, how she had held back despite her inclination to fall into his arms and lie with him forever.

Jenny adored him and, with her husband away, one thing could easily lead to another. Thelma wouldn't blame her. She'd met Jenny's husband, Roy, and hadn't thought much of him. A bully. A tyrant. Too self-assured for his own good. However, she felt that Jenny was too keen on this man. Oh yes, he was handsome and likeable; definitely came across as the answer to a woman's prayer. But there was also something elusive about him, even a bit too carefree and irresponsible. Not that what she said would have much impact on Jenny's feelings for him. Jenny was a dear friend, but slightly flawed. She asked herself what was Jenny looking for in a man? She reasoned that she was constantly seeking affection and something better than she had. Not always a good idea, Thelma thought. An obsessive need for affection could cause Jenny great pain. She herself had had plenty of that in her time.

'There you are, sir.' Thelma smiled as she handed Charlie Talbot the shiny black carrier bag emblazoned with the name Bertrams.

He touched the brim of his hat when he thanked her. Mrs Justin-Cooper merely smiled, more so for him than for Thelma.

He walked out with his arm around the woman who'd professed to be his aunt, though hardly as a means of assistance to an elderly woman. Mrs Justin-Cooper was older than him but not elderly. Neither was she in need of assistance. His action was one of affection. The nightdress was for her, Thelma decided. A gift from a young lover to his older mistress.

'Another satisfied customer, Mrs Dawson?'

Mrs Apsley's voice cut into her thoughts.

'Yes. The gentleman opened an account. He bought one of our Eleganza nightdresses, the sort a bride wears on a honeymoon. He bought it for his fiancée – so he said.'

They exchanged a knowing look. Sales assistants were not fools and could tell someone's status and when they were telling little white lies – like now.

'I see.' Mrs Apsley's comment was clipped, but said it all. Both her eyes and Thelma's followed the closing of the shop door behind the pair. 'I take it he introduced the lady with him as his aunt.'

Thelma smiled. 'Not quite. She introduced him as her nephew. How did you know that?'

Mrs Apsley smiled. 'Experience, my dear. Put it down to experience.'

Thelma had her own problems. She'd been attacked in January and it was now March and still her monthlies had not yet appeared. Although concerned for herself, she had enough compassion left over to be concerned for her friend. Charlie Talbot, it seemed, was not quite all that Jenny thought him to be.

Should she tell her what she suspected, or let sleeping dogs lie? And what exactly was it that she suspected? That Charlie Talbot really was engaged to be married or that he had a middle-aged mistress? Either way, Jenny would be devastated.

For the fourth time that day, she asked Mrs Apsley for permission to go to the toilets.

'I've got a bit of a stomach upset.'

'Something you ate?' asked Mrs Apsley.

'I think so.'

The cottage pie she'd had the night before had been delicious and not affected her stomach at all. Her reason was the same she'd had for the last month or so, to check to see if 'her friend' had arrived. Yet again, she was disappointed.

She'd heard it was normal for her monthlies to become more sporadic as she approached the 'change', though approaching forty didn't seem such a great age. Getting older and the midlife changes happening in her body did reassure her to some extent, but a nagging doubt remained.

8

Monday morning and yet again Jenny was having trouble with the gas jet beneath the boiler. For the fourth time that morning, she turned on the tap and then touched the circle of gas jets with a lighted match.

Cath interrupted her concentration, barging through the back door and asking if she knew there was an ambulance outside next door.

'Looks as though Mrs Partridge has had a nasty turn. When we asked, just as good neighbours what was wrong, 'er sister said she 'ad a weak heart and 'ad a funny turn.'

'Poor woman,' said Jenny, still facing the boiler. 'Was there anything else you wanted?' She sensed that there was. Cath was always running out of things.

'I've run out of sugar. Have you got a cup of sugar I can borrow?'

Setting the matches to one side, Jenny got to her feet . From a shelf in the larder, she took a stone jar containing sugar, scooped some out into an old cracked cup and passed it to Cath.

Cath uttered 'thank you' as she took it from her, cradling it with both hands. 'I'll pay you back later.'

'That's fine. Now to light this blessed boiler,' she replied, turning back to the wretched zinc boiler. 'I've got a load of washing to do.'

'I gets trouble lighting that thing too,' said Cath, nodding at the ugly grey tub. 'I hear some woman up in Leinster Avenue got 'er 'air blown off by one. It blew up. Just blew up. The 'ouse was badly damaged.'

'That's dreadful.'

'The back window was blown out too. You can't muck around with gas, so my Bill says. He reckons the council needs to check them a bit more regularly. He cleans our jets out 'imself and checks the tap turns off properly. Shall I get 'im to do yours?'

Jenny thought back to when Charlie had cleaned out the jets. 'Don't worry him about that. I usually open the window if the smell of gas lingers.'

'So do I, but you can't be too careful – that's what my Bill says.'

She finally agreed with Cath that it would be useful if he took a look. 'If he doesn't mind, that is.'

'Of course not.' Cath paused by the back door. 'You off out with that bloke in the car later?'

Jenny had suspected the question would be asked. Curtains had twitched the moment Charlie's car entered the street. His frequent visits would be noted and remarked on, though rarely within her earshot. Tonight would be the fourth time she was out with him. She'd given up suggesting she get the bus to the hospital. Charlie insisted he would take her and it had become their habit after that to go for a drink together. As usual, she was looking forward to it.

She guessed that Cath had expected to be invited to stay for a cuppa, but Jenny wanted to get the laundry out on the line before the girls came home from school at midday and a second load washed and dried before four o'clock at the end of the school day. That would then give her enough time to get ready to go out with Charlie.

Her heart raced at the thought of him, that floppy dark blond hair, those twinkling eyes, the way he pronounced words, as though they were toffee and flavoursome on his tongue.

Such silly thoughts, she told herself, shaking her head as she sorted out whites from coloureds.

The kitchen smelled slightly of gas, following so many attempts to light it. Thinking of seeing Charlie again superseded any idea of getting Billy Lockhart to service the jet. It could wait.

Tonight she was going out to see her dear friend Ruth again. On each visit, she entered the hospital side entrance with dread, hoping against hope that Ruth was still there, barely hanging onto life as resolutely as she always had.

Both Ruth and Isaac had been her only genuine friends at a time when she was living in dire circumstances, unhappy with her life and her marriage. Regardless of being out with Charlie afterwards, she owed Ruth those visits and only hoped the day was long off when she wouldn't be around any longer.

Bubble and squeak topped with an egg was the usual Monday midday meal when the girls came home from school. Slicing every sliver of meat from the bone, she'd made enough mince from the Sunday roast to make pasties. The bones and what remained of the meat clinging to them would make stew for Wednesday. Their weekly menu stayed very much the same from week to week. Not one scrap of food was wasted. Like everyone else, Jenny made the Sunday joint and leftover vegetables last as long as possible.

An afternoon of more laundry followed, until the girls came home from school at around four thirty.

After the girls had wolfed down their evening meal, they raced outside. Jenny shouted after them to be in by nine o'clock at the latest. 'I'll be home by then.'

The kids in the close played beneath the street lights until late. There was no traffic, no passers-by except those who lived there coming home from work or going for a drink at the pub.

It was not the most clement of nights. The rains of February had been replaced by the blustery winds of March. Jenny had to hold onto her hat as she ran to the car.

'In like a lion,' she said laughingly as she slid onto the warm leather seat beside him. 'Hopefully it will go out like a lamb.'

Charlie smiled. '*March brings breezes loud and shrill, stirs the dancing daffodil.*'

'April soon.'

'Something about showers and gillyflowers – whatever they are.'

'Primroses and daisies.' They laughed and recited more rhymes recalled from childhood as the car left the close and made its way from the estate and into East Street, Bedminster. He asked her how her family was. She told him the children were fine but refrained from bringing up Roy. Every so often she caught him glancing at her, mainly when he asked how she was settling in the house and was she happy. She said that she was especially sitting here next to him in the car.

He hesitated to say anything when she asked him about his family.

'We don't get on that well,' he said finally. 'They disagreed with my politics, especially my father.' He shrugged his shoulders. 'Cut me off without a penny, but there you are. My beliefs matter more than money. Anyway, I get by.' He paused as though deciding whether he should tell her more. 'I get by – I even get paid for issuing pamphlets and such like.'

Their conversation remained relatively light. She fancied that he was reluctant for any serious probing. They fell into talking about her neighbours, those she liked and those went out of their way to be disliked – Dorothy Partridge dominated the latter category, of course.

Their destination was reached too early as far as Jenny was concerned. As usual, Jenny was full of apprehension as they passed beneath the grim archway and into the hospital.

Her apprehension reduced when nobody came to tell them not to go in, that it was too late, that Ruth was no more.

As they approached the ward and nobody accosted them, Jenny felt her shoulders relax, her handbag less tightly gripped against her stomach.

A vase of daffodils on a table in the ward glowed in sunny splendour.

Before going any further, a small stout figure stepped into their paths.

All the apprehension Jenny had thought discarded came back to stiffen her shoulders and feel a deep sickness in her stomach.

'Ah. Sister,' said Charlie, his trilby held in both hands. 'We're here to see Mrs Jacobs.'

Although small in stature, the ward sister was large in superiority. She drew herself up, jutted her chin and told them they could not proceed.

'Mrs Jacobs died this afternoon. Did no one inform you?'

'No they did not.' Charlie didn't exactly snap but he did sound quite put out. 'We wouldn't have come if we'd known. It's most inconvenient.'

'She's dead?' Jenny went cold all over and her voice was as an icy breath, barely audible.

'I'm afraid so,' came the officious response.

For a moment, nothing was said. An odd cough, the sound of

metal on metal – medical utensils, dishes and bedpans on steel trollies echoed off the walls and high ceiling.

'Can we see her,' asked Jenny. Her tongue cleaved to the roof of her mouth. Her whole body felt too stiff to move.

'Are you relatives?'

'Yes,' said Charlie without giving Jenny time to answer. 'This is her niece. We've come a long way.'

The sister didn't contradict him, didn't question whether they were telling the truth, though they were the closest thing to family Ruth had. 'We await the undertakers.'

Jenny gasped. Charlie's arm snaked around her shoulders but gave no relief. She had not expected this. She'd hoped to see Ruth at least one last time.

'Do you still want to see her?' Charlie whispered.

Jenny answered promptly. 'Now we're here. Just to pay our respects and see that she's at peace. My aunt had a hard life. It would mean so much to me.'

A moment and then agreement. 'Of course.'

Their footsteps walking over the chestnut-brown lino sounded like a drumbeat, a slow dirge down the centre of the ward.

Jenny realised she hadn't asked whether Isaac had visited recently, whether he too had paid his last respects. She imagined him being devastated.

Curtains had been pulled around her old friend's bed. The ward sister pulled one back, just enough for them to enter. There were no chairs. Nothing except an empty bedside cabinet.

Ruth's complexion would have matched the whiteness of the pillow if it hadn't been for the greyness that had sucked her colour and sunken her cheeks.

Jenny held her breath and raised a hand to her mouth. Ruth had been like a mother to her and Isaac like a father. Warm, happy people, full of life and well built. Now she lay here, no more than a bag of skin and bone.

Jenny filled up and turned her head into Charlie's chest.

'I want to go,' she whispered against his overcoat. 'I want to go home.'

She felt his hand on her hair, smoothing it away from her face.

'Don't you want to see Isaac?'

She shook her head, her face hidden against his shoulder. 'No. Not now.'

Back outside, the wind that had blown them into the hospital brought the smell of mud and effluent from this part of the River Avon known as the Cut. Mildew and weeds came with it.

Charlie helped her into the front passenger seat of the car, where she sat numbly.

'Tonight of all nights, I think we need a drink.'

'I've changed my mind about seeing Isaac.'

'I'll go there tomorrow and see how he is,' he said as he threw the starting handle into the back seat and took hold of the shuddering steering wheel.

'And ask him for...' She paused, hardly daring to voice what had to be faced. 'Details of funeral arrangements.'

'Yes.'

For a moment, he sat looking through the front windscreen.

'Do you want to go for a drink?'

She shook her head. 'I'm not in the mood. I'd like to go home – if you don't mind.'

It was too dark to see his features, but she did fancy his jaw tightened. Like her, he was moved, shocked to find that Ruth had passed. Not that it was entirely unexpected. She'd looked ill each time they'd visited, but having a drink afterwards with Charlie had helped her cope, had lightened the whole evening. Had lightened her life in fact. But not tonight.

They were silent, at least for a while, then Charlie patted her hand. 'She was a good woman.'

Jenny managed a whispered a one-word response. 'Yes.'

She dabbed at her eyes on the way home.

The rain eased off. A sickle moon peered over tumbling grey cloud. The road ahead was still slick with wetness and empty of vehicles. The darkness was oppressive, the world chilly and damp.

Their mutual silence was suddenly split by the sound of bells. An ambulance overtook them, racing ahead, weaving its way through the sparse traffic.

The road ahead was dark, though the recent painting of kerbs, a precaution, so it was said, in case war was declared, did make a difference.

'I wonder where he was going in such a hurry,' said Charlie, his comment matching her thoughts.

Jenny stretched her neck to see further along the road ahead. 'Perhaps it's a road accident.'

'Could be anything,' returned Charlie.

'I can still hear the bells. It must be quite close.'

Charlie agreed. 'As though they're following us, but ahead.'

Her own words sent a chill down her spine. It really was as though the emergency ringing of the ambulance bells was keeping pace with them – or rather they were keeping up with it.

As they entered Coronation Close the sound was deafening.

'Oh no!' Jenny clenched her stomach.

The ambulance was parked up close to her house. Worse still, something bigger and equally worrying was parked in front of it.

Before her very eyes, firemen jumped down from a bright red

fire engine. People in the close were standing at their garden gates and front doors.

A policeman's bicycle was propped against Thelma's garden gate. The policeman it belonged to was standing in front of it, notebook and pen in hand.

Jenny gasped as she realised that the emergency vehicles weren't just close to her house, they were parked right outside it and a pall of smoke, gossamer like, surrounded her house.

'No!'

She reached for the car door, fear giving her the strength to push it open. As she did so, the smell hit her, the stink of rotten eggs, stronger than ever before. Along with it came the conversation she'd had with Cath that morning. An explosion – somewhere. A ball of fire. Someone's hair singed. Someone dead.

'No.'

That one word was no more than a breath, caught in the air. Nothing and nobody mattered – and that included Charlie who she left in the car – all she could think of was that her girls had been injured, perhaps were dead.

She dashed to her garden gate, only vaguely aware that Charlie had left the car and followed her.

A fireman's broad arm swept across, preventing her from going any further. 'Can't you smell it? There's been a gas explosion. Stand back.'

She pressed against the arm that restrained her. 'It's my house. What's happened to my house?'

'Your house? Was anyone in there?' asked the fireman, his look unreadable.

She smelled his sweat, the damp wool of his uniform, the strong scent of tobacco on his breath.

Jenny felt her legs give way. 'My girls are in there,' she cried.

'Tilly and Gloria. They're in there. Get them out. Please get them out!'

Charlie caught her before her legs totally gave way. He held her so tightly that she couldn't move her arms. Much as she wanted to rush into the house, escape was impossible. But her girls! Where were her girls?

'Have you found anyone?' Charlie asked the fireman.

The fireman shook his head. 'We got the gas cut off first. We're going in now. Luckily there was no fire, just a load of dust from the damage.' He jerked his stout jaw to where firemen disappeared around the side of the house.

Jenny felt her heart turn heavy. *Please God, don't take my girls from me.*

Tears filled her eyes as she waited for the firemen to reappear.

Just when she thought the end of the world had come, she heard someone shout her name.

'Jenny! Jenny!'

She turned to see Thelma pushing at the policeman who was trying to stop her from coming out of her garden gate.

'Get out of my way, you stupid sod,' she heard her say. Another shove, his helmet wobbled and Thelma barged past him.

Thelma gripped Jenny's shoulders so fiercely that Charlie was forced to relinquish his hold on her. Only concerned for her children, Jenny did not see the look of recognition that passed between Thelma and Charlie.

She became aware of Thelma shaking her, shouting something into her face.

'Your girls are fine. They're with me. It's only your boiler that's dead and gone,' she said laughingly, though it was far from being a laughing matter. 'And your kitchen window – and doors. Nothing that can't be replaced.'

Her girls were all right! Her house was damaged but it was

only a house. It was her children who mattered! The blasted boiler was now nothing but bits of jagged metal.

The whole scene, the very thought of it, was so surreal that Jenny burst out laughing. Although relieved, the tears continued to stream down her face and into her mouth. What if, she thought, what if... Yet again, she had a lot to thank Thelma for.

'Come on. Let's have a cuppa whilst this gets sorted out.'

Her dear neighbour had hold of her arm, guiding her across the road to the front door of her house.

All four girls were hanging out of the door, looking awestruck at what was going on.

'You're safe,' cried Jenny as she gathered her daughters into her arms, her tears now wetting the tops of their heads.

It occurred to her then to tell Charlie.

Beaming with relief, she looked over her shoulder to where she'd left him, but he wasn't there. The tail-lights of his car glowed from the far end of the close. Then it was gone.

'You all right?' asked Thelma.

'I expected him to stay a bit longer.' Jenny's relief that her daughters were safe was coupled with puzzlement. Charlie's swift departure had come as a surprise. Up until they'd arrived in Coronation Close, he'd been his usual attentive self. What had happened to change that?

There were lots of things Thelma could say, but she held back. This was not the time to mention Charlie's visit to the shop with Mrs Justin-Cooper.

'Never mind,' she said cheerfully. 'Your kids are hale and hearty. That's all that matters.' Thelma rubbed the two girls' heads.

A car stopped somewhere behind the fire truck and a man got out. An expanse of khaki-coloured trench coat flared out behind him like a single dull wing. He addressed one of the fireman. 'I'm from the council come to assess the damage. Can I take a look?'

The fireman said that he could.

Once assured it was safe, the council official boldly marched up the garden path and around the side to the back of the house. A fireman accompanied him, explaining before they disappeared that there was considerable damage. 'Could be a few days before...' The words disappeared with the two men.

Jenny exchanged a worried look with Thelma.

'Did you hear what they said?'

Thelma nodded, her arm tight around Jenny's shoulders, hugging her close. 'It'll be all right, love. They'll get it fixed in no time. How's your friend Ruth by the way?'

Jenny shook her head disconsolately. She was doubly devastated and Thelma saw it in her face.

'She's gone.' Jenny said it quickly. It was almost as though she had to push Ruth's death away to cope with this disaster.

Thelma understood immediately. 'I'm so sorry, and what with this on top of it...'

'I want to see the damage.' She took a step forward, but Thelma held her back. 'Be patient. The man from the council will inspect it and let you know how things are. Anyway, as that fireman said, it didn't catch fire.'

The two men appeared from out of the darkness that the side path of the house was always cloaked in. Their heads were together in deep discussion.

Jenny's eyes were wide with alarm.

With an air of old-world courtesy, the fireman introduced Jenny. 'This is the lady of the house. Luckily, both she and her children were not at home at the time of the explosion.'

'Can I go home?' she asked before the man from the council had time to open his mouth.

He shook his head mournfully. 'I'm sorry, but we must make it safe. The gas supply to the boiler was the problem. A faulty tap.'

Cath's voice rang out. 'Well, that ain't for the first time. You should be checking them boilers.'

Her husband Bill added his comment: 'I sorted mine meself – no thanks to the council.'

'You had no right doing that. It's council property,' said the official in a rather indignant manner.

Bill was right back at him. 'And wait to be blown up while you lot get 'round to doing something about it?'

Enjoying the argument and perhaps the possibility of fisticuffs, the crowd gathered closer. An official called out for everyone to calm down and disperse.

Jenny, dealt a double tragedy tonight, exploded with anger.

'Calm down? Calm down? Me and my children could have been killed. How can you expect anyone to calm down? As for you...' She turned on the man from the council. 'All I want to know is when I can put my children to bed.'

Faced with her anger and that of her neighbours, the council official took a step back, positioning himself slightly behind the fireman and the policeman, figures of authority he thought might protect him. Once behind them, he shook his head. 'Not tonight, I'm afraid. I must send workmen along to replace the pipework and boiler. Then there's the window and internal door to replace.'

'And when will that happen?' Jenny asked hotly.

'Within the next few days. I can't promise a date...'

'Oh Lord!' Jenny buried her face in her hands.

'There'll be no gas supply and no electricity either.'

She heard the words but did not come out from behind her hands. A poor shield against adversity but all she had.

'It's a precaution for your own safety,' added the fireman, his concerned frown hidden beneath the peak of his helmet. He felt sorry for her, sorry also for all the other victims of gas explosions. He really cared about the safety of those affected.

Thelma placed her hand on her shoulder. 'Don't worry. We can all shove up a bit at my place. Our Alice and Mary can share one bed and your Gloria and Tilly can share Alice's bed. You can share with me.'

'No, I can't, Thelma. You've got your George home and don't get enough time with him as it is. Me and the girls moving in would get in the way.'

A rarely heard voice intervened, wafting their way on steaming breath. 'Excuse me.'

Many neighbours had gathered to view the near tragedy that had befallen Coronation Close. The last person they'd expected to see was Dorothy Partridge's sister, Harriet.

Even at night, the darkness minimally lifted by the lights of emergency vehicles, it was enough to illuminate nervous hesitation.

'My sister's gone to hospital. Not for long, but perhaps long enough until the council have carried out the repairs. There's plenty of room if you need somewhere to stay.'

'She's staying with me,' said Thelma. 'If she wants to that is.'

Jenny was both surprised and touched, so much so that pent-up emotion brought tears to her eyes. 'That's so kind of you. Of both of you.'

She shook her head and the threat of tears became a trickle, pouring from her eyes, down her cheeks and into her mouth.

'Now what's this all about, girl. Everything will be all right,' said Thelma, her broad arm around Jenny's slender shoulders.

Jenny sobbed and sobbed. 'I have to say that it was the best thing in the world when I moved here. I've got the best neighbours in the world.'

Notwithstanding Isaac and Ruth of course.

Perhaps that was why Charlie had set off in a hurry. She'd remembered him mentioning calling in on Isaac.

'If you do get stuck at all, the offer's still open,' said Harriet.

'She'll be fine with me,' stated Thelma in a manner unlikely to attract argument. One arm was already around Jenny's back, pressing her towards the house Thelma shared with her two daughters and her son, George. 'And the girls will be needing fresh clothes. You heard the fireman. You can't go back into that house just now. My girls won't mind sharing their clothes. Me too for that matter.'

Jenny swallowed the very truthful comment that Thelma's clothes would be too big for her. Thelma's answer would be that it wouldn't take long to alter them to suit.

Instead of arguing, she thanked Harriet for her offer. 'It's very kind of you. How's your sister by the way?'

'Complaining. Dorothy is an expert at complaining.'

'You can say that again,' muttered Thelma.

'Is it anything serious?' asked Jenny, inclined to be more charitable. She hadn't been such a target for Dorothy's vitriol as Thelma.

A lowering of eyes, glance pointedly downwards. 'Women's problems.'

'Oh.'

That said it all.

'I hope she'll be home soon.'

'So do I. The house is very quiet without her.' A slight smile. 'Though that's not necessarily a bad thing. At least for a while.'

The ambulance that had raced past Charlie's car on the way here now left. There'd been nothing for the crew to do, but they had lingered when Maude had come out with a tray of tea and homemade cakes. Maude baked wonderful cakes from the cheapest ingredients. Apple cake was one of her party pieces.

Thelma's elbow nudged Jenny's ribs. 'Let's get inside. There's nothing can be done and I've got to get up in the morning. Business as usual at Bertrams.'

Before going, Jenny turned to Harriet once more. 'I really appreciate the offer. Thank you.'

Was that a flash of disappointment she saw?

'Perhaps you would like to come for a cup of tea tomorrow morning?'

'Yes. I would like that.'

Surprisingly, she received no condemnation from Thelma for accepting the invitation.

Their time once inside the house was taken up with sorting out sleeping arrangements, bedding and what the girls were wearing to school the following morning.

Thelma was like a whirlwind, dashing around and getting everyone organised.

After a quick supper of bread and jam, both sets of girls, giggling and chattering with excitement, were sent off to bed.

Thelma insisted they have a cup of cocoa each before turning in.

'And we can have a little chat. I've got biscuits. Do you want one?'

Jenny felt as though her eyes were rolling around in their sockets when she shook her head. 'Just cocoa will be fine.' Exhaustion was taking hold, sucking the adrenaline from her body.

Thelma insisted on three spoons of sugar.

Before they had chance to take a sip, George came in. It was explained to him why there was a policeman standing guard outside Jenny's house and why a fire engine had almost run him over at the end of the street.

'We've got three guests for a few days. I've sorted out who's sleeping where, but you be on your best behaviour,' his mother said to him.

'I'm never anything else, Mother. Never anything else,' he declared, a wide grin splitting his face.

'Right. Then you get off to bed. Me and Jenny need to have a chat.'

'What about?'

'Women's talk.' She jerked her head towards the stairs. 'So you get on up there.'

'Lavatory first,' he said.

Jenny had no idea what 'women's talk' Thelma had in mind and didn't relish the thought of it. She was way beyond talking about anything.

Shattered by the night's events, she rubbed at her head and slumped into a chair, the cocoa untouched. 'I'm so sorry, Thelma, but I can't manage it. All I want to do is close my eyes. I would have said goodnight to Charlie before he left, but when I looked he was gone.' She shrugged her shoulders.

Thelma pursed her lips. She badly wanted to give Jenny a good shake and tell her what she suspected of Charlie. Unlike Jenny, she knew why he'd shot off like he did. One look at her and he'd recognised her as the woman who had served him at Bertrams with his... She wasn't sure quite what word to use. Charlie wasn't the first she'd heard who was hitched up with an older woman. In her experience, the older woman paid the bills for her younger lover. That was the only thing that niggled. Charlie Talbot had set up a personal account. This confused her and as such she was glad she hadn't had the little talk she'd planned. Best she thought about it a bit more. There could be a simple explanation. On the other hand, there might not.

After Jenny took herself to bed, Thelma made cocoa for George.

He took a big slurp. 'Ma, you're a brick. Too generous by half.'

'I'm just being a good neighbour.'

'Course you are.'

George had had a drop to drink but still managed to focus on the paleness of her face.

'You don't look so well of late. Women's problems, is it?' He grinned as he said it.

'Cheeky sod!' She made as if to slap him, but George only laughed.

'Well, I'll be off to me bed,' he said, swigging back the dregs of the cocoa. 'You look as if you should be in yer bed too.'

'I'll be right behind you.'

He nodded and said goodnight.

Once she was alone, Thelma poured herself a glass of water. She sat back down in the chair and reached for her handbag. The laxatives were the same ones Cath had used. Every woman in the same circumstances she was in now knew about Penny Royal. Sometimes they worked, sometimes they didn't. She hoped they would work otherwise her life would be turned upside down.

9

On the following day, once Thelma had gone to work and the girls to school, Jenny crossed the road, desperate to know the plight of her beloved house. The policeman had gone. She looked to left and right just in case he was loitering somewhere. On seeing no sign of him, she pushed open the gate and followed the garden path around to the rear.

She gasped with shock. Her breath caught in her throat and tears stung her eyes when she saw the state of her house. The metal window frame had withstood the blast, but the window-panes lay smashed on the ground. The back door was still in situ, but the inner door was shattered. The saucepan rack that ran the full length of the wall and was above the boiler had taken the brunt of the blast. Only the length above the coal hole remained, the rest of it only fit for kindling. Pots and pans were scattered across the garden, warped and dented. The kitchen was a mess. The gas stove was covered in dust and splinters of wood.

My dustpan. I need my dustpan.

Daft thoughts, but she couldn't help the compulsion to clear the debris and sort out the cooking pots.

She would have no means to cook. No electricity either. But she did have a fireplace and there were candles kept for emergencies. They'd sometimes resorted to candles back in Blue Bowl Alley, the gas lighting having been unreliable. A coal fire in the grate had been a necessity. This house, she thought, and all the others in Coronation Close were luxurious in comparison to Blue Bowl Alley.

She knew she was supposed to be here. What was it the man from the council had said? It wouldn't be safe.

'Yoohoo. Are you all right in there?'

The sudden intrusion made her jump before she recognised Harriet.

'Oh my.' A pair of pale blue eyes scoured the state of the kitchen. 'My. It is in a mess, isn't it.'

Jenny sighed. 'I was hoping I could tidy it up enough to live in – or at least sleep in. We're a bit cramped over in Thelma's and I feel I'm imposing.'

'I can understand that. She's a good sort is Mrs Dawson.'

Harriet's attitude towards Thelma was at odds with that of her sister Dorothy so was mildly surprising.

'Do you want a hand tidying it up?'

'Yes. If it's no trouble.'

'None at all. I'm at a loose end without Dorothy around giving her orders.'

They set to with a vengeance.

Harriet took charge of the heavier jobs, fetching tools and setting the pot shelf back into place above the spot where the boiler used to be. The fragments of boiler had been removed. The ends of what remained of the lead gas pipes had been hammered flat to prevent any more gas escaping. The water pipes too. Debris and dirt were swept up with the aid of a sweeping brush, a hand brush and two dustpans. Harriet brought a mop and bucket from next door.

'The fresh air will dry the floor,' said Harriet as she pushed open the window. 'Oh dear,' she said, suddenly laughing. 'It never needed opening.'

Jenny looked ruefully at the glassless kitchen window where a pair of green gingham curtains hung in threads. She'd bought them at a second-hand shop in Bedminster. 'I loved these curtains. Now look at them. Fit only for dusters.' She screwed them up and flung them onto the draining board feeling some-what defeated, saddened and despairing. All her effort to make this a home, and now look at it.

Harriet stood watching her. Jenny could feel the sympathy reaching out like a kind pat on the shoulder, a reassuring hug.

'Come on, love. Let's go to our place and have a cuppa.'

Entering the house next door felt almost like trespassing. Such was her discomfort, Jenny half expected Dorothy to leap out and order her from the house.

Harriet seemed to sense her concern. 'Don't worry. Dorothy won't be home from the hospital for two days at least. I'm paying for an ambulance to bring her home. Lucky we can afford it.'

Crockery clattered in the kitchen as Harriet put a kettle on the gas, the pot, cups and saucers on the table.

Jenny sat feeling lost in the living room. Whilst she waited for the tea, she took in the details of number one, Coronation Close. Everything in the room was overly neat, to the extent of being pristine, untouchable and to some extent unusable. Not a thing was out of place. Cushions were set square in the two armchairs. One each of the same pattern – roses and a lady in a crinoline – sat either end of the settee. Another lady in a crinoline, painted in bright colours, tended a flower bed on the mirror above the fire-place. The brass fender and coalscuttle gleamed. The rug in front of the fireplace was Turkish in design. A pair of flat-backed Staffordshire dogs sat at either end of the cast-iron mantelpiece.

There were no pictures on the walls. Surprised by this, Jenny dared to get up and look around. Behind an ornate teapot of Oriental design sitting on the dresser was a photograph of two dour-looking people in front of a wide veranda running the length of a bungalow. A man in a turban stood slightly behind them holding a tea tray. She presumed they were her neighbours' parents.

Another photograph at the other end of the dresser was of a man in an army uniform. Glancing between the photographs, it occurred to Jenny that the man in the uniform resembled the man in the bungalow photograph. They were both thickset, though the former didn't look as dour as the latter. She decided they had to be related. Father and son perhaps.

There was also a wedding photograph and one of a young woman, her hair piled on top of her head, piercing eyes and a straight unsmiling mouth. Jenny presumed this was Dorothy when younger. If so, she'd been relatively pretty, not so pinched and bitter of expression as in later years.

'I've brought in biscuits. Custard creams.'

Harriet set down a tray on the table. The cups were flowery, delicate and gilt rimmed.

'Sugar?'

Jenny shook her head and whilst doing so couldn't help glancing across at the dresser. There was something disconcerting about those photographs, something that roused her suspicions.

'I take it the couple in front of the bungalow are your parents.'

'Yes.' The cup and saucer of milky tea was set in front of her. 'Sorry,' Harriet suddenly said, 'I should have asked if you preferred lemon. Most people who grew up in England prefer milk, but Dorothy and I grew up in India – as you've noticed from the photograph.'

'I'm fine with milk.' Yet again, her gaze strayed to the dresser. She was about to ask more but was asked a question herself.

'Have you heard anything from your husband?'

The change of subject was sudden.

Jenny explained that her husband was abroad so wrote infrequently. 'He's never been one for writing letters. Not even when he was serving in France. He served in the last year of the war and was lucky enough to come home unharmed. So many did not,' she added sadly. 'Hard to believe that it ended nearly twenty years ago.'

Nothing more was said. Jenny sipped at her tea. Over the rim of her cup, she noted that her companion's cup was suspended halfway on its journey to her mouth. The face itself had turned as rigid as that of a statue looking down on a tomb and the clear eyes were suddenly misted.

The comparison she'd made that Harriet resembled a statue had come out of nowhere. That's what she told herself. On reflection, it was deadly accurate. Cold and white as marble, she thought, as though she'd suddenly become shrouded in ice. As for the look in those pale blue eyes...

Yet again, Jenny's gaze strayed back to the photographs and the young man who looked so like his father. She presumed he was a brother, one who'd likely died in the war. The wedding couple she presumed was Dorothy and her late husband. She wouldn't ask. This was not the right time to open old wounds and sad memories.

All the same, her eyes returned there again. She just couldn't help herself – and then it struck her. Dorothy's husband looked just like the older man standing in front of the bungalow in India. Had she got this wrong? Were the couple Dorothy's in-laws? She was getting confused and decided it would be rude to ask any more questions.

Harriet had a faraway look, a small frown between her thick eyebrows. Jenny reminded herself that she was bound to be concerned about her sister, Dorothy still being in hospital.

She decided the time had come to leave Harriet to her own thoughts. 'I think I should be going.' She placed her cup and saucer back on the tray and got to her feet. 'I promised Thelma I would do some mending for her. It's the least I can do under the circumstances. Thank you for helping me – and for the tea.'

The ice-white face that had been so still lived again. It was like watching someone waking from a deep sleep. 'I was happy to help. We must have tea together again. I was glad of the company.'

'What will you do for the rest of the afternoon?' Jenny asked her as Harriet escorted her to the door.

'Read the paper. I like to keep abreast of the news.'

'I try not to,' said Jenny. 'It's too worrying, what with all that's happening in Germany. There's even talk of another war. Let's hope that doesn't happen.'

A dark, traumatic look came to Harriet's face. 'No. Let's hope not.'

10

Ruth's funeral occurred a week after the gas explosion and turned out to be a lonely event. Her husband, Isaac, was chief mourner. The only others besides Jenny were ex neighbours from Blue Bowl Alley and workmates from the fruit market. Each one of them offered Isaac their sympathy.

Jenny searched figures wreathed in funereal black for Charlie, but he wasn't there. She couldn't grasp why. He'd gone out of his way to take care of these people and to keep her informed as to how they were. Could it be that they'd only been an excuse to see her?

She asked Isaac whether he had seen Charlie. He shook his head sadly.

'He visited and gave me his condolences but said he wouldn't be able to come today. Politics.' The wetness in his eyes spilled onto the puffiness hanging under them. 'Getting involved with politics is a lonely task and dark too – and half the time thankless.'

Jenny was disappointed and also disbelieving that Charlie regarded politics as more important than seeing old friends in their hour of need. It hurt a little to think that it was also more important too than seeing her.

She said she would see Isaac again, to which he countered that she would not.

'I'm moving in with my sister in Whitechapel, London. She'll look after me.'

It felt to Jenny as though part of her past had broken away. Ruth was gone. Isaac was going. As for Charlie, it almost seemed as though he was in hiding. But why?

* * *

It had been two weeks since the gas explosion at Jenny's place. Council workers had repaired the damage, including installing a new boiler. Like the old one, it was a round galvanised drum but with new pipework and more efficient jets.

From its place in the kitchen, it provided hot water via a four-inch pipe through the wall to the bath. On Mondays, it was full to the brim with laundry and every window in the house still ran with condensation, as they always had.

Life returned to something like normal at number two, Coronation Close, although Jenny did need new curtains and other things to replace those that had been torn to shreds.

Thelma's answer was the jumble sale at St Dunstan's, which had turned out to be an unqualified success.

After a good rummage amongst a pile of fabric and bedding, Thelma threw Jenny a pair of flowery curtains, which she caught with one hand.

'A new pair for the kitchen windows,' she called out.

Thelma bought an ankle-length dress in pale mauve heavyweight lamé.

'You going to a ball, love?' asked the woman behind the counter.

'It's for the street party in May. I'm going as a film star. Hedy Lamarr, I think. Or Jean Harlow. A bit of taking out and it'll do me fine.'

The pale mauve and very sparkly dress wasn't the only one she bought. The others were larger than she presently wore. Some would need letting out. If the worst happened. Thelma stared at these the longest, trying to imagine how it would be and for the most part doing her best to wish it away.

If it comes, it comes, she told herself. *And it'll be loved. After all, it didn't ask to come into the world.*

She bit her lip at the thought of it, but she'd never been one for looking on the dark side of things. There was always a silver lining. That was her creed.

'You've got a load,' Jenny remarked laughingly. 'And they're huge. You'll be clothing the whole street at this rate.'

There was no way Thelma was going to admit that she had a new reason for buying larger clothes and plenty of them. She stuck to her usual reasons. 'The girls are growing up and it isn't every jumble sale you get such nice stuff as they've got here. And all donated for free.'

Rarely did Thelma allow herself to dwell on old memories. The past was like a narrow road to some things she'd prefer to forget. The future was a wider road and the present she could deal with. Some things in her past saddened her – as they did now. Ned, Alice's father, had been in the navy. He'd come back from war blinded when a torpedo had hit the magazine. He'd told her that the shells had shot heavenward like a whole series of rockets on Guy Fawkes Night. They were the last things he'd seen. They'd met some time after that and although he'd suffered from depression, she'd jollied him along in her inimitable way, assuring him that they'd have a great life together.

He'd not shared her positive outlook, not that she'd been aware of that at the time. Before she had chance to tell him she was pregnant – which she was sure would have raised his spirits – he'd climbed up onto the parapet of Clifton Suspension Bridge and thrown himself over. He might have survived if he'd landed in the mud, but not being able to see, he'd felt his way but not got far. When he threw himself over, he landed on the road.

For a few months, she'd been devastated but determined she couldn't be like that for long. She had George and Mary to consider. She'd also had the reason for her thickening girth to consider. A new life had been growing within her – just as it was now. But the circumstances of Alice's conception had been a different matter. She'd loved Ned and consequently loved the baby he'd given her. Finding herself pregnant at her age had unsettled her and put her in two minds of what she really did want. In a way, she didn't want it and had considered seeing a woman she'd heard of over in City Road. On the other hand, she knew she would wonder about how it would turn out as a grown man or woman for the rest of her life. A decision was half formed. As yet, she wasn't sure which way she would go. She needed a little more time.

Back in her living room, Thelma sorted through what she'd bought before putting everything away in a cupboard and getting ready to go out. Bert was taking her to the pictures and she was looking forward to it.

Nowadays, he had his own key. She was standing in front of the full-length mirror of her wardrobe when she heard him come in.

'Won't be long,' she shouted down.

Her dress was navy blue, her hat was red and her coat was

dark blue with a faint red check pattern. It was also a swagger design, fullness falling from the seam at the back of the coat, less so at the front.

Just for the tiniest moment, she took another look in the mirror and laid her hand over her stomach. Nothing much to show yet. Perhaps there never would be. At her age, there was always the chance that she would lose it. In the circumstances, she hoped she'd be out of the woods. But what if she wasn't?

She heard Bert call up the stairs, asking her if she was ready.

What would he do if this baby clung on and was born? Run for the hills. That's what. But in the meantime he was still around and she was grateful for that.

'Coming,' she shouted back down and plastered a smile on her face. Live for the moment. That's what she'd always done and that's what she would do now.

11

It was some time after she'd moved back into her house that Jenny was in Filwood Broadway and spotted a table and chairs in Robin Hubert's shop window. Thanks to the council, her repainted, refurbished kitchen was as neat as a pin. At the window hung the daisy-patterned curtains thrown in her direction at the jumble sale she'd gone to with Thelma. The bulky square table and chairs, the wood dark and too big to fit in the kitchen, took up much-needed space in the living room. When people called, they had to sit on the dining chairs. It was like that in most houses on the estate. Eating meals from a table in the kitchen would be a big improvement.

Gazing at the table and chairs in the window display, Jenny began imagining them in her kitchen. This set looked to be made of pine or some other lighter-coloured wood. She tried to guess at the price. Perhaps ten shillings? Perhaps fifteen or even a pound. Either way, she had a bit to spare this week. Roy's army pay came through like clockwork – over the back fence in the garden, Harriet from next door had told her it did when a soldier served abroad.

The surplus this week was partly due to that but also due to her own diligence. Like Thelma, she had begun making things. The rags left over were stuffed into a sack and sold to the rag and bone man when he came by on his rounds. As well as rags, he'd also given her money for some scrap bits of metal she'd had the presence of mind to store before the council workers could take them away.

For the past few weeks, she'd only waved to Robin from a distance. She'd heard he was living above the shop and that sometimes his children were with him, but not always. His marriage, it seemed, was still fractured. Sad, she thought. Robin deserved to be happy.

He'd wanted her to renew their old friendship, perhaps in time to become more than just a friend. No, she'd told him. She could have added not yet, but at the time had been adamant. Charlie Talbot had been on the scene and it was him that made her heart race.

Previously, there'd been a hand-painted sign hanging in the shop window proclaiming Hubert's Quality Second Hand Furniture. Now the same words were painted in green on a cream background on the fascia board above the shop windows.

There were always people, mostly women, looking in his window, turning over a ten-shilling note when they'd spotted something they needed. That was what happened now.

One woman was remarking to her neighbour that she quite liked the table and chairs Jenny herself was interested in.

'If it's the right price, I might 'ave it.'

Any hesitation on Jenny's part was swiftly ignored. She was a woman on a mission. Nobody else was going to have that dining set if she could help it.

A brass bell, a recent addition in Robin's shop, jangled as she pushed open the door and stepped inside, holding her breath, anticipating the smell of old furniture. She was surprised by the strong smell of beeswax.

Once inside and the door firmly shut behind her, she made for the window display and the dining set she had her eyes on. The women outside the window eyed her with a touch of hostility, even envy, as Jenny ran her hand along the table top.

'Can I 'elp you, love?'

Once she'd turned round and he recognised her, a bright smile spread from ear to ear and Robin exuded warmth, that of a man who was suddenly at total ease.

'Jenny.'

'Nice to see you, Robin.'

'You too.' He jerked his chin at the table and chairs she'd fallen in love with. 'That set in the window caught yer eye, has it?'

A flat cap sat like a plate on his thatch of dark hair. Her neighbour Cath had remarked to her that he looked like a gypsy. 'Not one of them selling pegs. More like that one in that song.'

'A gypsy rover came over the hill?'

Jenny smiled at the memory of that conversation and Cath's confirmation and air of romanticism about the song.

The women leering through the window who had also been interested in the set dispersed. Jenny fancied she could hear their grumbling and wondered what they were up to. They hadn't gone entirely away but stopped and stood some way off, looking at the shop window.

'You have an audience,' she said to Robin, her smile as wide as his.

'Well, you know me. If they can't get Clark Gable, they come for me.'

She laughed and he laughed with her.

'That table and chairs are just the right size to fit in my kitchen,' she said, brushing her hand along the top. The top of the table had a soft velvety feel around it and the colour resembled honey. The chairs too.

Robin tapped the front of his cap with two fingers, sending it to sit further back on his head. 'I hear you had a bit of an accident.'

She nodded. She hadn't been going to mention it, but news got round the estate quickly. 'The boiler I do the washing in. Apparently it had a faulty tap. There was nothing much left of it afterwards.'

She didn't mention that she'd been out that night and come home to devastation. That might lead to more questions, such as who she'd been out with. Neither did she tell him that she'd moved in with Thelma for a few days. He would have said why didn't you come to me. But she couldn't have. Tongues would have wagged; fingers would have been pointed.

Charlie had vanished and not been in touch. He might do one day, or he might not. Sometimes she admitted to herself that she missed Roy's maleness next to her in bed. But that was only sometimes. For the most part, she kept her desires at bay, threw herself into being a housewife and mother, dug in the back garden until her hands were blistered. Robin was saying that he was glad that she and the children were all right.

She replied that they were. 'We were lucky. The council repaired everything and repainted the kitchen.' She stopped trailing her fingers along the table and turned to face him with a happy smile. 'It looks so fresh and clean. Time, I think, to dispose of my old table and chairs – not that there's anything wrong with them,' she added quickly. 'Will you do part exchange?'

He laughed. 'You're taking advantage of my liking for you. You won't be asking to 'ave it on tick as well, will you?'

The small blush she'd had outside the shop intensified.

'No. I won't,' she replied, somewhat defensively. 'I've got

money.' She pulled her purse from her handbag. 'I can give you up to thirty shillings.' There was both defiance and pride in the way she said it.

'Jenny Crawford.' He tutted and shook his head, fists resting on his narrow hips. 'I wouldn't do it for thirty shillings.'

'Oh.' Her high spirits were dented. 'You wouldn't?'

He shook his head again, somewhat more vehemently this time. 'Would I rob a friend? Sight unseen, I'll take your old table and chairs in part exchange. The price will then be ten shillings.'

Her jaw dropped. 'Ten shillings?'

'Ten shillings.'

Robin is a good man, she told herself as she pulled out a ten-shilling note in her purse and handed it to him.

As he took the note, he closed his hand over hers. 'You know I'd do anything for you, Jenny.'

His comment came out of the blue and she was flattered.

'That's good to know. Can I have my hand back now?'

'Reluctantly.' He grinned.

Jenny kept her blushes under control and turned her attention back to the dining suite. 'It's such a lovely colour. Like honey.' She ran her hand along the back of a chair.

'It's pine. It came from a cottage in the country that was being pulled down.'

'It's lovely.'

He grimaced. 'So was the cottage, but it still got pulled down so they could build a longer runway – for aeroplanes. Airfields are sprouting up all over the place.' His grimace deepened. 'I'm trying not to think of the reasons why.'

Jenny didn't want to think why either. The newsreels at the Broadway Picture House painted a worrying picture of men in uniform marching in a place called Nuremburg, or a small man with a toothbrush moustache who had a vision for his country that seemed a bit unnerving to say the least.

Robin's eyes darkened and he frowned. The presence of Jenny Crawford helped disperse the concerns that plagued his mind. 'Now, about delivery...'

'I'm in all week.'

'No need to wait in all week. I'll be around tomorrow.'

* * *

That evening, Jenny told Thelma about her new dining suite that would fit in her kitchen. She also told her that the old dining suite would be collected and taken in part exchange.

'Robin's delivering it tomorrow. He's such a good friend.'

She immediately regretted mentioning how good a friend he was, fully expecting Thelma to rib her about how Robin would like to be more than a friend.

'That's nice.' Such an uncharacteristic response. It seemed Thelma's mind was elsewhere.

'You look tired,' Jenny remarked. Of course that could be all it was, but she couldn't help thinking there was something else. After all, nobody was as energetic and steadfast as Thelma Dawson! But of late her energy had seemed depleted.

Just as she was thinking that, Thelma broke out of her musing, a bright expression flashing like lightning in her eyes. 'It's the street party making me so tired. There's still so much to do.'

'And lots to look forward to,' Jenny agreed, though she didn't entirely believe it to be the reason.

The brightness intensified. 'Yes. I'm doing my best to persuade Bert to come, but he won't come without his mother.

Says he can't leave her alone by herself on such an important day.'

'She hasn't met you.'

Thelma shook her head and looked contrite.

Jenny took it one step further. 'He hasn't told her about you?'

Thelma pulled a face and shrugged her shoulders. 'I'm afraid not.'

Jenny thought it over. Thelma and Bert had been close friends for at least eighteen months, their relationship beginning in the months prior to her arrival in the close. 'Isn't it about time she did know? Don't you think he should tell her? You could write to her.'

'Hah,' returned Thelma, slapping her thigh. 'Like that old cow over the road in number one? You know I shouldn't say this, but I hope and pray that she doesn't come out of hospital ever again. Anyway, it's a coward's way out. If Bert won't tell her about me, then the only alternative is for me to visit her and tell her myself.'

Jenny's jaw dropped. 'You'd really do that?'

This was hardly what she'd had in mind and fancied there was a specific reason for Thelma's flagrant and slightly unnerving statement. Surely it would set Bert's mother against Thelma.

They might have discussed it at further length if George hadn't come barging in the back door, cap set off centre, cheeks flushed and the smell of booze on his breath.

He greeted his mother and Jenny with a cheeky grin, dipped into his pocket and drew out a pair of silk stockings still in their cellophane wrapping.

'What you got there?' asked Thelma, surprise and disapproval etched on her face in equal measure.

He laughed. 'You can see what it is. Stockings. Bought them for one and eleven from a bloke in the pub.'

'Who are they for?'

'A girl,' he replied, his grin expanding into a smirk that Jenny felt bordered on lascivious.

Thelma asked if she had a name and why hadn't he told her before. 'And when's she coming for tea?'

The drink made him wobble a bit, but the smug expression remained. 'I can't bring 'er to tea. I ain't met 'er yet. I give 'er the stockings and she gives me...'

Thelma was up like a flash. She grabbed the stockings, opened the dresser drawer, shoved them in and shut it. She looked furious. Two steps and she was inches from his face, wagging her finger and shouting that she was having none of that in her house. Giving a girl a pair of stockings purely to get his wicked way with her. 'You could ruin a girl's life.'

George almost fell over, just about keeping himself upright by grabbing at the dresser, steadying himself only to have Thelma have another go at him.

'I know what you're up to. And I won't have it, George Dawson. I bloody well won't have it.'

The man that George Dawson had grown into vanished. He was again the little boy Thelma had brought up by herself, praised when he did right and shamed when he did wrong.

Befuddled by drink, he looked unsure what to say or what to do.

Thelma made the decision for him, pointing a manicured, red-painted finger at the living-room door. 'Get to bed, George Dawson. And don't let me see you until you're sober.'

Amazingly, he did as she ordered, looking confused and instantly sober.

Even after he'd gone, Thelma's anger remained. Her face was flushed, her shoulders rigid, her eyes downcast to the hearth-rug that couldn't possibly share any blame.

'Thelma. I'd better be going.'

Thelma shuddered as she came to, blinking at Jenny as though she'd forgotten she was there. She clapped a hand to her heart, sat down. Her breathing was erratic.

Feeling instantly concerned, Jenny urged her to take deep breaths. 'Do you really think he would do what you said – you know – give a girl a pair of stockings in exchange for sex?'

Thelma sat back in her chair. For the first time since Jenny had known her, she looked defeated and incredibly angry. Was it all down to George? Jenny wasn't convinced. Thelma had acted a bit strange for some time. She couldn't put her finger on it with any great certainty. In time, Thelma might disclose what was troubling her.

When Thelma at last raised her eyes, Jenny had expected the forthright look to be back. To her dismay, they were moist with tears.

'Oh Jenny. I don't know what to do. It wasn't my fault and I'm all at sixes and sevens...' Her bottom lip quivered, the words dried up and she sobbed.

Jenny felt at a loss. Ever since she'd known her – which admittedly wasn't that long – she'd regarded Thelma as – not exactly formidable – but pragmatic, the kind who could sort things out when nobody else could.

'What is it? What's wrong?'

Thelma sniffed, got out a handkerchief and blew her nose. She shook her head, held it a bit higher, then set her jaw firm. 'Sometimes I hate men.'

There was nothing Jenny could say except that sometimes she did too – which seemed a bit lame.

Thelma's watery eyes held hers as she said, 'I'm expecting.'

Jenny's jaw dropped as she processed several thoughts, questions that popped into her mind.

'Is it...?'

Thelma shook her head vehemently. 'Bert's? No. Bert is a gentleman – one of the few I've ever met.'

'Then who?'

Thelma blew her nose again, took a deep breath and began to outline what had happened to bring her to this sorry state.

'Do you remember that blizzard back in January on the night when George was due home?'

Jenny nodded silently and waited for Thelma to continue.

'I was late home from work because I'd had to walk.'

'The bus broke down. I remember you saying.'

'That's right.' She paused. 'That was when it happened. I didn't know him. He helped me down off the platform and then offered to accompany me through the snow. If I'd put my boots on that morning instead of my court shoes, I might not have been slipping and sliding all over the place. Anyway, he took my arm. Seemed kind of him at first – until we got to the top of Donegal Road where the houses fall back behind the trees. You know where I mean? That little cul-de-sac set around the green. Just a path going round. It was pitch black there.'

She looked down at her handkerchief as she twisted it around one thumb and then the other. Her eyes remained downcast.

'I screamed and shouted, but nobody would have heard in that storm. The houses were too far away and there wasn't a solitary soul around.' She raised her head. Her eyes, still glistening with unshed tears, looked at Jenny. 'It wasn't my fault, Jenny. There was nothing I could do to fight him off.'

'Of course you weren't to blame, Thelma. Of course you weren't.' She swallowed. 'Have you told anyone else? George? Bert? Anyone?' She didn't mention the police, who tended to take a hostile view. What was she doing taking the arm of a man she didn't know on a pitch-black night? She was asking for it. That's what they tended to say.

Again, a shaking of Thelma's head. 'I've only told you and the truth is... I'm not sure I've got the heart to get rid of it. I'd feel so guilty, but on the other hand... What shall I do, Jenny? What shall I do?'

Taken aback, Jenny looked down at her hands. Never had she seen Thelma look so dejected or so confused. On the surface, her dear friend and neighbour was full of confidence. Beneath the surface lurked a more uncertain person, a soft centre.

She thought about Cath buying the laxatives in the chemist. It had worked for her. She mentioned it to Thelma.

She shook her head. 'I've already tried them. It didn't work.' She took a deep breath. 'There's a woman in City Road. I might have to go to her, but time's marching on. I'll have to go soon or keep it. Poor thing didn't ask to come into the world, did it? The woman in City Road could get rid of it for me – for a price.'

Jenny didn't mention that she knew that woman, had made use of her services when she'd found herself pregnant again and unable to face the consequences – especially with Roy the way he was.

She bit her bottom lip, then cautiously said, 'I've heard of that woman, but could you do it. Could you really do that?'

The broad shoulders shrugged from beneath her favourite green satin blouse. 'I don't know.'

Silence reigned until Jenny finally advised her to sleep on it.

'It's a big decision, but it's your decision Thelma. Remember that any time of the day or night I'm there if you need me.'

12

Thoughts of Thelma and her little problem were still in Jenny's thoughts the next day. She recalled the snowstorm on the night George had come home and that Thelma had arrived home late. It had been somewhat surprising, given how much she'd been looking forward to his return.

Since then, she'd told nobody about what had happened to her except for Jenny. How far gone must she be? Three months? If she did decide to get rid of it, she'd have to do it soon. The thought of it cast a gloom over the morning, one spent in general housework and some mending, but it was hard to concentrate. It also kept thoughts of Charlie from her mind. For the most part, she now accepted that he was out of her league.

In between household tasks, she got up and looked out of the window across to number twelve, Thelma's house. Her gaze travelled across the green and around the close to the other houses, grouped in a horseshoe fashion, the narrow access road keeping them apart from the green and the trees in the middle. Thelma had been so looking forward to the coronation street party and still was. Busying herself in the preparations was no doubt keeping her predicament from her mind.

Jenny was just about to turn back to the pile of freshly ironed bedding. It had taken the last two hours to iron and was now ready to be put away in the airing cupboard. The airing cupboard was at the side of the fireplace in the living room. It was whilst she was doing this that her attention was suddenly drawn to the sight of an ambulance coming into the close and pulling up outside number one.

The doors of the ambulance were thrown open. A figure emerged swathed in blankets and was taken into next door by two ambulancemen. Snatches of conversation drifted in her direction – the Crittall windows kept out little sound and not enough wintry weather.

She couldn't see from her living-room window but presumed that Harriet had answered the door. Her immediate conclusion was that Dorothy was home from hospital.

So how would it be inside that pristine house now she was home? Not warmer, she thought. Dorothy didn't come over as a warm person though she sympathised that she'd been in hospital. She didn't so much feel sorry for Dorothy as she did for Harriet, who had admitted that things were much more peaceful without her. She wondered how long it would be before Dorothy was healthy enough to return to her old ways. Thelma was the number one subject of her malice, though she wasn't the only one.

I might be next, Jenny thought to herself. How long would it be before Dorothy learned that Harriet had invited her for tea within the hallowed portals of number one, Coronation Close? She couldn't see her liking it. Dorothy wasn't the sort to welcome visitors, though Jenny had seen the vicar call in.

Poor Harriet. She felt sorry for her. She'd been so nice, so open until mention of the army that is.

Well, the ice had been broken. With an air of resolution, Jenny determined to knock on her door now Dorothy was home, perhaps take in a few homemade rock cakes. *One good turn deserves another*, she thought – at least as far as the amiable Harriet was concerned.

And what about the things that had happened in her absence? Would Harriet tell her sister any of it? She presumed she would learn of the gas explosion, though doubted she would approve of her sister's act of kindness inviting her in for tea and most definitely not inviting her to move in for a while.

Today wasn't the time to present herself at the door of number one. Besides which her new table and chairs were being delivered.

Just after lunch, Robin arrived, his van pulling up outside in a puff of blue smoke, the crunching of worn gears enough to set teeth on edge.

She waved at him from the front door. He waved back, then beckoned her.

'You take two chairs; I'll take two, then we'll handle the table between us.'

Being smaller, the new table and chairs were easy enough, but heaving out the old oak table took some doing, but a quick shout to George, who was on his way out, made the job a lot easier. The chairs were not such a problem.

Jenny stood there admiring her new furniture, feeling lighter for several reasons, mostly because there seemed to be much more room. A shaft of springtime sunshine chose that moment to show its face. What with its fresh paint and pine furniture, the kitchen gleamed.

Jenny sighed with happiness. It really was like a picture in a magazine. There was so much more space. Without the dining table clogging up the centre of the living room, the second-hand armchairs and settee were accessible. A floor lamp with a parchment shade was more easily seen. The bamboo table on which the wireless balanced looked less crowded, hidden as it had been against the wall. The dresser drawers and cupboards were easier to open.

Undoubtedly, the living room was much improved, but as far as Jenny was concerned, it was the kitchen that took centre stage. The light-coloured country-style furniture and daisy-patterned curtains and the sunshine coming through the window made it glow. In fact, it seemed more like May than April, inside the house as well as outside.

In the garden, early buds had appeared on the apple tree, vegetables were sending green shoots through the dark earth, along with the peeping heads of cowslips, remnants of the meadow that used to be from the time when the estate was fields. The smell of spring was in the air.

Absorbed in her thoughts, Jenny forgot that Robin was still there, one elbow bent and resting on the door surround, a slight smile tweaking his lips as he watched her looking so pleased with everything.

Receiving no reaction from her, he eventually asked, 'How about a cuppa after all that 'ard work?'

It was as though she'd awoken from a deep sleep.

She laughed in a light-hearted, distracted manner. 'Oh, Robin. I'm so sorry. I forgot you were there. I'll fill the kettle.'

Robin continued to watch her. He loved her laughter, loved the fact that in some small way he'd brought her happiness. Amazing, he thought, what a bit of old furniture could do.

She wasn't to know that he'd paid more than he'd sold it to her. That was for him to know and keep locked away. Like his love for her. That too was locked away, ready to be declared when the moment was right. He couldn't guess as to when that would be, but one thing he had in abundance was patience. He would never have put up with Doreen so long if he hadn't had patience.

Water gushed from the tap into the kettle. As she filled it, he got out a box of matches and lit the gas. The kettle went straight onto it.

'I'm so grateful,' she said to him. 'You've been so kind. I'm sure you would have got more than ten shillings for it.'

'We're old mates,' he said, unwilling to admit anything. He pulled out one of the new chairs from beneath the table. 'If you can't 'elp an old mate, then you ain't worth a light.'

He lit up a cigarette. Jenny provided an old tea saucer to use as an ashtray.

She was wary of asking whether he was still living apart from Doreen and how often he got to see the children. Best, she decided, to stick to details of his furniture business. His personal life was a mess, his marriage broken. She feared going there.

Pouring tea into his cup, she asked how the business was doing. 'Any plans to expand?'

After swigging his tea, he wiped his mouth and looked pleased with himself when he outlined what he was planning. 'I'm reopening the pawnbroking business. There's a need for it around 'ere, so might as well jump in.'

'Will you be able to manage?' she asked whilst pouring a second helping of tea and spooning sugar into his cup.

'I'll need to employ someone. I can't do it all meself.'

She didn't ask about his wife helping. She already knew the answer to that. As it turned out, he mentioned her first.

'I need to make more money. Doreen wants a toaster and loads of other things besides.'

'That's expensive.'

'Yeah, and even though we're separated, she says I've got a responsibility to keep 'er just as if we were still together. I told 'er to use a toasting fork like everybody else, but she weren't 'aving none of that. She wants a toaster that she can plug in. And one of them irons that plugs in to the light socket.'

Jenny puffed out her cheeks. 'Goodness. I'd like one too, but for now it's the old way.'

In the world she knew, there were two heavy irons placed on the hobs at the side of the fire. Or on the gas. Either way, that was the accepted way of ironing and hadn't changed much for over a hundred years or more. Take one off, put the other one on; once the heat had gone out of one, it was put back on the gas and the one heated taken off and used. It took hours, but that was how it was.

She didn't like to say that Doreen was very grasping, but Robin said it for her.

'She sees advertisements for modern things and thinks she can have them.'

Setting his cup in the saucer, he took off his cap, leaned forward and ran one hand through his hair. He looked exasperated and worn out.

'I told 'er that if she wants all that stuff she 'as to get a job or 'elp me in the shop. I made the mistake of suggesting she run the pawnbroking side of the business.' He shook his head dolefully. 'No chance. Blew up. Said she weren't going to handle dirty people's dirty clothes and stuff. I said to her that it was mostly family valuables: watches, clocks, jewellery... I didn't mention a woman bringing in the old man's suit on a Monday and retrieving it on a Friday. That's the bread-and-butter side of the business, little things for small money that 'elps people out, but suggesting it was all gold and silver, watches, clocks and stuff cut no ice anyway. When Doreen makes her mind up...'

Jenny noted the sudden sloping of his shoulders, the continuous shaking of his head. He looked beaten, worn down by work and the demands of his wife. The poor chap didn't know what to do. That much was evident. Doreen sounded a right Tartar. She vaguely remembered seeing them courting together. Her laugh had been too loud and the way she'd clasped Robin's arm to her side had been possessive – I've got you and you're not getting away.

Before he'd arrived, Jenny had vowed not to encourage him in any way, but this was a man deserving of her sympathy. It was hard not to resist reaching out and stroking his arm. She curled her fingers into the palm of her hand to restrain from doing it.

Robin emptied his cup and once his whistle was wetted went on to say, 'I hear she's been carrying on with the landlord of the place she's living. Gettin' a discount on the rent, I should think. Quite a big one.'

His sneer was both contemptuous and despairing.

He must be missing his children, Jenny thought. Children always came first, no matter how bad the marriage. Deep down, she knew Robin would be back with Doreen like a shot just for their sake, but it seemed Doreen had other plans. She didn't want to be tied down, he said to her. To which Jenny replied, 'Well, she should have thought of that in the first place before she married you.'

She couldn't help her heart going out to him. Against all that she'd promised herself, she weakened, reached out and lightly touched his hand. 'I'm so sorry, Robin. If there's anything I can do...'

The kiss on the back of her hand came sudden and unexpected.

Jenny broke the connection and drew back.

'You shouldn't have done that.'

An apologetic but plaintive look came to his face. 'I needed to. You should know that. I've always loved you, Jenny. Me old mum, bless 'er 'eart, used to say that I should 'ave married you and I would 'ave, if Roy hadn't come along and swept you off yer feet.'

Her blood was racing and her heart was beating like a drum behind her ribcage. How long had it been since a man had kissed her? Charlie! Some weeks ago now. He'd made her blood race too, more than any other man ever had. But time had drifted on. She still wondered why he'd shot off that night and not got in touch, but thinking about it was too depressing.

And here was Robin making his feelings clear with a kiss on the back of her hand.

'History, Robin. It's all history.'

He looked directly into her eyes. 'We've almost got the same history. I only wish we could go back and do things differently. Don't you feel like that sometimes?'

'Time only goes forward, not backward.'

She didn't protest when she felt his blunt, strong fingers caressing hers. Her throat felt tight. She swallowed. She thought about saying that Roy wouldn't like it, but the new Roy was unlikely to care. He had his own brand of love, though perhaps in his own way, he still loved her.

'How about you come to the pub with me on Saturday night?'

Her first inclination was to refuse. Tongues had wagged when she'd been seen going off with Charlie in his car – though she had made it clear that they were visiting the hospital to see a sick friend of mutual acquaintance.

Another lonely weekend loomed. Yes, there were her female friends and although she valued their friendships, it wasn't enough.

She nodded, her eyes downcast as she said yes, she would

love to. It wasn't so much that she was being bashful; she didn't want him to see the sudden brightness in her eyes.

'I'll pick you up in the van,' he said, his eyes as bright as her own, hardly daring to believe his luck.

'No.' She shook her head. 'I don't want to set tongues wagging. I'll get the bus. We can meet in town. That would be best.'

'On the steps outside the Hippodrome? Say seven?'

'Yes. That would work for me.'

She could see he was tempted to kiss her again before leaving, not her hand this time, but her lips. To his credit, he controlled himself and desisted.

'I'll be seeing you.'

She smiled warmly and watched him whistling his way down the garden path, hands tucked into his pockets, his customary habit, cap at a jaunty angle on his head. Instead of opening the front gate, he vaulted over it as though leaping with joy. Once on the pavement, he patted his van on the roof as though it were a pet dog, got in and drove away.

He looked a lot happier on leaving than when he'd arrived and so was she.

13

It was a Saturday and on Monday Thelma's son George was going back to sea.

'He's going away aged twenty and when he comes back he'll be twenty-one,' she declared solemnly.

A farewell tea was enjoyed by all the family, plus Bert, who had been invited because he'd offered to do her a favour.

At one time, Thelma had met Bert on the other side of Melvin Square at the beginning of Daventry Road. That was in the days when she'd worried about what the neighbours might say. Nowadays, she didn't give a hoot and especially not this evening. Besides, this evening he was taking George to the station and afterwards taking Thelma for a drink, probably at the Shakespeare Inn in Victoria Street.

There'd been no further mention from Cath about her old man seeing Bert out and about when he should have been home, and she wasn't letting herself worry about it.

Alice and Mary had agreed to do the washing up whilst Bert and their mother took George to the station.

Whilst Bert did his bit, wiping the dishes the girls were

washing up, George got his mother alone in the hallway. He looked concerned.

'You sure you're all right, Ma? You look a bit paler than usual.'

Thelma laughed it off and made an excuse. 'That's because I forgot to put on some lipstick. See?'

She got a lipstick from out of her handbag. Before applying it to her lips, she took in the face that looked back at her. George was right. She was paler than usual. It might have been better if she had changed from red to pink lipstick, though that had been purely an excuse.

'As long as you're all right, Ma.'

'Fine,' she said as they hugged and kissed before she reached for her coat.

On their way to the station, George was sitting in the back seat. The incident with the stockings had been forgotten, not that her flying off the handle had had the desired effect. When she'd searched for the stockings he'd intended using to bribe a young and unknown lady into him having his wicked way, they were gone from the dresser drawer.

Desperately needing to part on good terms, she chose not to mention the fact. Who knew when she'd next see him?

'Now you've got everything,' she said to George over her shoulder.

'All present and correct, sir!' He gave smart salute as though she was admiral of the fleet, or captain at least.

'Cheeky devil,' she said, touched but tearful as she turned back to the front. Her boy was off again. Just as well in a way. He wouldn't know about her dire predicament. Whatever would he think, a young man with a pregnant mother? Come to that, what would Bert think? At some point, she would have to tell him. It was just a case of when.

She vowed that when she got back home she would take more

Penny Royals. She prayed that this time it would work – before it was too late.

Her eyes watered as she looked ahead to the road down from the estate, through Bedminster and along the Bath Road to Temple Meads Station, the main terminus in Bristol.

The night was fine, the gothic-style spires of the station silhouetted against an indigo sky. Ragged clouds drifted across the moon.

Bert drove his car to where half a dozen taxis were lined up, their drivers talking in a group beneath the canopy outside the station. The tips of cigarettes glowed in the dark. The cabbies glanced their way before going back to their smoking and their conversation.

Thelma and Bert escorted George up the incline, over the crumpled flagstones of the forecourt and into the station.

Bert offered to buy platform tickets for himself and Thelma. George told him not to bother.

'It's not worth it. My train won't be long.'

Thelma was disappointed but acknowledged his wishes. However, the yearning to hang onto him as long as possible was overpowering.

'I'm going to miss you like mad,' she said, as she hugged him and rained kisses on his cheeks.

'Ma, I'm too big for all this. People are looking.' George looked and sounded mortified, face pink with embarrassment.

Thelma was unrepentant. 'You'll never be too big. Let your mother have a last cuddle before you go away. I won't take no for an answer.'

Amid the steamy station where grit from locomotive fireboxes hung in the air and stuck in the throat, she saw him exchange a knowing look with Bert. She'd welcomed the fact that they'd had a few heart-to-hearts during George's leave. She'd wanted them to get on. Bert knew what it was like to have a doting mother. Thinking of her made her finally unlock her arms from around her son. She wouldn't want to be regarded as clinging. That would never do.

More tears ensued, though she tried to hold onto them until George had waved goodbye and disappeared through the portal and onto the station. He was off to Portsmouth to join his ship and from then goodness knew where.

'Looked smart in his uniform didn't he, Bert?'

Bert, knowing very well how she was feeling, wrapped an arm around her and gave her a bigger hug than she'd given her son. 'He did indeed, my love. Smart lad that. I wouldn't be surprised that promotion could very well be on the cards for your George whether he stays in the Merchant Marine or joins the Royal Navy, and quite frankly I for one think he deserves it. A fine boy, but then that's no major surprise. He's got a fine mother. You should be proud of him – proud of yourself too.'

'I am,' said Thelma, much comforted by Bert's words and the warm arm that lay heavily around her shoulders and held her close.

She continued to dab at her eyes when they were sitting in a city centre pub – The Shakespeare, a long narrow bar, bench seating ranged along the wall, small round tables at regular intervals.

A drop of brandy helped her recovery and so did the honky-tonk playing of a piano, though at times the pianist seemed to miss as many notes as he hit. The row of pint glasses, most still full, might have had something to do with that, she thought and managed a smile.

As with any city-centre pub, the air was thick with smoke and the smell of strong beer. There were few who weren't smoking a cigarette and one or two were taking puffs on a pipe.

Seamen, Thelma thought, judging by the thick fug they exhaled into the air. Black Navy Shag was a big favourite with men who went to sea in boats.

Raucous laughter took her attention to a woman sandwiched between two men. She was looking from one to the other. In one hand, she held what looked like a port and lemon or perhaps a sherry. Her other hand was out of sight. When it hit Thelma what she was doing – something far too physical to be done in public, Thelma felt her face reddening.

'What a hussy,' she said, perhaps a trifle too loudly.

If the woman heard, she didn't care. She was enjoying herself with her drink, her cigarettes and her men. Thelma studied her, noticed the three-inch feather in her hat, the fox fur snuggled around her shoulders. It was too warm for a fox fur. She guessed it was being worn for effect rather than to keep the chill off.

'Fancy another?' asked Bert.

Thelma shook her head. 'Just for once, I'm going to say no.'

'Tired?'

She smiled a wan smile and nodded. 'It's been a long day. Thanks for giving him a lift.'

'My pleasure.'

At that moment, she felt more cherished than she'd ever felt in her life. Bert wasn't the sort to charm a woman, but he was kind. He wasn't exciting, but he was dependable, and that, she'd long ago realised, was more important than anything.

They had a cuddle and a kiss in the car before entering Coronation Close.

'You feel lovely and cuddly,' he said to her. 'I do like a cuddly woman.'

She pushed away from him. 'Are you saying I'm fat?'

'What's wrong with that? I'm saying I don't like scrawny women. They're not healthy.'

She realised she'd been too defensive and regretted it. Bert knew nothing of her predicament and, as yet, nobody could tell. But deep in her mind the worry gnawed at her insides.

'Sorry,' she said, giving him a quick kiss on the cheek. 'Didn't mean to snap. Am I forgiven?'

'Course you are.'

He gave her one final lip-smacking kiss.

At the end of the street, she got out and headed for home. It was gone ten o'clock and the street lights had gone off, consequently she hurried to her front gate, a shiver of apprehension going with her. Dark nights had never worried her that much, but memories of that snowy night had made her nervous.

As instructed, the girls were already in bed. A handful of Penny Royals were swallowed with a glass of water. She still couldn't stomach cocoa before retiring. Tonight, she just wanted to snuggle down under the bedclothes.

Before doing so, she checked on the girls and found them both sound asleep. Like her, they'd got used to George being home and had been sad at his going and it touched her heart. She badly wanted to stroke each dear head but restrained herself. They needed their sleep and so did she.

Once between the covers, her bedroom now to herself, she reached across and turned off her bedside light.

Her head hit the pillow and she slept.

* * *

Thelma didn't know what time it was when she felt the first pain. It started sharp and got steadily sharper, made her gasp and reach out for the bedside light.

The bulb blinked into life. Suddenly, she needed the bathroom. Sliding the bedclothes back as far as her belly, she brought one leg, then the other out of bed. The pain was intense, yet she welcomed it, hoped it would bring forth what she so much wanted.

Part of her was scared, the other regretful, but whatever her feelings, the girls mustn't see it! That was her first response. The girls must not know.

On weak legs, she made her way downstairs. The blood wasn't flowing too strongly just yet, but she knew it would. There was a heaviness bearing down between her legs. More blood was bound to come.

Everything she needed – water, soap, a flannel and sanitary pads – was down in the cupboard in the bathroom.

She reached for the switch that would turn on the light on the landing so she could see her way downstairs, then stopped. It might wake the girls up.

Grasping the banister, she made her way down the stairs one cautious step at a time in the dark. Once downstairs, she turned on both the living-room and kitchen light, then the bathroom. There was respite there, coolness, somewhere to sit whilst she collected herself above the pain.

For an hour, perhaps more, she sat there, her head resting against the coldness of the cistern pipe behind her, eyes closed. What she'd longed and hoped for had finally happened. The child born of a rape on a snowy night would not be born. Of that she was now sure. But all the same, the tears came, streaming down her face whilst the blood streamed from between her legs.

As she sat there, she cursed the man who had caused this to happen. Selfishly determined to have what he wanted, he had not considered what she wanted. Neither had he considered the life or death of the child conceived of his violence. For all the hurt, she cursed him. For all the worry, all the pain both for herself and for the baby that would never be born, never live. She cursed him and swore under her breath, desperate to keep the noise down, but so wanting to tell him face to face of the pain he had caused. Not that it was at all likely that she'd ever run into him again. Even if she did, she wouldn't recognise him, except perhaps for his smell, the tobacco, the sweat ingrained on his skin and his clothes. In the meantime, her life had been saved and the life of the baby had never begun.

Despite everything, the pain, the mix of emotions, both anger and fear, she forced herself to cope. She averted her eyes as she wrapped up the bloodied mass ejected from her body. Still gripped by afterpains, she made her way into the living room. The fire had burnt low, but the coals were aglow. Carefully, almost reverently, she placed the newspaper and its contents onto the fire. Once the paper had caught, she turned her head away. It was over. For both of them.

14

It was the first week of May and the time for celebration was drawing near.

'It's almost as though the very air has changed,' remarked the man who was known as Harriet and lived in number one Coronation Close with his supposed sister, who was actually his wife. 'I hear we're having a street party. They've been organising it for months, since before the abdication of King Edward in fact. Seems very apt to my mind, seeing as we live in Coronation Close.' He paused before suggesting to Dorothy that she might like to attend.

She sniffed. 'Dancing and eating with these common people? Whatever next?'

He took a deep breath before daring to continue, to rebel against his wife, to make the decision as to what he wanted to do. 'I'm going to join in. I think it could be very enjoyable.'

Dorothy looked at her husband with daggers in her eyes. 'You can't. People will see you and you know what will happen then. Someone will be suspicious. Someone might recognise you. The police will come knocking at the door and they'll take you away. They'll put you in prison. They might even shoot you.'

He breathed a great gasp of exasperation. 'They will see me as Harriet. They've never seen me as anything else.'

'How could you demean yourself like that! Mixing with those people.' She sniffed contemptuously. 'The lowest of the low, all of them!'

'That's unfair. They're just ordinary working-class people. Salt of the earth, some would say.'

'Well I wouldn't! They disgust me. As for you...' Dorothy made a huffing sound and turned her head away. Her period of hospital rest had not done anything for her anxiety or the moments of overpowering anger, one of which had caused her to fall down the stairs in the first place. She'd blamed one of her headaches. She was always having headaches and 'spasms', as she called them.

Unwilling to disclose any of this, she had instructed her husband that should anyone ask why she'd gone into hospital, it was due to women's problems. Describing her illness as such encapsulated so many things, yet really said nothing very much.

Dorothy was obsessed in how she was perceived by her neighbours. In her own mind, she regarded herself as a cut above them. The fact that she and her husband Harry were living a lie didn't count, simply because nobody knew about it. Flanders and France were still like a sore wound in the public perception. Over the long years since he'd deserted, living a lie had become merely a truth born of expediency.

Uppermost in her mind was the fear of her neighbours finding out about their true circumstances, including her moods, her mental state, her outbursts of temper.

She turned suddenly and glared at him. 'Don't go telling

people I'm mad or anything like that. Or I'll tell them what you are. A deserter. A coward.'

Harry had heard it all before, though never with quite the intensity as of late. The fact was that she was getting more vindictive, more anxious.

With the aid of a walking stick, she headed for the green Moquette armchair set in front of the living-room window. From here, she had an unobstructed view of the comings and goings of her neighbours.

'Get me another cup of tea. I could be here some time.'

'Would you like me to turn on the wireless set?'

Dorothy shook her head. 'No. I can't concentrate on that and our neighbours. And fetch me a pen and paper.'

Harry groaned. 'Not another letter! No, Dot. No! I forbid you to write another one.'

Dorothy laughed. 'Forbid! Forbid? Don't give me orders, Harry Partridge. I'll do what I like.'

There came a series of tuts from the other side of the room, where crockery was being loaded onto the dresser. Harry shook his head. 'I just cannot understand how you can be so cruel.'

Dorothy turned away from the window, pinpricks of colour on her wan cheeks, her eyes glittering from inside deep wells. 'Cruel? How about the cruelties that were done to us? We can't even be open about our relationship. We couldn't be from the first. Your mind was addled back then. You shook with fear and jumped like a rabbit when a door was slammed. If I hadn't taken charge of matters, you would have been dragged in front of a firing squad for cowardice. As it is, you're still in danger of a prison sentence – and where would you be then? Where would I be for that matter?'

She knew her barb had hit home, that the fear felt for years was undiminished. And wasn't it down to her that they were still together? That she'd shielded him from the consequences?

Nobody knew their secret and they never would. To all intents and purposes, they were sisters, both war widows, and that was the way things would stay.

Shoulders hunched over the draining board, head lowered, the cruel words seared into his brain. Harry contemplated all that had happened. He recalled how he'd felt back in that terrible war and although he knew he would never be quite the same he regarded himself as better than he had been. But he worried about Dorothy. She too had been affected by the war, how they'd had to live such an unnatural existence. That, he decided, was what had made her the way she was.

Unlike Dorothy, he hadn't held himself entirely aloof from their neighbours. Although not intending to, he had got involved, principally with Mrs Crawford next door. First, he had rescued her from a beating by her husband, and then that creep from the council. Both circumstances had gone some way to resurrecting the man he'd always been and still was inside. Recently, he'd even begun greeting neighbours he recognised when he passed them out shopping. At first, they'd looked surprised to hear him speak. He'd purposely kept his voice as soft and as light as possible. Dorothy insisted that he would be Harriet until the end of his days. She hadn't been amused when he'd mentioned that the undertaker was going to get a shocking surprise once he saw him naked. It had made him chuckle. Dorothy had scowled.

Dorothy stretched her neck. In times past, her slim and sinuous neck had been likened to a swan. Age and a malice acquired from circumstances that had embittered her had made it scrawny.

'Her from across the road is home. It must be Wednesday afternoon. Half day at Bertrams on a Wednesday afternoon.'

'It is Wednesday afternoon.'

She didn't answer. It was as though she hadn't heard or had not taken in what he'd said. She was doing that more and more of late. Not in a big way. Not yet. But, day-by-day, a little piece of her was disappearing. What would he do when one way or another she had left him? He stared out of the kitchen window at the well-kept borders, the neat rows of vegetables, the six-foot canes around which the young runner beans were climbing.

Dorothy's voice carried from the living room. 'Never mind about that tea. She's out there at number five. I can't see what she's up to from here, but I need to keep my eye on her. Can never tell what she's up to.' It was a struggle to get up from the chair, but Dorothy was nothing if not a determined woman and refused to give way to the onset of infirmities. 'I'll go out and finish cutting the privets and see what's going on.'

* * *

Thelma was intent on what she was doing, banging hard on the door of number five. She hadn't seen Mrs Russell since the weekend when she'd taken her a meal. The old dear had lived alone for a while and although she had a son, he worked away. Thelma could only call in on those days when she wasn't at work. Weekends or Wednesday afternoons, but since George had been home, her visits had been less frequent.

However, she was not so wrapped up in her task that she didn't notice a curtain flickering across at number one.

'Nosy old cow.'

Thelma had gone into Mrs Russell's last Sunday week with two fresh faggots that she'd made that morning. Mrs Russell had been slumped in her chair. Within reach on the floor at her side were half a dozen bottles of brown ale.

Can't blame her, Thelma had thought. At her age and all alone, what else was there.

'Are you all right, Sybil?' she'd asked.

The old lady had shaken her head in a way that made it seem as though her neck was too fragile to support the effort. 'I didn't want to wake up this morning.'

'Now come on, Sybil. Don't be so down. Life in the old girl yet,' she'd said. 'Do you like me blouse? I could make you one if you like.'

Sybil had seen the blouse before and had always taken a keen interest in how she looked.

Thelma had sat a while and made conversation. 'Heard from yer son lately?'

'No.' She didn't seem that concerned. It was as though she'd given up on everything including life itself.

Thelma wished she'd called in since Sunday, but what with her own little happening... But at least her girls hadn't known about it. She'd staggered over to Jenny's, told her what had happened, got fresh sanitary towels and sworn her to secrecy.

Too many days had passed since the last time she'd called on the old lady. She felt guilty about it. Even on that Sunday visit, Sybil had taken a while to answer the front door. Today, no matter how much she knocked, there was no response. Panic began like a tickling in her stomach and spread like a chill throughout her body.

On the other side of the road, she was aware of the front door of number one opening. Shears in hand, Mrs Partridge appeared. Her hair pulled back from her forehead and a tight bun on the nape of her neck was held in place with a hairnet. Her crossover apron – the most ageing item of clothing ever invented in Thelma's opinion – was floral and rust coloured. Her neck was encircled with a white collar, more suited to a child's dress than a grown woman. Her facial features looked more pinched than usual. Well, she had just come out of hospital. One arm appeared stiff as she attacked the top of hedges that didn't look in need of trimming.

Thelma glared at her.

Some time ago, she'd overheard Dorothy speaking to the rent collector in a very loud voice. 'Mrs Russell drinks. She goes up to the off licence at the pub with a big shopping bag, and when she gets back, it's full of brown ales. I've heard them rattling. I wrote a letter to the council about it. Disgusting it is. Plain disgusting!'

The conversation and Dorothy's vitriolic voice had stayed with her, causing Thelma to grind her teeth and mutter under her breath. She felt Dorothy's eyes at her back. She was out there snipping away, determined to see what was going on. Even without seeing her face, Thelma could feel the malice winging across from the other side of the road. The sensation was like that when a wasp is hovering around and determined to sting. She gritted her teeth some more. Even the pain of the miscarriage was as nothing compared with putting up with Dorothy Partridge.

Despite all the hammering, the door in front of her remained firmly closed. Out of the corner of her eye, she espied Cath hurrying in her direction, metal curlers bouncing beneath a plaid headscarf. Her arms hugged a dusky pink cardigan together around her midriff. Her skirt was faded and she slopped along stocking-less in a pair of old slippers. She was looking old before her time, not that Thelma would say so. Every so often, she offered to do her hair or offered her a lipstick or powder compact not quite yet empty enough to throw out.

Cath stopped by Mrs Russell's front gate. 'Blimey, Thelma, your 'ammering on that door is enough to wake the dead. Somefin wrong is there?'

'Have you seen anything of Mrs Russell of late? I haven't had the time to call in and check on her what with one thing and another.'

'Can't say that I 'ave.'

Apprehensive and feeling a big need for support, Thelma's gaze strayed across the road. 'What about Jenny?'

Cath shook her head. 'I don't think so.'

Mrs Russell kept herself to herself and although she rarely appeared outside or joined in to gossip with the other women, they did keep an eye on her.

Neighbours curious to find out what the noise was all about were coming out of doors now, wandering over to stand at the garden gate of number five. All except Jenny Crawford.

Thelma guessed where she might be but wasn't going to mention it. Jenny had only gone out once with Robin Hubert, but she did dally with him up at his shop in Filwood. Dallying was about it for now. The girl was still mooning after that Charlie Talbot bloke. He hadn't come to the shop again after Thelma saw him that time with the rich woman. So far, she'd not mention it to Jenny and wasn't sure she ever would.

Thelma stepped back, bent her head back and looked up at the front bedroom window. She shouted as loud as she could. 'Sybil? Sybil, are you in there? Are you all right?'

Realistically, it was a daft thing to do. If Sybil hadn't heard her banging the knocker, she wasn't likely to hear her shouting.

Apprehension churned in her stomach. 'I don't like this.'

'Should we fetch a policeman?' Cath shivered.

'Not yet.' She made her way along the narrow concrete path in front of the living-room window and looked in through the crack in the curtain. 'Can't see a bloody thing.'

It wasn't like her to swear and feel so helpless, but she was beginning to feel frustrated.

'Did I tell you I ain't in the club any more,' Cath said suddenly. 'Auntie Monthly is back.'

Thelma tensed. She hadn't said anything about her own predicament to Cath. Only Jenny knew and she'd keep the secret.

'Good for you. Now make yourself useful and look for clues.'

'Clues?'

'Things that might give us a clue as to whether she's all right or not.'

'No milk bottle left on the step,' Cath said hopefully, totally unaware of what was going through Thelma's mind. 'The milkman 'as been. P'raps she didn't order any.'

'Possibly. I think the milkman only leaves a bottle of pasteurised every other day.'

'Right,' Cath said slowly, folding her arms across her chest, eyes still fixed on the doorstep. 'So what next?'

Thelma didn't hesitate. 'This is what we're going to do. I'm going round the back. You're going to stay here and give that knocker a good bash.'

Thelma marched around the side of the house.

The path was well swept, the garden well cared for, thanks to the efforts of Sybil's son, a keen gardener, not surprising seeing as he worked in the gardens of a stately home in Wiltshire. A yellow climbing rose clinging to a drainpipe and just coming into bud nodded in welcome. The unrelenting sound of Cath knocking echoed between the two semis from around the front of the house.

It did occur to Thelma that Sybil had gone out to the shops to buy some groceries, her drink and a newspaper.

Thelma cupped her hands above her eyes to better see through the kitchen window. A plate and a cup and saucer sat on the draining board. She couldn't be sure, but it looked as though they were waiting to be washed. There was also an egg cup. She frowned at that. The egg cup hinted that it had last been used this morning – or yesterday morning?

Clenching her fist, she hammered on the windowpane. The window frames were metal, the panes a series of squares, twelve in all. Thelma knew this for a fact. She cleaned hers once a week and always counted. The higher the number, the closer she was getting to the end of her task.

The opening parts of the windows were casements, one panel of square panes sitting to either side of a central non-opening piece. The handles were the key, but they were on the inside and she was outside. Some handles were stiff. Some had got a bit loose over time.

On a whim, she hammered extra hard at a single square pane adjacent to a handle. If it was loose, it might open. If not...

It didn't open.

Perhaps she might have left and made a promise to herself to come back the next day if she hadn't seen there was a light left on and the bedroom curtains were still drawn. The thing that further clinched it was Paddy.

At first, the feeling of something brushing her leg made her jump. Paddy meowed and looked up at her with big yellow eyes. Words were not needed to know that he was hungry. Sybil always put the cat out last thing at night and let him back in first thing in the morning.

'I gets up early, round about five. You don't sleep so well when you're older you know,' she'd once told Thelma.

No she didn't know. Thelma wasn't yet forty and that wasn't old. But Paddy and the memory of what Sybil had uttered made her mind up.

After the sound of knocking from round the front ceased, Cath appeared looking pensive, a look that turned to amazement as she espied the piece of stone Thelma had picked up from the garden.

'Thelma, you're not going to...?'

The sound of breaking glass preceded anything more she might have said.

'Give me your headscarf.'

Cath duly obliged and, with great care, Thelma wound the headscarf around her left hand. Once she was one hundred per cent sure she wouldn't get cut, she slipped her hand cautiously through the broken pane and pulled the handle downwards.

As the window swung outwards, bits of glass fell onto the concrete path. Bigger pieces became splinters and shards.

'Finished,' she said to Cath, handing her back her headscarf.

Cath gave her headscarf a good shake but declined to put it back on. 'Better wash it first or I might cut me head.'

'Right. Give me a hand with that dustbin.'

Together they dragged the bin across from where it was and positioned it beneath the window.

Thelma held out her hand. 'Help me up.'

One hand on the window ledge, and Cath holding onto the other, Thelma climbed onto the dustbin. Steadying her balance first, she placed both hands on the window ledge, then on the frame.

'Here goes.'

One knee was placed where her hands had been. The other would have been placed more firmly if Paddy hadn't chosen that moment to barge in under her torso, leap onto the draining board and down onto the kitchen floor.

Thelma fell head first into the deep china sink. One hand landed on a frying pan sticky with grease and the smell of old bacon fat.

'Damn,' she said, as her hand slid in the cold lard.

'You all right?' Cath shouted behind her.

'Yeah. Just that bloody cat. I was nearly doing the dishes with my nose.' She chuckled at her own joke and wondered what anyone would think on seeing her legs sticking out of the window, suspenders straining to keep stocking tops up and even a glimpse of her knickers.

Her amusement was short-lived. No matter the noise made, there was no sign of Sybil. The old girl was a bit deaf, but she would have certainly heard the smashing of glass.

Thelma took a deep breath. She needed to check upstairs. Sybil might have taken a turn. She might be unconscious. She might even be dead.

'I'm going to look upstairs,' she murmured over her shoulder. 'You get round to the front door and I'll let you in before going upstairs. No need for you to climb in.'

'Whatever you say, Thelma,' said Cath, not relishing the thought of climbing through the window herself. Her stockings were the only pair she had left. She couldn't afford another pair until the end of the week when Bill got paid and she didn't have a spare pair, even ones with ladders in that she made do as long as she could. She charged off along the side of the house to wait at the front door for Thelma to open it.

Thelma made her way through the kitchen, into the living room and then the hallway. Her face was tight when she opened the front door, though still conveyed energy and the will to brave the problem and sort something out.

'Come on in. Let me close the door and keep the draught out. There's no sign of her down here, so we might as well go straight upstairs. I noticed the bedroom curtains are still drawn.' The stairs went off immediately opposite the front door. With one foot on the bottom stair, Thelma shouted up: 'Sybil! Are you up there?'

'Do you think...?'

Thelma gave Cath a withering look. 'Well, we won't find out by standing here, will we?'

Facing resolutely up the stairs, Thelma led the way, a reluctant Cath following behind.

Cath asked nervously, 'What if she's...'

'Oh, for goodness' sake.'

Being sharp was not usually Thelma's way, but the reason she had broken the window was because she was thinking exactly that. She just did not want to worry Cath. Hopefully, Sybil might only have collapsed or been ill and unable to answer the knocking at the door. In her heart of hearts, she didn't believe that but hadn't wanted to come in here alone.

Upstairs, the doors to all three bedrooms were open. Old suitcases and cardboard boxes occupied the box room. There was a double bed in the largest bedroom, a three-quarter width one in the other. The latter had no bedding on it. The pink eiderdown on the double bed looked untouched, as though made but never slept in.

Thelma frowned as her concern deepened. Was she mistaken in believing the worst-case scenario and smashing the window? Where was Sybil?

Cath turned on the spot, keen to get away just in case they did find something. 'She's not 'ere. Let's go.'

'Wait a minute. I want to make sure.'

Leaving Cath trembling out on the tiny square of landing, Thelma entered one bedroom, then the other, walking round each side of the bed before getting down on her knees and looking beneath. The rooms were empty.

For a moment, she stood thinking things through. 'Where are you, Sybil Russell!'

She let Cath lead the way back downstairs.

Nothing had changed. The living room was empty. The kitchen was empty.

And now... thought Thelma. There was only one place she had not looked.

A door led from the kitchen into as small a back porch as the hall at the front of the house. Off that was the door to the bathroom.

The dark wood glowered at her as if daring her to open it. The round Bakelite handle was there to be turned, but she was reluctant. She had a very nasty feeling.

Behind her, shoulder to shoulder, Cath gasped. 'The bathroom!' She sounded horrified.

'That's right. The bathroom.'

None of the bathrooms of these houses had locks on the doors, the premise being that they housed families so were not needed.

At the very moment Thelma's fingers touched the doorknob, Cath, averse to being impolite and scared to death, reached around her and tapped on the door. 'Sybil, are you in there?'

The silence was deafening in a way that it can be when the worst is expected and they were certainly expecting the worse.

Thelma turned the knob.

Both women gasped with horror and covered their mouths with their hands. Sybil was lying flat out beside the bath, her head in a pool of blood.

'Oh Lord,' breathed Cath. Trembling like a leaf, she covered her eyes as well as her mouth with both hands. 'What we gonna do?'

'Have you got any pennies on you?'

'I didn't bring me purse. I thought...'

'Never mind. I don't think you need pennies for an emergency. Get to the phone box and dial 999. Ask for the police and an ambulance. Explain what's 'appened. I'll stay.' Shaking her head, she backed out of the bathroom and closed the door. 'Poor old Sybil.'

Half an hour passed before the local bobby arrived on his bicycle. Thelma showed him the body.

'It looks as though she fell. She told me weeks ago that she'd been feeling a bit wobbly of late,' she explained.

'Excuse me, madam, but we're the ones who will deduce what happened.'

He was being stroppily superior but was not to know that Thelma could give out as good as she got. Like a battleship, her bosoms heaved above a pair of crossed arms, her look lethal.

'No, son, and you are not a doctor or a nurse. You wouldn't know that she'd been feeling a bit unwell of late. You were not the one taking in a hot meal when you could. Oh, no, you were out and about on your bicycle ringing your little bell and telling kids you'd box their ears if they didn't behave themselves!'

'Yes. Quite,' he said, licking the end of his pencil and writing a few words in his notebook. In an effort to placate this woman who looked likely to floor him, he attempted brevity and dared to chuckle. 'No cure for what she's got now.'

Thelma frowned and really did look as though it was his ears that would get boxed. 'That's not funny.'

He ran his fingers through the chin strap of his helmet, cleared his throat and headed outside to await the arrival of reinforcements.

A plain-clothes policeman arrived in a police car, confirmed it was an accident and asked for details of next of kin.

Cath had been in such a state that she had not called for an ambulance. As it was, the police said to leave it to them. They would arrange for an undertaker to collect the deceased and take her to the chapel of rest.

A crowd gathered around Thelma once she was outside the house and the police had gone. Leaning on the garden gate, she told them all the details.

She shook her head sorrowfully. 'I knew something was wrong. Poor old love fell and hit her head on the bath. Nasty things them baths. Cast iron.'

Sighs of sympathy circled around her. Silence fell when the hearse arrived.

'The police are getting in touch with her son and with the council,' said Thelma once the hearse had pulled away.

'Poor old love,' said Mrs Lovell from number three. 'I was friends with her mother. She used to live there too. Lovely woman she was. Died a few years back.'

Thelma had also known Mrs Carr, Sybil's mother, and had thought her a right cow. She didn't say so.

'Whatever she was, it don't do to speak ill of the dead,' said Maude, who had arrived like a lot of others to see what was going on. A piece of white rag – by way of a handkerchief – appeared from her apron pocket. After giving her nose a good blow, she swiped at the brown line of snuff trickling from one nostril. 'May angels take her to heaven and give her rest.'

The sentiment was a trifle elaborate, but some of the women gathered muttered amen, while others expressed their wish that she rested in peace.

Maude jerked her head sideways to number one. All the excitement over, Mrs Partridge had disappeared, the front door firmly closed. 'You'd 'ave thought next door being close to the same age might 'ave kept an eye on 'er.' Maude tutted and shook her head. 'Poor old dear used to hang out on the gate sometimes, not often mind you, just now and again for the chance of speaking to someone. Someone to share 'er troubles with. A kind word goes a long way.'

There were murmurs of agreement.

Unaccustomed as she was to having an audience and thoroughly enjoying it, Maude carried on. 'Some woman from the council called on 'er a while back. Upset 'er it did.'

'Council inspector, I bet,' spat Thelma, not holding back on her contempt. 'Somebody told them she had a drink problem and the place was going downhill.'

'That's rubbish!' Mrs Lovell stamped her heavy feet, her ankles thick and veined above man-size slippers. 'Sybil was tidy and, anyway, she didn't drink that much. Not so much as a bloke, and certainly nowhere near what my old man chugs back, that's for sure!'

Thelma narrowed her eyes and glared across at number one. The curtains were drawn. Not only that, but...

'I don't believe it.' Face crumpled with disgust, she pointed an accusing finger. 'The cheek of the old cow! She's already got a sympathy card up in the window and drawn the curtains!' It was the custom that neighbours put up a black-edged sympathy card and drew their curtains – usually on the day of the funeral. Dorothy Partridge had jumped the gun. Thelma was beside herself. 'The old bat never spoke to poor old Sybil except to moan about the cat doing its business in 'er garden. Talk about hypocrite! The old mare!'

The eyes of the gathered women turned equally outraged expressions to the frontage of number one.

'Flowered curtains too.'

'Like a bleedin' cemetery.'

* * *

On the day of Sybil Russell's funeral, all the curtains in Coronation Close were drawn as a mark of respect and everyone had caught up with Dorothy and placed a black-bordered card of sympathy in their front windows.

A crowd of mostly women had gathered outside the garden gate, not that there was anything to see. Sybil's coffin was going straight from the funeral parlour to the cemetery and the only mourner was her son.

Steve Russell, who'd always been a shy lad, kept his head down and merely nodded at the voiced condolences as he made his way down the garden path to the bus stop.

One or two of the older women tutted.

'T'ain't right. Going to his mother's funeral on the bus.'

Thelma was more pragmatic. 'What's the point of a car for one? Sybil told me she did a penny a week insurance with the Royal Life and London. Pennies might make pounds eventually, but it takes time. It couldn't have amounted to much.'

Murmurs of agreement and comments about paupers' funerals ensued.

A number of the women gathered wore black headscarves, cardigans, skirts or dresses. Most were teamed with a pair of slippers. Nobody was going to put on their best funeral shoes just to wait around out in the street.

The exception was Thelma. A black skirt stretched across her ample hips, a black blouse with white piping across her equally ample bosom. Besides black court shoes with a sensible heel, a black felt hat with a net veil sat pertly on her head.

Someone suggested she should have gone on the bus with Sybil's son, seeing as she was dressed for it.

Thelma tutted. 'Oow, no. That would only 'ave led to gossip that I was after 'is inheritance. A penny policy is a penny policy.'

Titters of laughter rippled around her. Everyone knew that a penny policy just about paid for the cost of a hearse, the vicar and the burying expenses.

'Not a bad-looking chap, though,' said another neighbour.

As the neighbours dispersed, Thelma knew looks were exchanged behind her back. Whispered comments would follow behind closed doors over cups of tea. It didn't matter that she might or might not be a widow. She'd entertained several gentlemen callers since moving into the close some five years ago but had remained living alone with her daughters.

When she'd first moved in, she'd had a job at Edwards and Ringers, the tobacco factory in Redcliffe Street, within sight of St Mary Redcliffe church. After that, she'd worked in the sweet factory. Since then, she'd gone up in the world, working as a senior sales assistant in an up-market dress shop. There was bound to be gossip and she accepted that. They never said as much to her face and she believed having such as her with forth-right views living amongst them brightened their lives. She was like a bird of paradise living in a pigeon loft, vividly interesting and thus well liked.

Once the hearse and Steve Russell were gone, Jenny offered her closest neighbours a cup of tea.

'By way of a wake. Just for us. I've made tea and rock cakes. A few sandwiches too. Only fish paste, but it was all I had in the larder.'

Thelma followed her into the kitchen. 'Bought it up in Filwood Broadway, did you?' She kept her voice low, but the inference was obvious.

'I can buy fish paste anywhere.'

Thelma smiled and gave her a nudge. 'You know what I mean.'

'Yes I do. If you must know, Robin asked if I could go in and do a few hours in the pawnshop for him. I said I'd think about it.'

After saying that, she busied herself handing out tea plates to everyone.

The women of Coronation Close packed into Jenny's living room munched and sipped at the food and drink on offer. In between, they chattered like magpies, the noise almost too big for the room.

Out of sight and sound in the kitchen, Jenny asked Thelma how she was.

'Fine now. Full of vim and vigour. And are you all set?'

'Set?'

'For the coronation, of course. I've finished my costume. I've managed to get a blonde wig too, snitched it off one of the mannequins in our shop window. Well, not exactly snitched. I did ask Mr Bertram and he said that under the circumstances, it being the coronation of the new king, then I was welcome. As long as I remembered to put it back once I'd finished with it. I'm going to dress up as Jean Harlow.' One hand on her hip, Thelma sashayed around Jenny's new kitchen table. 'Come up and see me some time.'

Jenny laughed. 'That's not Jean Harlow, that's Mae West.'

Thelma dismissively flapped one hand. 'Who cares. Anyway, I've written down everything we still need to do.'

'What are you two chatting about? Are you going to join us or what?' Maude was standing in front of the living-room window pulling back the curtains and letting the daylight in. 'And this can go,' she said, tearing the black-edge bereavement card from the window. 'Let's think about something jolly. I've 'ad enough of funerals and I ain't looking forward to me own.'

Thelma placed herself in the middle of the room and clapped her hands. 'Maude is right. It'll soon be the coronation. To ensure things run smoothly, I'm going to write out a programme and a rota of who's doing what. I'll oversee the costumes. Each of us is bringing some item of food, crockery and cutlery. Now who wants to judge the kids' fancy dress? I think we should have two judges.'

Ivy and Mrs Lovell volunteered.

'Any games?'

Jenny shook her head. 'No. The kids will sort that out themselves – once they've stuffed themselves with cake and jelly.'

'I did try to get Bert to organise the men.'

'Do we need them?' asked Maude.

'To lug the tables out onto the grass.'

'And Bert won't do it?'

Thelma grimaced. 'He's not coming.'

A host of surprised eyes turned in her direction.

'He ain't gone and...'

'Dumped me? No. Maude, he has not.' Thelma sighed deeply before explaining. 'He can't leave his mother by herself, not on such a memorable day.'

'Understandable,' said Mrs Lovell, wiping more snuff from her nostrils. 'A man should look after 'is mother. My Stan's promised to look after me. When 'e comes out of prison, that is.'

Nobody mentioned that not only might it be some time before Maude's son came out of prison, but it was also likely that it wouldn't be long before he was in there again.

Cath confirmed that Bill would take charge of tables and chairs. 'And the kids can 'elp, that's if they want their coronation tea. They're looking forward to jelly and blancmange.'

'Dancing,' Jenny said suddenly. 'We need music to dance to. I doubt the lead from the wireless will stretch that far and we might not be able to hear it.'

The rest of them agreed that what they needed was a gramophone with a wind-up handle. And a whole load of records of course.

Heads shook disconsolately.

'Not one of us has got one?' Jenny queried. 'I thought one of us would have one.'

'Perhaps that chap up in Filwood Broadway might have one.' Thelma's eyes met Jenny's.

Jenny resisted blushing at the reference to Robin but said she would ask him, though she couldn't recall seeing one in the shop. Keen to divert any curiosity around Thelma's comment, she added, 'How about we put up a notice at the end of the close asking if anyone's got one they can spare for a day?'

Thelma had to agree that the idea was promising. 'Someone might oblige.' She couldn't help herself adding with some amusement, 'That's if your friend up in Filwood find one for us.'

'I noticed Mrs Partridge didn't put in an appearance at the funeral,' Maude remarked. 'Unusual for 'er. She does like a funeral and 'er being the first to put up a sympathy card in 'er window.'

There were murmurs of agreement.

'You'd think as a churchgoer she would have done,' proclaimed Mrs Lovell.

'To my mind, there's more charity outside the church than inside,' Thelma pronounced. Not that she'd spent much time inside a church herself.

'Perhaps Harriet, the sister, is ill again. Have you noticed that sometimes you don't see anything of 'er. I asked 'ow she was when I saw Mrs Partridge in the queue at the Co-op in Melvin Square,' said Cath as she passed around the plate of biscuits.

'What's wrong with her? Looks strong as a carthorse, though she sometimes gallops away like a racehorse if she thinks you're going to speak to her,' Thelma commented.

Cath looked a bit peeved. 'Nerves, so Mrs Partridge said.'

'And what does that mean?'

Cath shrugged. 'I don't know, Thelma. It could mean anything.'

Thelma scowled with disapproval. 'Darn right it could.'

Jenny frowned over the rim of her teacup. There was something she could add but held back. She had often wondered if anyone had seen her going into number one and taking tea when Dorothy was in hospital. Nobody had mentioned it, so it seemed she'd not been seen. If Thelma had been home, it would have been a different matter.

'Another biscuit, Thelma?'

Thelma declined. Her skirt was already tight across her belly. Still, at least it wouldn't be growing with an unwanted pregnancy. In a way, it saddened her, but in another it had come as an almighty relief.

As she sipped her tea, she thought about Mrs Partridge's sister. She'd once seen her head bobbing above the bright yellow chrysanthemums and dark red dahlias in the front garden of number one. Rows and rows of vegetables grew in the back garden – beans, cabbages, potatoes, carrots and parsnips. It took a lot of energy to have such a productive garden. Would somebody who suffered with their nerves be capable of such a feat?

'Another empty house in Coronation Close. I wonder who'll move in,' said Maude, interrupting her thoughts.

Everyone else began chipping in with who might or might not be their new neighbour.

A soft, loving look came to Cath's face. 'Hope it's a family.'

Thelma placed her cup into its saucer and left it to balance on the chair arm. 'They've got to clear Sybil's stuff out first, not that there's much in there to clear out. She didn't have much. I expect Steve will be back to do that – or her sister. I think she's got a sister in Taunton.'

'The painters and decorators will go in first. Freshen it up,' said Maude.

'There's nothing we can do about it. We've got a street party to organise. Now, we're all going to dress up, aren't we?'

Thelma asked everyone in turn what they were coming as, starting with Cath.

'A rabbit.'

Thelma and Jenny exchanged looks of surprise.

'You might be a bit hot dressed as a rabbit.'

'Only the ears. I'm going to make some ears.'

'Are you also going to make a fluffy bobtail?' Jenny added with a laugh.

'Yes.' Cath beamed, her eyes bright with intent. 'And my Bill is going to wear his granddad's top hat and stick a label in it saying ten shillings and sixpence.'

'Oh. The Mad Hatter from *Alice in Wonderland*,' said Jenny.

Thelma laughed. 'That's a good 'un. I thought when you mentioned him wearing his granddad's top hat that he was coming as an undertaker.'

'Course not,' said Cath, turning red. Everyone knew that Bill's father had been an undertaker whose drinking problem had ended with him being found fast asleep in a coffin lined with silk-covered padding.

'I thought I might come as Snow White,' said Jenny. 'I thought a few of the kids might want to dress up as the seven dwarfs.'

Everyone agreed that she had the right looks for it, with her creamy complexion, dark hair and slim figure.

Once again, it was remarked as a shame that Bert wasn't coming.

'It can't be helped.' Thelma spoke with conviction, though sincerely wished he was able to come. Half of her still believed he would. She'd even made him a John Bull waistcoat from a Union Jack flag she'd bought at a boy-scout jumble sale.

'What about you, Maude? What are you coming as?'

Maude, aged before her time with arduous work and too many children, pulled herself up in her chair and looked loftily from one to the other. 'Her glorious majesty Victoria; Queen and Empress.'

Jenny clapped. 'You'll make a great Queen Victoria. Who knows, we might even get someone to play Prince Albert.'

'Wish I'd thought of that,' said Thelma. She thought of Bert and smiled. 'Bert would have made a good Prince Albert, but there, he's not coming and that's that.'

15

'There's something pressing on her brain.'

The words the doctor had uttered on the occasion when Dorothy had been taken to hospital came back now.

Harry watched over her, took care of her as the soft-hearted man that he was. Some days were better than others. On some days, she sat in a chair, not seeing him, not hearing him, not saying a word. On others, she was almost her old self, cooking, cleaning and running down the neighbours as she'd always done.

He found her stiff and cold one morning. Shocked to the core, he immediately sank onto the dressing-table stool, not quite able to believe she was gone from his life.

The woman she had become was a world away from the one he used to know. Once upon a time, she'd been young and he'd loved her. Of late, she'd become a woman to be tolerated and understood after everything they'd been through together. He'd become more and more frustrated but couldn't really hate her or even dislike her. She'd been the mainstay of his life, the support he'd needed when his mind had been torn by war. She'd protected him. He had to give her that. But living in a world where he couldn't appear as the man she knew had damaged her view of the outside world. The old Dorothy who he'd fallen in love with would have been on friendly terms with their neighbours. The one burdened by the constant fear of discovery had warped into something bitter and twisted.

Thanks to the bloody war!

After closing her eyes, Harry left the house and walked out of the close, around the corner to the telephone box. Placing pennies on the cold metal shelf with one hand, he retrieved the details of the undertakers from his pocket.

They were polite and respectful, asking the name, the address and a general outline of the cost of their service. Once the preliminaries had been discussed, they promised to be around to collect her right away.

On his way home, he leaned against the wooden post on which the Coronation Close sign was perched immediately outside the boundary of his home. From there, he looked at the house, not wanting to go in whilst she was still there lying so silent and cold.

He spread his hand on the wooden post, leaned his head against it, closed his eyes and gritted his teeth. Eventually, he got a grip.

Disconsolate, he looked up at the name, Coronation Close. As with all street signs thereabouts, it was hand-painted atop a wooden post. Tears stung his eyes as he contemplated the sight of Dorothy up the ladder cleaning it. She'd been proud of that sign, proud of the fact that it had replaced the name Truro Close on the accession of the new king. Not the same king as now of course, but Edward the Eighth. *And now we have George the Sixth*, he thought to himself.

As he blinked away the tears, he spotted a note pinned on the pole, a simple little note asking for the loan of a gramophone.

He'd bought their gramophone way back, thinking it would ease both their hearts. He'd bought the records too. Dorothy had complained that she didn't want any of that modern music in her house. Her house! So he'd stored it away in the spare bedroom.

It was in a wooden case, a handle on one side. He had a whole box of records for it. Dorothy wouldn't approve of him lending it out, or perhaps she might. She'd wanted it out of the house as though they had no right to music, to anything that cheered their life, a life destroyed by his experiences on the battlefield. Now she was gone, he would arrange for it to be out of the house – if only for a brief time – or perhaps longer. He had a lot of thinking to do.

Tucking his hands in his pockets, his head bent, he made his way up the garden path and back into the house. Dorothy had to be laid out. It was usually the undertaker's job, but he couldn't bear the thought of a stranger's hands on his wife's body.

Laying her out on the bed they'd shared for most of their married life – a marriage and a man and a woman ruined by war – he first took off the faded maroon dressing gown she was wearing. After that, the high-necked cotton nightdress. Both items were flung onto a chair. He would dispose of them later.

The brown suitcase he took down from the top of the wardrobe contained her wedding dress. A couple of mothballs fell out and rolled away when he shook it out. So did a dried bunch of lily of the valley that had once been freshly picked and formed part of her wedding bouquet. She'd been happy then; laughing, passionate, a different person from the one she'd become.

By the time he'd dressed her, the hearse had drawn up outside and a heavy hand was knocking on the door. Harry went down to let them in.

Not much went unnoticed in Coronation Close and the

arrival of an undertaker was no exception. Curtains twitched. Faces full of curiosity appeared at windows. One or two women made their way to their front gates. Heads came together as they discussed what was going on.

Harry followed the funeral directors and the temporary coffin out to the hearse. His head was bowed, hands folded in front of him. He felt the inquisitive eyes, the looks of puzzlement, even of hostility.

He wanted someone to speak. Wanted to speak himself but where to start?

Softly spoken words came from next door.

'I'm so sorry. What happened?'

Jenny joined him at the front gate and together they watched as the hearse pulled away, Dorothy Partridge on the way to the Chapel of Rest and onwards to her final resting place.

There was a lot to explain. Although his jaw worked in a chewing action and his lips attempted to form words, none came out.

He flinched on feeling her hand on his arm.

'How about we go inside and I make you a cup of tea?'

At first, he didn't respond.

'Harriet. Come with me.'

Suddenly, like a veil lifting or a dam bursting, he loathed the name that had hidden his identity for so long. His dry mouth prevented him from correcting her, from declaring that his name was Harry – Harry Partridge. But he would tell her. Soon, quite soon.

There seemed to be no strength in either his voice or his muscles as Jenny took his arm and guided him up the garden path and into her house.

Once inside, she settled him in a chair.

He smelled her fragrance as she leaned forward, stroked his

face an action of sympathy and told him she would put the kettle on.

For a moment when stroking his cheek, she looked surprised but made no comment. He realised the problem was that he hadn't shaved that morning.

'Never mind the kettle. Please. Sit down. I need to talk to you.'

Looking both sad and surprised, she sat on the armchair opposite him, her fine fingers clasped in front of her.

Over time, he'd softened the deep baritone of his voice. He now let it flow.

The truth came flooding out; he told her of the trenches, the soup of mud and blood sucking at his boots, friends there one minute and gone the next. Body parts raining down along with artillery shells.

She listened without comment, her knuckles whitening with the enduring tightness of her clasp. She was horrified and unsure she would ever sleep again for fear of nightmares.

He went on to tell her how he'd fled the carnage, found his way home but never returned to that scene of hell on earth.

'I deserted. I don't recall how I did it, all the way from over there to over here. But I did. Dorothy saw the state of me and vowed I wouldn't be going back, that if I did I would die – or go mad – or be shot for cowardice. That was how it was. If you didn't fight, you were a coward.'

Jenny's lips moved but had become too dry to speak.

'So I became Harriet. It was Dorothy's idea.' He shook his bowed head, his gaze fixed on his feet, though not really seeing the clumpy shoes, the thick lisle stockings. 'Even today they still hunt deserters. How long before it's forgotten and forgiven, I don't know. Perhaps never.'

'And now that Dorothy's gone? What will you do now?'

He shook his head. 'I don't know. The funeral won't take place until after the coronation. Out of respect, the undertaker said.' He gave a little laugh. 'Out of respect for the king that is, not for my wife.'

'Oh, Harriet...' She reached for his hand and her eyes were moist with understanding.

He raised his head a little but maintained his downward gaze. 'I've already told you. I'm not Harriet. My name's Harry.'

She nodded and apologised. 'So what will you do now?'

He presumed she meant would he stay here now his wife was gone. It might also mean would he continue to masquerade as a woman so he wouldn't be arrested.

'I need to think things through. I'm not sure about anything yet.'

She didn't ask how Dorothy had died or if it was as a consequence of her being in hospital a while back. He was grateful for that. Dorothy had lived for him and they'd lived for each other. There was no one else except some far distant relatives in India and her cousin on a farm in Gloucestershire. By virtue of their predicament, they'd seen none of them for years.

He told her about the far-flung relatives. 'The trouble is I would have too much explaining to do. I couldn't bear it. They probably think I died in the war. It would be difficult to tell the truth. I could only do that if...' His voice fell away.

'You can't stop living, Harry. How about making a start and coming to the coronation party? As Harry or Harriet. The choice is yours. It might help.'

He looked into her bright eyes, the lovely face that so reminded him of the way Dorothy had once been.

He shrugged. 'I don't know. I'll think about it.'

16

Such a topsy-turvy world, thought Jenny as the bus left Melvin Square and went on its way to the heart of the city.

She couldn't help thinking about Harry and Dorothy. It was difficult to imagine but at one time, they'd been just an ordinary couple. They'd loved each other – or at least it seemed that they had. In a way, they'd had more than she'd had with Roy and it made her yearn for something similar. Would it ever happen?

Tonight was a step in that direction. Thelma was keeping an eye on the girls and had told her to go and enjoy herself. She'd agreed a date with Robin, and pushing a vestige of guilt aside, she determined to make the most of it.

As arranged, they met on the steps of the Hippodrome. The lights of the theatre burned bright and Jenny felt almost as though she were standing on a stage herself. Surely an actress never felt as nervous as she did.

Nestled against the wall at the corner of the entrance was a good spot. She could see everyone from here, the rattling trams, the new omnibuses, the cars and lorries adding to the volume of traffic around the central island of what was still called the tramway centre.

She saw Robin striding across the road from the central island, his tousled hair slicked back and the usual bounce to his stride. Not only was he wearing what must be his best suit, he was also wearing a white shirt and tie. She'd never seen him quite so dressed up before and briefly wondered whether he felt a trifle uncomfortable. The thought that he was trying to impress her brought a smile to her face. She was still smiling when he was standing in front of her.

'You came then.'

There was surprise in his voice, but also relief.

'I had to. I have to ask you something important.'

He beamed. 'Really? What's that then?'

His deep voice made her feel warm inside. Like a pot of tea brewing beside a fire grate of glowing coal.

'Do you happen to have a gramophone? We need one for the party.'

He shook his head. 'Sorry. Can't 'elp you there.'

'Shame. Never mind. Something's sure to turn up.'

'I'm glad you came. I never thought...'

'That I would?' She laughed. 'I could do with a bit of fun. It's been a stressful week.'

'Care to tell me all about it?'

She thought of Harry. His secret would remain with her.

'No. I wanted to thank you for offering me some work. The money will come in handy.'

'You're keeping your word?'

He looked and sounded surprised.

'Of course I am.'

'Well. That's fine and dandy. This calls for a celebration, a drink or two at least.' His laughter died. 'Unless you want to go in and see the picture that is.' He nodded at the poster advertising that Douglas Fairbanks was starring in the current film.

She smiled. 'You invited me. It's up to you.'

He was undecided for only a moment. 'I fancy going for a drink – so we can talk. Is that all right with you?'

'That's fine.'

They ended up in the bar of The Garrick's Head on the other side of the centre. The atmosphere was warm and full of smoke. Rough-looking men hogged the bar at one end. At the other, men in smart suits sat on upholstered benches, eyeing the men at the other end who in turn eyed them back.

'A small shandy,' said Jenny when Robin asked her.

He made his way to a gap at the bar between the two opposing factions. There were a few other women in there grouped at one end.

'Cheers,' he said on sitting back down.

'Cheers.'

'I'll pay you cash in 'and. I can't be fairer than that, can I.'

She smiled, sipped at her drink and shook her head. 'You can't be fairer than that.'

He looked somewhat sheepish for a moment, his long fingers caressing the pint glass.

'You know how I feel about you, don't you?'

She nodded. 'That's the problem. We've always been friends and at present we can't be anything other than that. You're married. I'm married.'

He wrung his hands as he considered what to say next.

The nervousness she'd experienced whilst standing on the steps of the Hippodrome had melted away. Now there came a different kind of nervousness. She was enjoying the night out, but wary of him taking things further. Dare she allow it to happen?

'You're right. I only wish things could be different. The only reason I don't divorce 'er is the kids. She said that if I want a divorce, I've got to be the guilty party, the one who's committed adultery.'

'But you haven't!' Jenny was shocked and sad for him.

'No. I haven't. And that's it, Jenny. I don't want to drag you into this. Not so much because it would end your marriage, but because I will not drag your name through the mud. You know what people are like.' He shook his head. 'I would never do that.'

'So we remain just good friends.' She hadn't given in to Charlie and she had no intention of falling for Robert. Being friends was all she could offer him.

He looked disappointed.

She felt compelled to reach out and stroke the back of the head he hung so low. She only just about restrained herself. However, she felt compelled to give him hope, small as it might be.

'I'll come and work for you, but not until after the coronation. Arranging this street party is taking up a lot of time.'

His head sprung up. His look brightened.

'Jenny, you've made my day.'

She was glad for him, though at the same time wondered if she hadn't been a bit rash. Tongues might wag and his wife Doreen was likely to take advantage of any situation that would get her what she wanted.

17

Cath Lockhart tucked the bedclothes beneath her chest and made herself comfortable. Next to her, in the double bed that squeaked with every move, lay the person she loved most in life.

Bill was breathing gently, apparently asleep.

Cath stared at the far wall, thinking through the events of the day. The bedroom was plain and the walls were unadorned by pictures. A washbowl and jug sat on the tallboy, the blue and white pattern matching the chamber pot beneath the bed. The bathroom being downstairs at the other end of the kitchen meant that old methods sometimes held sway.

She eyed the rounded shoulders lying next to her.

'I wonder what Mrs Partridge died of. It was a bit sudden when that hearse drew up.'

'It's none of our business,' grumbled Bill, annoyed to have his sleep disturbed. 'Anyway, she was an old cow and good riddance, I say.'

'Bill! You shouldn't speak ill of the dead.'

'I ain't spoke ill, but let's face it, it's unlikely she'll be in 'eaven.

More likely going downwards, I shouldn't wonder. With 'er drawers on fire!' He chuckled.

Cath frowned. What Bill said was true, but she couldn't help being curious. 'I might knock on the door and give the sister my condolences.'

'Might invite you to the funeral.'

'She might do, but that won't 'appen until after the coronation. All shops are closing for the day and that includes undertakers. Ain't gonna be burying anyone until the big celebration's over.'

'Well, that'll be something else for you to celebrate when the time comes.'

'I wonder if Mrs Russell's old place is taken yet?'

Bill grunted a wordless response.

'I was wondering. Our David is on the council list. He could apply for it – if it ain't gone yet.'

David Otley was her brother and she loved him dearly. Unfortunately, Bill didn't like him. He was a police constable and a bit full of his own self-importance. Besides that, he was too straight and upright for his own good. Break the most trivial law and he'd get out his notebook. A summons would ensue even for a close friend or relative.

His wife was a bit common and Cath got on all right with her. Only one kid so far and another on the way. He had to be in with a chance of getting a council house.

'I could ask Bert. He would know. Might even be able to put in a good word for our David. Wouldn't that be nice,' she said with a final sigh.

She sensed a stiffening of the rounded shoulders before he rolled onto his side, his heavily lidded eyes flickering when he looked at her. 'Why can't he get a police house? Don't they have some that come with the job?'

'Only in villages. There's not many, if any, in the city.'

Bill sighed. 'You won't be popular if Dave moves in, so let's not mention it again, eh?'

He turned his back to her, determined to get his sleep, but Cath was persistent. She relished the thought of her policeman brother moving into the street. It would certainly put a few noses out of joint.

'I thought I could visit 'im, just to put 'im in the picture.' She hesitated. 'Or you could write.'

'Cath, forget about it and get to sleep.'

She paused only long enough to think it through and then said, 'I think the best idea is for me to speak to Bert. I could stress in no uncertain terms that I don't want just anyone moving in Sybil's old place. We want somebody law-abiding and upright.'

'I don't think the rent collector has much say in the matter of who moves in.'

'I suppose not. I just thought...'

There was no response from the person with whom she'd shared a bed for a considerable number of years.

'I can't sleep.'

A strong arm appeared from beneath the covers and rested on top. 'If that's the case, go down to the kitchen and get me a cup of tea.'

There was hesitance before her feet touched the floor, the legs to which they belonged enveloped in a thick flannelette night-gown. She sat on the edge of the bed wondering what she could say to him to keep him awake and talking.

'I want to tell you something I saw when I went shopping today.'

Bill flopped onto his back. 'Don't keep me in suspense.'

A little pause, then, 'There was a man. He was wearing one of those plastic facemasks. It covered one side of his face. I doubt there was much left of his face beneath that. Poor soul, I thought. Poor bloody soul! And then... and then...'

Bill's response was abrupt. 'The war's over. Let's forget it, shall we?'

Tea forgotten, Cath snuggled down, wrapping herself into his back. Bill had been in a reserved occupation during the war – working for the Great Western Railway. GWR the anachronism also termed God's Wonderful Railway. He'd been glad of that, otherwise she had no doubt he would have ended up in prison, a conscientious objector. 'War is the last resort of idiots.' He said he'd read it somewhere but couldn't remember where. Not that she'd cared. It was something to celebrate that he was still alive. There were plenty who were not.

* * *

Midnight had come and gone. At number two, Jenny blinked into the darkness. Try as she might to get to sleep or at least concentrate on arrangements for the forthcoming street party, sleep eluded her.

Was it a mistake to promise Robin she would work for him after the coronation? It seemed only a small thing but could lead to bigger things. They were both lonely. Would they be able to help themselves? She consoled herself with the fact that she'd held off Charlie Talbot so should be able to cope with Robin.

Thinking of Charlie made her wonder again why he hadn't been in touch. Perhaps he'd had an accident. Perhaps a relative had been taken ill. So many thoughts. So many possibilities and so many shared secrets.

What Harry Partridge had confided to her whirled around and around in her mind like a fairground roundabout that wouldn't stop. The difficulties and unhappiness of his life had begun in the Great War. Only now that Dorothy, the woman she now knew was his wife, had gone had he opened up and shared his secret.

The poor man. Such a lot to go through. Such a lot to suffer.

What would he do now? Continue his existence as a woman? If he chose to do so, she would not betray his secret. What right did anyone have to condemn how he lived? Anything that helped him cope with what had happened had to be a good thing.

Down to the war. It was all down to the bloody war.

18

May had not been the sunniest of months and Coronation Day, May the twelfth, would be no exception. The weather forecast said so and for once turned out to be right. A brisk breeze blew, strong enough to send petals from the apple tree tumbling like confetti across the back gardens.

The very air in Coronation Close seemed to be vibrant with excitement and expectation. Everyone had been up early, keen to prepare the food for the feast and excited that later they would be in fancy dress.

Unusually for her, Thelma's hair was still in curlers, but she just couldn't resist overseeing the erection of trestle tables and sending the men to fetch more chairs, more tables and ladders so they could tie more bunting between the trees.

'Not enough,' she shouted, running up and down, making sure table legs were level, insisting on yet more tables. One extra table provided was normally used by its owner in his job as a painter and decorator for wallpapering, another was dragged from out of a garden shed.

'Better too many than too few,' Thelma declared. She looked

around, her eyes falling on those she didn't consider were doing enough.

'Anyone would think it was 'er who was being crowned,' Maude murmured to Mrs Lovell.

The tables and chairs were all set out, but still Thelma wasn't satisfied. 'We might not have enough. We need more. Ah,' she exclaimed on spotting Robin Hubert pulling up in his van. No new suit today, just his waistcoat worn over a white shirt with no collar and rolled-back cuffs.

'I've brought a couple of trestle tables. Thought you might need them.'

'You deserve a medal,' Thelma called out as she toddled unsteadily over the soft grass on high-heeled shoes, not yet wearing her fancy dress costume. She grabbed his face with both hands and landed a smacker on his mouth. 'Robin, you're a sight for sore eyes.'

'Never had a customer do that before,' he said, grinning from ear to ear.

'I know you'd prefer it to be Jenny, but give it time, old chap,' she whispered in his ear. She jerked her chin in the direction of Jenny's house. 'She's in her kitchen making sandwiches.'

When he got there, Jenny was covering a meat plate full of sandwiches with a damp tea towel. She was wearing a pale green pinny over a dark blue dress. One of her cheeks had a light dusting of flour. Her eyes were bright and she looked happy.

'Robin. You made it.'

'I did indeed. Brought a couple more trestle tables.'

'What about a gramophone. I know you said you didn't have one, but we were living in hope.'

He shook his head. 'No. 'Fraid not. I had a couple a few weeks ago but they went. Everyone wants a gramophone so they can dance in the streets.'

As she crimped the edge of an apple pie, Jenny shook her head, still smiling but disappointed. 'We tried everywhere. We even tied a notice to the sign at the end of the street and put a postcard in Mrs Bellamy's shop window.' Jenny sighed. 'We'll just have to put a wireless on and hope that everyone can hear it.'

'We could try it now. How about I switch it on and twirl you around a bit?'

He made as if to take her in his arms, but she waved him away.

'Be off with you. I haven't got time. There's all this to put out on the table and we still need to take the chairs out.' She called for Tilly and Gloria. 'Chairs please!'

The sound of giggling came from upstairs, but there was no sign of the girls.

Hands on hips, Jenny shook her head in exasperation. 'They're in their own little world.'

'Never mind. Leave it to me,' said Robin. He grabbed two of the dining chairs he'd only lately sold to her. 'You know very well that I'm used to lugging furniture.'

It wasn't long before he came back for the other two to find that Jenny had finished sandwich making. The apple pie was in the oven and she was taking off her pinny.

'I'll light that gas for the pie later. I need a breath of fresh air,' she added, tucking a freshly laundered and pressed tablecloth under her arm.

Strings of bunting made in those long winter evenings by Thelma and the others fluttered from the trees. Cardboard crowns made by the children and hung from the trees danced in the breeze.

Thelma stood at the head of the T-shaped arrangement, arms folded, nodding with satisfaction. 'Looks like there's room for everyone. And a bit of room to dance too.'

Once the furniture was in place, the women spread out their carefully laundered tablecloths. Most were white. One or two that bordered on grey were diplomatically placed between the whiter ones. Not that it mattered much. It was the food everyone was waiting for, especially the kids.

Cath's husband, Bill, and Fred Wiltshire, his neighbour, carried out a crate of brown ale and placed it at the far end of the table. It was followed by another crate containing ginger beer and lemonade for the kids. Another crate of brown ale followed, then another.

Jenny eyed them laughingly, at the same time shaking her head. 'That's them taken care of. What about the ladies?'

'I've got us a couple of bottles of sherry. We'll be all right.' Thelma pulled a face. 'Shame we couldn't get hold of a gramophone though.'

Jenny shook her head. 'Robin did try. He said everyone was after one. We just weren't quick enough.'

Thelma sighed. 'Never mind. We've done the king and queen proud. I think they'd say that to us if they were here.'

Jenny agreed with her. When it came to royalty, Thelma was strict on detail. Besides her family, they were the centre of her universe.

'Time to get ready,' Thelma trilled in a sing-song voice. She sounded like a young girl about to go to her first dance.

* * *

Jenny came back wearing an ankle-length slim line dress in dark green velvet. She wore a cardboard crown, made at the same time as the crowns swinging from the trees.

The girls trailed behind her, giggling. Gloria was a fairy princess complete with wand made by Jenny from a twig plucked from the apple tree, wound around with a piece of silver tinsel left over from last Christmas. At the last minute, Tilly had refused to put on her costume, saying she felt too stupid. 'I'll just be myself,' she'd said, and went off to see what Thelma's daughters, Alice and Mary, were wearing. Both girls wore dresses of red, white and blue and paper crowns that looked as though they too might have been made from bits and pieces left over from Christmas.

'Do I look all right?' Thelma asked Jenny.

Jenny's jaw dropped. So did everyone else's for that matter.

The blonde wig Thelma had purloined from Bertrams was shoulder length. The dress she'd made from the pale lilac sparkly material from the jumble sale clung to her voluptuous curves. Jean Harlow had been far slimmer than Thelma, but Jenny couldn't help thinking that her neighbour had more presence.

'You look wonderful.'

Maude came over in her black silk dress. She was wearing an old lace curtain on her head beneath a small crown. She didn't look a dead ringer for Queen Victoria but close enough. At least her clothes were the right colour.

Glamorous and full of herself, Thelma began cavorting around, swaying her hips in her tight-fitting dress and high-heeled shoes.

There was laughter and raucous comments as she exhaled a cloud of smoke from an ebony cigarette holder clenched between pouting red lips. At the same time, she belted out 'My Old Man Said Follow the Band'. The kids joined in, though not all of them knew the words.

Such was Thelma's enjoyment that she didn't at first hear Cath say something or feel the sharp nudge of her elbow.

'Thelma!'

Thelma stopped dancing around and took notice of what Cath was saying.

'Ain't that Bert's car?' she asked, nodding her pointed little chin to where the small black car she knew so well had driven against the kerb.

It was Bert's car all right. Thelma's dropped jaw turned into a wide smile.

'He said he wasn't coming.'

Bert got out of the driver's side door and, without acknowledging anyone, went around and opened the passenger door.

A woman wearing a feathered hat and a floor-length black lace dress emerged, straightened and reached for his arm. She leaned on an ebony walking stick with her other hand, held her head high and in a majestic manner headed towards them.

Even from the middle of the green, they could see the luminescent glow of a multi-layered pearl choker around her neck and pear-shaped pearl earrings of an old-fashioned style hanging from her ears. A black net veil covered her face tucked severely beneath her chin.

Cath took a deep breath. 'She's come as Queen Mary.'

Although she'd never met her, Thelma knew this was Bert's mother. She shook her head. 'No she has not. She's come as herself.'

Remembering that his mother didn't approve of smoking, Thelma stubbed out the burning cigarette and handed the whole thing to Jenny.

She tottered over on her high-heeled shoes, hoping Bert's mother wouldn't think she was a tart. If she'd known she was coming, she would have worn something more sedate.

'Good morning, Bert.' Her smile for his mother was enough to break her jaw. 'And this must be your mother, Mrs Throgmorton. Pleased to meet you, I'm sure.'

Pale eyes swept over her from head to toe.

Crikey, I must look like a right floozy, thought Thelma, and once again regretted her outfit.

She went on to explain. 'It's fancy dress. I'm supposed to be Jean Harlow, the film star. I'm not really blonde. It's just a wig, see?'

She swept the wig off her head then put it back on again. Her own hair was a mass of hairpins and hairnet.

Realisation and acceptance was slow coming. A slight nod, hesitant but a nod all the same. Hopefully of approval.

Bert looked apologetic as he explained why they were both there. 'Mother wanted to see something of the celebrations because...'

'It might be the last time I will see a new monarch crowned,' his mother interrupted. 'I firmly believe I should make the most of it.'

Christabel Throgmorton spoke down her nose, as though addressing an audience or school assembly. Not surprising in Thelma's estimation, recalling that Bert had mentioned she'd once been a schoolteacher.

'Would you like a cup of tea?' asked Thelma. 'Or perhaps you'd care to sit down?'

She pulled the best-looking dining chair out, her smile still fixed on the face of Bert's mother.

Mrs Throgmorton gave no sign of accepting the offer but looked around her, eyeing the tables, the chairs, the crates of brown ale...

'This is Thelma, Mother. My lady friend,' Bert introduced.

His mother scrutinised Thelma anew. The pale eyes suddenly flickered from behind the net veil as though she'd had thoughts that had led her to a conclusion.

'Cuthbert tells me you collect celebratory items. I would like to see them.'

Her voice resembled those of the customers at Bertrams; wealthy women who could afford anything they wanted. Gloves, scarves, hats or evening gowns. Thelma shook the image away and, adopting her brightest smile, said, 'Yes. You'd be most welcome, madam – sorry – Mrs Throgmorton.'

Still holding his mother's arm, Bert attempted to go with them. His mother stopped him.

'No need for you to come. Go and make yourself useful.'

She didn't exactly snap, but the sharpness of her voice was in the manner of an order.

Holding the hem of her evening gown with both hands, Thelma led Mrs Throgmorton to the gate and up the garden path to number twelve.

As she did so, she prepared herself for what was to come. Her stomach was in knots, tight with apprehension. No doubt she would be told in no uncertain terms to break off her relationship with Bert. That her sort, a widow with three children, two of whom were born after her husband died, was not a suitable match for her son.

She decided to take her in the front door rather than go round the back and through the kitchen.

The key made a grinding noise as she turned it. Thankfully, the hallway was tidy; not too many coats hung on the pegs behind the door. Sometimes it was impossible to open the door very wide thanks to the bulk of coats.

On opening the living-room door, they were met by the smell of lavender-scented polish. There was no fire in the grate, but it had been tidied up and the brass fender gleamed.

Earlier that morning, she'd kicked off her slippers and left them where they'd landed. She moved quickly to pick them up and place them to the side of her favourite armchair.

Mrs Throgmorton took steps from one end of the dresser to the other, her eyes raking Thelma's crockery collection. For her part, Thelma was reminded of an army officer inspecting his men, though in her case it was the mugs, cups, plates and saucers, each one commemorating a royal event. Her gaze transferred to the pictures on the wall. Thelma had moved them around the night before. The picture of King George the Fifth and his queen had been relegated to the right of what was now the main picture: King George the Sixth and his queen, Elizabeth.

The loftily held head of Mrs Christabel Throgmorton bent to one side as she scrutinised each one again before going back to the dresser.

'King Edward the Eighth is missing.'

Thelma took a deep breath. She'd worshipped that man and he'd let her down. What would Bert's mother think of that? No matter. She decided to stick to her guns and declare how she felt.

She shook her head and hissed in her breath. 'I couldn't bear to look at him. Not after what he did. So I smashed the lot. Anyway, Bert bought me one for this king and his queen. As for Edward, well, seems he didn't care tuppence for anyone – except that American woman.'

Should she have said that? Never mind. It was out and couldn't be retracted.

Mrs Throgmorton's back was turned to her. Suddenly, her shoulders shook in what Thelma feared was anger.

Oh dear, she thought to herself. *What have I done?*

As it happened, when Mrs Throgmorton turned round, she was shaking with mirth.

'So did I. Did Cuthbert not tell you?'

Astounded, Thelma shook her head and laughed with her. 'No. He didn't.'

'Edward the Eighth failed in his duty.'

'I totally agree with you. I felt so let down.'

'So did I. Shall we have tea now?'

It surprised Thelma that there'd been no condemnation of her relationship with Bert. No motherly possessiveness or comment inferred or otherwise that she wasn't good enough for her son. Inference was not enough. She needed to hear approval from Mrs Throgmorton's mouth.

'You don't mind me and Bert... well... going out together?'

'Would it make any difference if I did?'

'No, perhaps not. Will he still be required to be home by ten o'clock?'

A frown appeared on the high forehead, deep enough to send her eyebrows plunging between her brows. 'He's a grown man. He can come home whatever time he wishes.'

What should have been a final settlement of the issue left Thelma feeling confused. Right from the start, Bert had insisted that his mother required he come home by ten o'clock. She'd accepted this, but now she'd been told that it just wasn't so, in which case, why had he said it was?

* * *

There had been a flurry of activity when they'd gone into the house. It had escalated by the time they came back out. Chattering, running around, dashing backwards and forwards with platters of sandwiches, bowls of blancmange and homemade trifles. Now, to Thelma's amazement, there was dancing and she could hear music.

A gramophone had been set up on the pavement, the sort contained in a walnut cabinet.

Thelma was both surprised and delighted. 'Where did that come from?'

'From him,' Jenny said softly.

Thelma's gaze followed hers to where Bill, Robin and the other men were standing in a huddle, conversing sullenly with a man wearing a tight-fitting uniform identifiable as being from the Great War.

'He looks familiar...'

Before Jenny could explain, Bert left the group of men and came over, looking just a little pensive. She guessed he was wondering how she and his mother had got on.

She obliged him. 'Your mother and I have had a nice little chat,' Thelma said to Bert, keen to find out what was going on. For now, she'd not mention him lying about having to be home by ten o'clock. 'Now she could do with a nice cup of tea.'

Jenny was beckoning her over. She nodded at the man in uniform. 'This is Harry Partridge.'

Thelma looked confused.

Jenny explained. 'Dorothy's husband. We knew him as Harriet. It was the war,' said Jenny, her soft voice a little sad but also happy.

'The war,' said Thelma, her luscious lips set in a hard straight line. 'It always bloody is. We are having a surprising day today.'

Jenny agreed. There was no time to explain anything more about Harry, and besides, everyone was out to enjoy themselves and make this day the celebration of the century. The street party was in full swing. Explanations could come later, perhaps tomorrow. Thelma agreed with her.

'I just want to eat, drink and dance till I drop.'

19

Although Coronation Day had passed, the bunting remained fluttering from the trees. Full size Union Jacks festooned across the red brickwork of houses dripped water in the rain. The green was empty now of tables, chairs and people.

An air of sadness hung grey and heavy in the dull weather. Not only were the celebrations over, but Harry Partridge had declared that he was giving himself in.

'I've written,' he said, his head hanging so low that his chin rested on his chest.

Just before he reckoned they would come for him, he invited Jenny and Thelma to call at number one.

'I need you to help me out,' Harry had said. 'If you could call in.'

'And the gramophone?'

'It's yours. And the records.'

Jenny thanked him.

In the space of a few days since Dorothy's death, it seemed his wide frame had diminished.

'I need to put my affairs in order,' Harry informed them. 'I've asked for time to attend my wife's funeral before they come for me. I've not heard anything, but think they'll oblige.'

So here they were, staring at each other wondering what this was all about. Thelma was apprehensive about entering the house. She'd never been invited inside before.

'Imagine what she'd have to say if she knew I'd stepped into her house.'

'She won't know, Thelma.'

Despite their obnoxious neighbour no longer living there, it still smelled as though recently polished. The living room curtains were drawn across the back of the black-edged card stuck in the window declaring her death. The house had an aura of never having been lived in – bereft of everyday aromas and warmth.

Harry's hair was slicked back with oil. He was wearing a pair of serge trousers, striped shirt and maroon pullover. He also wore a tie. Some men still did wear a tie indoors. Matter of pride or just habit?

'This way.'

They followed his sluggish footsteps upstairs, turning left at the top into the front bedroom.

It seemed like sacrilege to both Jenny and Thelma to be in Dorothy Partridge's bedroom. It was surprisingly warm. A sudden break in the clouds and rain brought a shaft of sunlight in through the window. Perfume from flowers in the front garden came in with it.

He'd stripped the double bed and piled the bedding at one end, the remaining space taken up with a pile of voluminous dresses, some flowered, but most plain and big enough to hide Harry's broad frame.

He picked up a dress of dark blue with a lace colour and cuffs, scrunched it up in both hands then threw it aside. The old-fashioned style did nothing to accentuate the contours of an ordinary woman's body, but Harry was a man. He always had been. 'I don't want the coppers seeing them.' He meant of course the clothes he used to wear as Harriet.

Jenny swallowed as the pressure of tears threatened.

Thelma shifted from one foot to the other, looking awkward but also sad. If only they'd confided in her... or someone, although, on reflection, they couldn't possibly have done that. Harry would have been arrested long ago. She felt bound to apologise. 'I wish I'd known. I might have been less... you know...'

Harry shook his head. 'You've nothing to be sorry about. Our circumstances altered me and Dot. That's what war does. I hope there will never be another one, but who knows. Germany's on the rise again, and that bloke Hitler...' He shook his head mournfully. 'So many died back in the trenches. So many scarred in body and mind.' He hung his head. 'Myself included. The war to end all wars, we were told. But if it happens again... all in vain. For what did they die?'

Thelma hated the question. Hated what it stood for, a past that had ruptured the world and the dreadful possibility that it might happen all over again. If it did, there was the possibility of her own children being involved, especially George. He was of the right age, the same age his father had been when he was killed. Nausea churned her stomach. She needed to change the subject.

'So what do you want us to do with it all?'

'Take all my clothes. The wife's too, if you like. The bedding too and the furniture.'

It seemed odd to hear him refer to Dorothy as his wife. To her neighbours in Coronation Close, she'd been a malevolent presence best avoided, a woman who'd not had the time of day to give anyone – except the rent man, seeing as he represented authority,

even if only in a small way – or Roy, due to his uniform and polit-
ical views. Being a wife made Dorothy Partridge seem more
human, increasingly so now she was dead than when she had
been living.

What had she been like before the war and changed circumstances? wondered Jenny. Dorothy as a young woman, smiling
instead of scowling – as in that wedding photo on the dresser
downstairs. A wife. Once a sweetheart. A bride. Both her and
Harry destroyed by war.

Banishing the vision and the questions, she asked about the
furniture.

Harry shrugged and spread his palms. 'You and the neighbours can take whatever you want. Ask Mr Hubert to take the
rest. I don't want anything for any of it. Just make use of it. Hopefully, it will go some way to making up for the things Dorothy
did.' He hung his head. 'I'm not going to need any of it where I'm
going.'

They knew without him having to say that he was going to
prison. Deserters were still regarded as the lowest of the low,
cowards who should have preferred to die. But did anyone prefer
to die? Nobody.

The garden gate made a clanging sound, pushed open by two
policemen, their helmets bobbing up and down as they
approached the front door.

'I'm so sorry,' said Jenny. Harry jumped at the gentle touch of
her hand on his. 'I can't thank you enough for what you did for
me, what with Roy and that awful man from the council. I much
appreciated it. And don't deny you didn't hit Roy. I know it was
you.'

Moist eyes and sad smiles were interrupted by the police
constables' heavy-handed knocking at the front door reverber-
ating through the open window.

'Be right there,' Harry shouted down. To Thelma and Jenny, he said, 'It's been a long time coming, but I'm ready. I'd better go.'

He picked up a canvas haversack, enough to hold only a few items.

'I've told the rent man and your man Bert that I'm moving out.' He spoke directly to Thelma. 'He'll make sure everything is done that has to be done. I won't need to come back here, not even for the funeral. Everything's taken care of. I'll leave you with the spare key. Here.' He passed the key to Jenny whilst Thelma looked on.

They watched him leave; a solitary, sad figure sandwiched between two burly policemen.

Jenny stifled a sob. Thelma sucked in her lips at the same time as blinking away the tears from a past best forgotten.

'I can't deal with this tonight,' said Thelma once the policemen and their prisoner had disappeared.

'You go on home. I'll make a start.'

'No. Leave it. Fancy going to the pictures? I don't know what's on and quite frankly I don't care. I just need to get out.'

After everything, Jenny agreed that they needed a break.

'Let's round up the girls and make it a family event. Bert too.'

How they all got into Bert's car was a miracle. Thelma eased herself into the front seat beside Bert, and Alice just about managed to squeeze onto her lap. Jenny was in the back squashed in alongside Thelma's daughter, Mary, plus her own girls, Gloria and Tilly.

They trooped in just as the matinee performance had ended and the evening performance began. Some who'd already watched part or all of the matinee stayed seated to see it again. Blue fronds of tobacco smoke curled upwards. A family group to one side of them licked fingers made greasy by the pigs' trotters they were eating. Several people made a night of it that way, evening meal eaten as they watched their favourite film.

A hush descended as the lights of the Broadway Picture House dimmed, signalling the start of the evening performance. The plush velvet curtains slid back and the screen lit up. Gaumont News.

There were cheers for the royal family both during and after the coronation. The next news report pictured the German Condor squadron arriving in Spain to assist Generalissimo Franco combat those who favoured democracy over autocracy. The faces of German pilots smiled from the screen and waved from the cockpits of their fighters.

The news commentator announced, 'Adolf Hitler comes to the aid of his fascist colleague, Generalissimo Franco.'

Bombs erupted on screen. A horde of aeroplanes, like angry bats, rose and fell against what looked like a bright blue sky – not that they could tell for sure. As with most films, the news was in black and white.

At the sight of fleeing refugees and wounded men, women and children, a hushed silence descended, then erupted with boos and catcalls. Somebody shouted, 'Bloody Germans.'

Jenny almost swallowed her tongue. She turned her head away so she didn't have to watch it. Thelma's eyes met hers. Even in the darkness, she could see that her friend and neighbour was thinking the same thing as she was. Harry had hinted at another war starting in the not too distant future. They didn't want to believe it, but that didn't mean that it wouldn't happen.

20

Thelma and Jenny blubbed a bit as they sorted out the clothes that had once belonged to Dorothy Partridge and her husband Harry, now imprisoned as a deserter.

Thelma gathered up the large dresses, stating they would cut down into matching dresses for the girls. Some of it they decided to give away – especially Dorothy's dresses. Nobody in Coronation Close was as skinny as she'd been, or as tall for that matter.

The furniture had been distributed as per Harry's wishes. Before he'd left Jenny had suggested she write to him with details of where it had gone. Harry had declined, saying he had no use for any of it and anyway he wasn't sure where he was being incarcerated. He'd write to her when he knew.

'If he gets round to it,' Thelma had declared sadly and Jenny was inclined to agree with her. Harry had a lot of wounds to deal with and not all of them were visible. It would be some time before he felt confident enough to put words to paper.

Aided by a tall school leaver with broad shoulders and in need of a job, Robin had come along to collect the stuff nobody else wanted. There wasn't much of it left. The neighbours had not looked a gift horse in the mouth and swooped on the things they could find a use for. Some, useless at present, might be at some point in the future.

Once the van had been backwards and forwards with two or three loads of furniture, Robin lingered, cap on the back of his head and a hopeful look in his eyes.

'Call in when you're around the Broadway and we can talk about you coming in to give a hand. Two mornings a week would be a big 'elp.'

From experience, Jenny knew two mornings a week wouldn't really be of much use to him. Mondays and Fridays were the busiest days of the week and required all day cover, perhaps even a few more midweek.

There was a moment when they had to squeeze past each other as he manoeuvred a piece of furniture out from the living room into the hallway. They laughed as they did, both stuck against either side of the door jamb. As the piece of furniture popped out from between them, they collided. His arms were around her, his lips hot on hers.

She surprised herself. She didn't hold back. His kiss was soft and warm, full of a passion she'd never been party to.

'Mr Godwin. Are you ready with that last piece?' shouted the young lad helping him.

'Be right there.'

They sprang swiftly apart. The moment was lost but would be remembered.

Jenny's cheeks were still pink when she went outside and met up with Thelma.

'He's sweet on you. Anyone can see that,' said Thelma. It was also Thelma's opinion that she should take the job on. 'It fits in with the girls' schooltime, not that it matters much. They're getting older.'

Later that day, she stood watching them playing on the green with their school friends. Was it her imagination or had their legs got longer, their bodies curvier?

She turned away and shook her head. She didn't want to think of her girls growing up and away from her. From their father too. Gloria occasionally asked when her daddy was coming home on leave from the army.

'I haven't seen him for ages.'

Tilly never asked such a question. In a way, Jenny was saddened by this, but on the other hand, Tilly had never got on with her father.

* * *

Jenny was standing at the counter in the cooperative store where Fred Stacey, the brown-coated manager, was pushing the bacon slicer backwards and forwards.

'And a pound of cheese,' she said as Fred wrapped the pound of back bacon in greaseproof paper before slipping it into a brown paper bag.

'Want any bacon bones? I got a lot of bacon bones. Think me customers must 'ave won the pools, with all the bacon they've bought of late.'

Fred hadn't necessarily sold a ton of bacon but was of a generous disposition and made a habit of giving away the bacon bones after slicing away the meat. Men got a slice of bacon for breakfast before work and the bones made the basis of a meal for the kids. He was also in the habit of giving away the rind from truckles of Cheddar cheese for grating onto bread and toasting.

Jenny thanked him. 'Just enough to make a stock for some vegetables.'

'Free to my most beautiful customers.' He winked.

She smiled. 'Fred, you're a flirt and a fibber, plus a bit short-sighted. Mrs Russell from our street was getting on for eighty if she was a day.'

'All me customers are beauties!'

His big belly jiggled as he laughed and the cheese-cutting wire made a twanging noise as he stretched it above his head before applying it to a truckle of Cheddar cheese.

'Cheeky devil,' said one of the women in the queue behind her.

Titters of laughter, feet shuffling through the sawdust-covered floor as they edged forward, keen to get a bag of free bones before they were all gone.

A woman Jenny didn't know nudged her in the ribs.

'I 'ear a woman died in Coronation Close. You live there, don't you?'

'Yes. I do.'

'I 'ear the 'ouse where Mrs Russell used to live is already taken.'

'So I believe.' She'd heard the house was let and the new residents would shortly move in.

'But there'll soon be another one?'

'I suppose so, once the council clear it out.' The woman, who smelled of grease and unwashed clothes, gave her another nudge.

'Wouldn't mind either of them 'ouses meself.' She took the cigarette she'd been smoking out of her mouth and threw it on the floor, grinding it into the sawdust with the sole of her shabby shoe.

Jenny gave no response. She exchanged a quick look with Fred as he handed her the bones and the other purchases she'd made.

'Might be seeing you,' the woman called after her as she left the store.

Jenny pretended she hadn't heard. Dorothy Partridge hadn't been the ideal neighbour, but at least she'd been clean. A smell of ingrained dirt, biscuit crumbs and sweat was enough to make it obvious that the woman who'd nudged her wasn't so particular.

As she left the shop, she had a feeling of being watched from the other side of the green. Without looking over, she knew Robin was standing in the doorway, waving to her.

She stopped to study the display of knitting yarns, needles, bobbins and knitted babywear in Rigby's shop window. A series of knitting patterns were taped on the inside of the glass. She read what it said, something about lightweight wools for summer matinee jackets, and a heavier wool for winter ones. Bootees too. And hats. And mittens. None of it was relevant to her, but she read it anyway.

It was a crowded window with highly reflective glass. Robin's face appeared in the reflection beside hers.

'Were you going to ignore me? If so, it saddens me. Are you coming on over for a cup of tea?'

She wanted to say yes and she also wanted to say no. His kiss had excited her, but still the old guilt lingered.

Her eyes fluttered away from the window. She half turned, glancing up and down the road, just in case anyone from her street was watching. She saw nobody she knew.

A slight blush coloured her cheeks and she averted her eyes. It was best that way, best not to see the warmth in his eyes, the way his brandy-coloured hair flopped onto his forehead and curled over the nape of his neck.

'How's your wife?'

He shook his head, his lips pursed with exasperation.

'Still living rent free – so I hear.'

'I'm sorry. That was unfair of me.'

'Moved in with the latest fancy man. Still expects me to maintain 'er and the kids though.'

Jenny looked at him, appalled. 'Is he keeping her?'

He nodded. 'Keeping her in the high life. She always said that was what she wanted. But they're my kids, Jenny. They're still my kids. I 'ave to do me best by them.'

For a moment, from the broken wording of his voice, she thought he was going to break down. His sigh was deep enough to erupt into sobs. She felt so sorry for him.

'I'm so sorry.' She made her mind up there and then. 'I'll take you up on that offer. We could have a chat.'

Of course he nodded and said he would like that. Uncaring of whether anyone was watching or not, she went with him along the path that cut through the grass to his shop.

21

Thelma passed the letter she'd received from George to Jenny.

'Read it.'

Jenny began reading it to herself.

'Out loud,' Thelma instructed. 'So Cath can hear.'

Jenny took a deep breath and began to read. 'Dear Ma, I've got married. Her name is Gina. She's Italian. I met her in Naples. She gave me lessons on the mandolin. I now have my own one. Hope to see you before the end of the year. You'll meet my wife then. Much love, George.'

Jenny laughed. 'Congratulations are in order. Shame we couldn't take part in the celebrations, but no doubt we will when he brings her home.'

Her attempt at reassurance appeared futile.

Thelma's frown was a deep vee above her nose and there was hardness in her eyes. 'She's foreign. An Italian girl.'

Cath remarked in all innocence that she'd heard Italian girls were very pretty. 'Dark and smouldering.' She giggled.

Thelma's frown deepened. 'And what would you know about Italian girls? Have you ever met one?'

A squashed-looking Cath fiddled with her fingers. 'Well... no... Bill said...'

'And what would Bill know about Italian girls, might I ask?'

Cath hung her head.

Jenny felt obliged to intervene. 'Was Bill ever in the navy?' she asked.

Cath nodded. 'Merchant Navy. Went all over the place when 'e was young. I waited for 'im. We'd promised each other we'd marry and so I waited.'

On receiving a withering look from Thelma, she didn't say anything more.

Thelma was as a block of white marble. Her eyes were glazed, her red mouth a tight line of indignation and she could have cracked walnut shells with her jaw. Her hands and fingers were clenched so tightly, Jenny was unsure whether the crimson fingernails were varnish or blood.

Jenny latched onto the more positive side of the news. 'As long as they're happy,' she offered. 'That's all any of us want from marriage – isn't it?'

Rarely did Thelma show signs of weakness, but she did now. A handkerchief came out from her sleeve and she dabbed at her eyes.

'I wanted him to marry a local girl, one who'd move into a council house nearby so I could see the grandchildren regularly.'

'Come on, Thelm. Give them a chance. They've only just got married.'

'My name's Thelma.'

Cath blanched when Thelma threw her a withering look; she didn't like her name being shortened.

'Thelma,' Cath corrected herself. 'Fancy another cup of tea?'

'No.' Thelma got up from her chair. 'I've got some ironing today. Can't go into Bertrams looking like a bag of rubbish.'

Cath gave no sign of seeing the shaming look that flew her way. 'Point taken. I've to do a bit too. My John's left school and is going for a job interview tomorrow. 'Ope 'e gets it.'

'He's a nice boy, your John,' Jenny said brightly. 'I'm sure he will.'

'My John's a good worker. Used to look after the milkman's 'orse when 'e was a nipper. Can't wait to get out in the world and earn some money. Says 'e wants to be rich someday.' She laughed; happiness restored. She was always happy talking about her children. 'You coming, Jenny?'

Jenny wanted to linger and try to reassure her friend. She also wanted to confide in Thelma about her own problems, but she went anyway.

Night had not yet fallen. The air smelled of cut grass, privet flowers and the scents from the roses that had once been Dorothy Partridge's pride and joy. The house was still empty, awaiting its new tenants.

Mrs Russell's house had already been let to a Mr and Mrs Arkle, who had four children of various ages.

At present, there was no sign of the dark-eyed, dark-skinned Arkle boys, the eldest of whom had to be about fourteen. The father Frank had a nut-brown skin, a shiny pate fringed with dark hair and a wide girth. He spoke in a booming voice, no doubt as a direct result of his job selling fruit and vegetables from a barrow in Bedminster. His wife, Rosellia, didn't speak a word of English but smiled and nodded a lot when you spoke to her – as if she did understand. Word had it that she was Spanish.

Not once did it occur to Jenny that the new neighbours might be the reason for Thelma taking a dim view of her son's marriage. Thelma had been looking forward to George eventually leaving the sea and settling down at home. Home might not now be

Bristol but somewhere in Italy, his wife's country. Mrs Arkle reminded Thelma of the fact.

'I'll be off then,' said Cath.

Jenny heard her, but her thoughts were elsewhere. She was looking to where the street sign stood as firm as ever, though not so clean as it had been.

'You know what, Cath, I got used to Mrs Partridge cleaning that sign. I wouldn't want it to get too grubby. I might even take to cleaning it myself.'

'You'll need a stepladder.'

'A chair would do.'

'I suppose it would.'

'Oh blast. I've left my cardigan behind. See you tomorrow.'

She didn't wait to see the possessive look on Cath's face. The truth was she'd left the cardigan behind on purpose. It was the only way she could think to have a quiet word with Thelma.

Thelma was standing in the back doorway, Jenny's lemon cardigan held outright in one hand. 'I thought you'd be back – and not only for the cardigan.'

Jenny took the cardigan. Together, they stood by the back door, their backs against the warm brick walls watching the moths and insects in a haze of sunset.

'You must let him go, Thelma. George, I mean.'

Thelma crossed her arms, her glare rigidly fixed on the flying insects at the end of the garden. 'I know who you mean,' she said grimly.

'Even if he does decide to live over there when he comes out of the navy, he's a grown man. You left home yourself and got married, didn't you?'

Thelma sucked on a cigarette, blowing the smoke into the evening air whilst jerking her chin upwards, her head back. 'I didn't leave home. Home left me. I grew up in an orphanage – a children's home. I never knew my mother. For all I know, she never knew my father – being of a certain profession.'

It would have been easy to be speechless, but Jenny refused to show any sign of surprise. Yes, she was surprised, but she was also determined to give Thelma all the support she could. Condemning her background was irrelevant.

'I didn't know. All the more reason for supporting George – and meeting his wife. They're married, Thelma. He's old enough to know his own mind.' She shook her head and flattened herself more firmly against the back wall of the house. The warmth of the brickwork was soothing.

Thelma flicked her spent cigarette into the ashbin. 'Oh well. Not much I can do about it.' She sighed deeply. 'Who knows? I might get married. Old Bert does like his home comfort.'

'And what about his mother?'

'She's not so bad.' Thelma smiled.

For the first time since reading out the letter, she seemed more relaxed and even a little wistful.

'She's invited me for tea on Sunday.'

'You might end up with her as a mother-in-law.'

Together they burst out laughing. It was a joke, but a possibility. Who knew indeed!

Before leaving, Thelma insisted on showing Jenny the lovely teapot given to her by Mrs Throgmorton. 'She gave me a coronation mug after the street party. Now she's given me this. A coronation teapot. Bert brought it over by way of a birthday present from both of them.'

'I didn't know it was your birthday.'

Thelma grinned. 'My birthday's in February. Or at least I think it is.'

For a moment, the shadow of the orphanage darkened Thelma's features then was gone.

'It was to celebrate her birthday, by way of an invitation if you like to the tea party. Oh my!' Thelma clutched at her stomach. 'I'm so nervous, Jenny. I've never been to her house.'

'She seemed nice enough at the street party.'

Thelma placed the teapot back on the dresser and covered her face. 'Don't remind me! I was in fancy dress – Jean Harlow. That dress! It clung to everything!'

They laughed together.

'I'd better wear something a bit more restrained on Sunday. Will you help me choose what's best to wear?'

A cheeky grin lifting one side of her mouth, Jenny looked at Thelma appraisingly. 'As long as you don't wear that Jean Harlow dress. Not suitable for Sunday tea. Not suitable full stop!'

Thelma saw the funny side. 'Would be funny though, wouldn't it.'

'Funny but not wise.'

'I'm nervous.'

'Of course you are. I know it's useless telling you not to be. She isn't going to eat you.'

'No. No. Of course not.' Her breasts rose to meet the hand that patted her racing heart.

'She's just an old lady.'

Thelma pulled a disbelieving expression. 'She's more than that! She's Bert's mother.'

'Forget that if you can. Enjoy the moment and when you get back, you can tell me all about it.'

22

The day of going to tea with Bert and his mother arrived and Thelma was a bag of nerves. Whilst waiting for Bert to collect her, she rushed in and out of the bathroom.

'Do I look all right?' she asked Alice, who of course said yes.

Still in need of reassurance, Thelma turned to Mary, her other daughter.

After rolling their eyes at each other that yet again she was seeking some flattery , her two daughters repeated that she looked very fine indeed.

'He's not going to eat you, for goodness' sake.'

Thelma pursed her lips at the mirror murmuring, 'That might be nice.'

Time and time again, she touched up her lipstick, though it didn't need it. Then she rubbed it off, thinking it perhaps a bit too bright. Another perusal in the mirror and she put it on again.

Her girls were preparing their own Sunday tea and had invited Gloria and Tilly. No doubt Jenny would come too. Thelma hoped Jenny would be here when she got back so she could pour out everything that had happened. She'd asked Bert why she was being invited.

'I thought your mother didn't hold with you going out with women. She's always wanted you home at ten.'

He didn't flinch when she said that. She'd wanted to say that she knew he didn't go straight home but held back. On the one hand, she was curious, but on the other, she didn't want to lose him. The thought of that surprised her, though, on reflection, she'd been let down before and although she'd got over it, she wasn't sure she could cope so well if Bert gave her the shove.

The car horn sounded. Bert had arrived.

Thelma, her eyes shining, took a deep breath, popped the lipstick into her handbag and snapped it shut.

'Well, here goes,' she whispered.

The girls watched her from the front door. The day was warm and she was glad she'd opted for a navy jacket, matching skirt and white blouse. It suited Sunday, she'd thought on scrutinising her appearance. The rest of the clothes she'd tried on and discarded remained on the bed upstairs. Not for long though. The girls would tidy up after her. They were good her girls, responsibly mature for their age too.

Holding one gloved hand against her stomach did little to settle the collywobbles. Her gloves were cream and matched her handbag. Her shoes were two-tone – navy and white. The whole outfit gave her a crisp and clean appearance – a bit like a Sunday school teacher, she thought and almost giggled. As if she would ever look like a school teacher – or behave like one either.

She was smiling and still feeling giggly when she got into the car.

'You look happy,' said Bert and, judging by his expression, took pleasure from it.

'I hope your mother's got the best china out.'

He looked surprised. 'We always have the best china out on a Sunday.'

'Not specially for me then.'

The smell of tobacco wafted over her when he laughed. 'You're a card, Thelma Dawson. A right card!'

It sounded approving.

* * *

Homefield was an end terraced house with an arched entrance porch, bay windows and battalions of gladioli nodding pink and purple against the pebble-dashed walls. Many such houses had been built by private builders in the twenties. Thelma had only ever entered one such house. One of her posher school friends had lived in one in Bedminster Road, across from where the Malago, a tributary to the river Avon, tumbled and chortled between grassy banks. All she remembered from then was being in awe, though, thinking back, the bathroom had been long and narrow, the kitchen much the same.

The friendship hadn't lasted long. The girl, whose name she'd long forgotten, had been very popular so had bequeathed her friendship like a princess throwing bread to the poor. The last Thelma had heard of her she'd married an insurance clerk. In a way, it was spiteful, but Thelma hoped the marriage had ended up as uninteresting as it sounded. Real friends lasted forever. Her friendship had been as fleeting as a moth flitting through candle-light. Nowadays, she had really good friends and appreciated them.

Bert put his key in the front door and let them in. A long passage ran from the front of the house to the back.

Now, Thelma thought, will we be in the living room or the parlour? The parlour – or front room – was normally kept for special occasions or special visitors. The question was whether she was a special visitor or only fit for the back room.

'In here,' said Bert as he opened the first door they came to.

The parlour! My. She was favoured.

The room had beige wallpaper, and a brown and burgundy rug in front of the fireplace relieved the parquet flooring. The beige three-piece suite blended with the walls. A gas fire sat in the grate of a walnut fire surround surmounted by a central mirror. To either side of it were two cherubs holding porcelain candlesticks.

Seated in one of the armchairs, Mrs Throgmorton raised her head but didn't get up.

'My dear. Do sit down.'

Thelma sat where indicated. A low table divided the space between her and her host.

'Thank you for the invitation,' said Thelma. She gripped her handbag tightly in her lap and found herself wondering whether she'd got it wrong. There were no porcelain cups and saucers on the table. Nothing in fact.

As on the first occasion they'd met, Mrs Throgmorton was wearing a pearl choker and earrings. Other than that, her outfit was less ostentatious, a pale green twinset, a box-pleated skirt.

Thelma swallowed her nerves and forced her fingers not to grip her handbag quite so tightly. This was just a woman. Just because she was Bert's mother...

'Cuthbert. Make the tea. I've set out two trays. One for tea, one for cake. I've cleared the coffee table,' she added, indicating the low table.

So that's what it is, thought Thelma. *A coffee table. I must have one of those, quite something different to a big old dining table filling up the room.*

'Is there anything...?'

'Cuthbert. I want to speak with Thelma alone. Now go and do as you're told.'

Bert leaving the room was disconcerting and his meek response came as something of a surprise.

Thelma's trepidation increased. Here she was sitting across from Bert's mother ready to be interrogated and perhaps warned off?

Mrs Throgmorton wasted no time. 'My son has a secret life. I can tell from the look on your face that you didn't know that. He meets up with you and then he goes on to his obsession. I've tried to dissuade him. Tell him he'll never get anywhere. But he turns a deaf ear.' She sighed, leaned back and closed her hooded eyes, the wrinkles around them flattening in the process.

Thelma didn't know what to say. Cath's husband, Bill, had been coming home from work late at night when he'd sworn he'd seen him. Cath had been adamant. Thelma had told her she was mistaken. She'd not mentioned it to Bert, fearing what she might hear. Now, his mother had mentioned an obsession and Thelma dreaded what this obsession might be. Gambling? Drinking? From what his mother had divulged so far, it didn't seem very likely that another woman – or numerous other women – were involved. For that at least, she was grateful, but then what about the other likely sins?

It was no good. Her curiosity overwhelmed the trepidation she had feared before coming here. Nervousness flew swiftly out of the window.

'What exactly are you talking about?'

She was rewarded with a thin-lipped smile and a flash of what looked like amusement in the all-seeing eyes.

'The place he goes to after he leaves you. He used to carry out his work in the shed at the bottom of the garden until I complained about the sound of the wheel – turning, turning, turning!'

Mrs Throgmorton sighed, turned her head and rested her brow in her slim-fingered hand.

At first, it seemed that she was sobbing, and then the truth hit. She was laughing, a low controlled laugh. What was more, Thelma realised that the joke was on her. Her ignorance. Her stupidity.

Thelma leaped to her feet, a picture of pure indignance. 'Look. I didn't come here to listen to riddles. Either put me in the picture and not subject me to your ridicule, or I'm off home! We passed a bus stop on the way here...'

'Please.' Mrs Throgmorton raised her hand and focused her eyes. Thelma read honesty, but also the same warmth she'd thought she'd seen in her own living room.

Bert chose that moment to come in pushing a two-tier tea trolley. Thelma had only seen the likes of such things at work, pushed by the tea lady, the rattling cups and saucers surrounding a large tea urn. This one was much smaller, made of wood and adorned with crisp white paper doilies.

Slowly, her mind no longer reeling with worrying possibilities, Thelma sat back down.

'I was about to tell Thelma about your obsession and your deafness to my insistence that you give it up.'

'Oh yes, Mother,' said Bert without looking up. He concentrated on pouring tea, adding milk and sugar, offering Thelma a slice of Victoria sponge, a jam tart, a cucumber sandwich.

An amused smile creased Mrs Throgmorton's lips as she accepted her tea. She took a sip.

'My son sculpts and pots. Thankfully, no longer in the shed. He's got a proper studio now. And a kiln. Isn't that right, Cuthbert?'

Thelma fancied she saw a splash of colour come to Bert's cheeks. The poor love. He looked embarrassed that his secret was out. But why? Why had he been so embarrassed to tell her that he didn't go home to his mother after leaving her, that he went to his studio?

All the suspicions she'd had were drowned in a mouthful of tea and never had a slice of Victoria sponge tasted so good.

'I didn't know you were artistic.'

Bert looked away. 'I don't like people to know. They might make fun.'

'Fun? But why. Even if you're no good at it, if you enjoy it...' She fancied she had hit a raw nerve. Perhaps hinting that he wasn't much good was the wrong thing to do.

'I'd like to think I might get a job throwing pots one day, making jugs and mugs.'

Mrs Throgmorton shook her head. Mirth was still in her eyes but coupled, so Thelma thought, with love. It came to her that she was a strong woman – just as she was. As for Bert, well, he was different – she'd never quite known how different. How must it be, she wondered, to be clever with clay but having to do a mundane job, tramping around the streets making sure others did their job? Before that, he'd been one of those he now checked on. It must have been doubly bad back then.

Placing her cup back into her saucer and brushing cake crumbs onto her plate, Thelma asked Bert when he would show her his work.

His jaw worked and his eyes were downcast as he thought about it.

Eventually, he looked her way. 'I'll pick you up tomorrow night and we'll go straight there. How would that be?'

'Wonderful.' Thelma beamed, surprised and bemused that he should feel a need to hide what he did. 'Quite wonderful.'

23

'You'll enjoy the day out,' Thelma insisted. 'You need to get out and about a bit more.'

Jenny wasn't sure she needed to at all, but Thelma was insistent.

'Get the bus into town. You know where Bertrams is. Wait for me outside and we can go for a bite to eat in the Busy Bee teashop. They do a lovely apple pie with cream. Or a custard slice if you would prefer that.'

Jenny flashed her a dimpled, mischievous look. 'I might miss something in Coronation Close. The new people are moving in next door today.'

'You can get to know them in time. Coronation Close is hardly the centre of the earth, you know.'

'But I live there. It's my world.'

'I'll show you around the shop. Mr Bertram won't mind.'

The idea quite appealed. Because there was the possibility of bumping into Mr Bertram himself, besides all those posh customers.

Jenny wore a dark green jacket and skirt Thelma had told her to wear.

'That costume makes you look dark and mysterious,' she'd pronounced.

Jenny was unsure, but Thelma had a way of delivering advice as an order.

Teaming it with a white blouse with a crisp collar, she set off to meet her friend and neighbour.

* * *

It wasn't the first time Jenny had stood outside Bertrams double-fronted window displays, but she'd never thought to enter. The prices were far above her pocket and the women she saw go in and out were elegantly dressed in the latest fashions. Some alighted from chauffeur-driven cars, the glinting paws of fox furs falling from shoulders. Others walked with their heads held high, their stride full of confidence and entitlement. Jenny wondered whether they'd left their cars – chauffeur-driven or otherwise – close by.

Thelma had told her to be here by one. The plan was that she would come out and take her in for a quick look. Jenny had no watch with which to check the time, but a black figured clock hanging from wrought-iron brackets from the next building told her it was slightly past that. She wondered whether Thelma had already popped out, saw she wasn't there and went back in again. The shop sometimes got very busy – 'hardly enough time to go to the ladies,' Thelma had declared.

Jenny looked up and down the street. There was no sign of her.

'Right,' she said, as yet another square-shouldered, fur-wearing woman pushed open the door to the shop. 'Here goes.'

* * *

Of all the days. Thelma had kept glancing up at the wall clock. Jenny would be outside waiting for her. She couldn't go out. Not yet. Not until that dastardly rat and his elderly floozy had gone.

Whilst Charlie Talbot smoked, his slinky, sultry companion sorted through silk handkerchiefs. He carefully averted his eyes though must have known that Thelma was looking at him.

'Have you any finer ones? These are not quite what I'm used to.' Her manner was aloof and at the same time condescending. Thin red lips curled over her utterances as though she was spitting lemon pips.

Thelma had observed her from the moment she'd entered and decided that it was not Mrs Justin-Cooper, the other woman she'd seen him squiring. This one was older, had tightly curled grey hair but amazing bone structure. With hair of that colour, she had to be in her sixties. Her face and figure were well maintained. *A good corset*, thought Thelma, *does marvels*.

'They're the very best we have,' said Thelma, a rictus smile fixed on her face. The woman she could cope with; the same ilk as most of Bertrams' clients. Wealthy, married and bored. Charlie Talbot was another matter. What was he to this woman? She thought she knew, but dear Jenny had no idea. She'd come across women like this before. Come to that, she'd also come across men like Charlie Talbot. A gigolo, a younger man who latched onto older, wealthy, lonely women, accepting gifts, escorting them to wherever they wanted to go – and all at the woman's expense.

How could she tell Jenny? She couldn't. She didn't want her to see him. The pain would be too terrible.

When her gaze yet again strayed to the clock, she felt Charlie watching her. Her suspicion was confirmed when, for the briefest moment, their eyes locked.

Thelma looked away. He'd let Jenny down on the night of the gas explosion. He'd left her there and, without saying a word, had disappeared, never got in contact again. A relief to Thelma, it meant she didn't have to expose what he did, what she believed he was.

As it turned out he'd never got in touch with Jenny again and for that she was grateful. Never would she have to explain to Jenny that he squired wealthy women. He'd disappeared and that had been it – or so she'd thought. Now here he was again.

She glanced at the shop door and prayed that Jenny wouldn't appear. If only they'd arranged another day for her to visit. What a predicament. All Thelma hoped was that she didn't come barging in and see him, the man who she'd thought herself in love with who had scarpered without any explanation or a swift adieu.

Whatever fates were floating about, they didn't hear her prayer. Unknowing what she would face, what surprise was in store, there was Jenny, swanning through the door in her dark green outfit set off by the crisp white blouse. She looked a picture, and judging by the shocked expression on Charlie's face, he thought so too.

'Excuse me.' Thelma didn't give the woman time to demand more handkerchiefs. Neither did she give time for any exclamation from Charlie. She darted off and placed herself between Jenny and the two people standing at her counter. She so didn't want her hurt. She'd do anything she could to stop that happening. 'Jenny! Come along here with me. There's something I have to show you.'

Ignoring Jenny's gasp of surprise, Thelma grabbed hold of her arm, intending to frogmarch her along the passageway to the back storerooms and the small closet that contained the staff WC.

Hardly a place to be shown to the general public, but that wasn't her intention.

Jenny glanced over Thelma's shoulder. 'Shouldn't you be serving those people?'

'I'll get someone to take over my customers. I won't be a moment.'

The arm she'd grabbed suddenly stiffened. It was too late. Any attempt to drag Jenny away proved futile. She stood immovable, staring at the two figures standing in front of the counter. The woman was still shuffling through the drawer of silk handkerchiefs, unaware of what was going on. Charlie, on the other hand, was looking transfixed, staring at Jenny, two people across a room oblivious for now of everything else. A cashmere coat hung nonchalantly around his shoulders. The smoke from his cigarette rose languorously upwards towards the downturned brim of his hat.

'Jenny. I didn't expect to see you here.'

A puzzled look on her face, Jenny's lips parted slightly. There was a tightness in her chest and her breath seemed to catch in her throat.

'Charlie.'

It was all she could say and came out hushed on a zephyr of breath.

Thelma tugged at her arm. 'Come on, Jenny. I'll get my coat and we'll go for that tea and cake we promised ourselves. Sarah's here. I can go now.'

Sarah Brown was Thelma's underling, just learning the job, brightly enthusiastic but entirely insensitive to what was going on.

'My colleague Mrs Dawson is off out to lunch with her friend. Dressed by us by the looks of her. Doesn't she look wonderful?'

The woman's cool grey eyes raked Jenny from head to toe.

'Very smart. I'd quite like an outfit like that, though in blue rather than green – to match my colouring. Can Bertrams supply something similar?'

Sarah explained that even if they didn't have the outfit in stock, they could employ a seamstress to make one for her.

This was the last thing Thelma wanted to happen, Jenny was the centre of attention and as such could not avoid looking at Charlie and his companion and coming to the obvious conclusion.

'Order one for me, will you?'

'There will be a deposit incurred if we have to employ a seamstress.'

'Put it on my account.'

Whilst she busied herself handing over a deposit for an outfit she would find they didn't have, Charlie took his hat off and nodded at Jenny.

She smelled the familiar scent of cigarettes, hair oil and good-quality clothes.

'Nice to see you again. How are you?' He kept his voice low.

'Very well.'

He glanced over his shoulder at his companion before continuing. 'I'm sorry I haven't been in touch. I've been a bit busy.'

'Oh.'

'I've opened up an office just off the alley where you used to live. Most of the houses around there have gone or are going. I've been installed there where I decant advice to people with problems.'

'What kind of problems?'

He shrugged his shoulders sideways. 'This and that. Housing mainly. But other needs too.'

'She doesn't look as though she's in need,' said Jenny, indicating the woman with a sharp jerk of her chin.

He gave a little laugh. 'She isn't. Her husband's a councillor. He asked me to take her shopping. She doesn't drive, but I do.'

'That's nice for her.'

She was aware of Thelma fidgeting beside her, shuffling her feet and making tutting noises. She only stopped when one of the sales assistants asked her where she could find more carrier bags as she'd ran out.

Huffing and puffing, Thelma left to find what they could not.

'I don't think your friend approves of me.'

'I'm not sure I do. You left me to handle a very difficult moment in my life and never got in touch.'

'Tell you what. How about you call in on me when you leave here? Here's the address.' He handed her a small white card. On it was printed an address not far from Blue Bowl Alley in the Pithay.

Beyond his right shoulder, Jenny could see the councillor's wife taking another look at the drawer of silk handkerchiefs before pushing it aside. 'No. Definitely not. I'm not even sure they're real silk.'

Handbag scooped onto one arm, she approached with an air of finality, of superiority, of all the things those of her class felt entitled to, including looking down her nose at lesser mortals.

'Ah. Charles, my darling. There you are. We have one more shop to call in on before I let you go. I saw a simply sweet pair of crocodile shoes in Lamberts. They're not likely to have my size, but I'm sure they wouldn't be too insufferably long in getting a pair made.'

There was something predatory and possessive in the way she locked her arm into the crook of Charlie's arm. She acknowledged neither Thelma, who had now returned from her mission, nor Jenny, but with a self-satisfied smile looked straight ahead.

On reaching the fine mahogany double doors, she stopped

dead. Shrugging her fox fur more securely around her shoulders, she glanced meaningfully at the door handle, then at Charlie.

Without preamble, Charlie opened the door for her and stood back until she'd glided through. He turned then and looked directly at Jenny. His expression was laconic, but not in the least apologetic. 'Nice to see you again. Perhaps we could get together some time. Have to go now. Toodle-pip.'

The door made a whooshing sound as it closed behind them, like a brush swept over a rough stone floor.

'Get together? What does he mean by that? He's not been in touch with you for ages and now he's suggesting you get together. Take a tip from me. Keep yourself to yourself. He's not worth bothering with.'

Though she heard what Thelma had said, Jenny couldn't quite take it in. She stood agape. She didn't understand his attitude. Where was the warmth? Where was the passion she'd dreamed there would be? But what happened in dreams didn't always come true or look so good in the clear light of day.

'My mouth is as dry as the bottom of a birdcage,' Thelma remarked, directing Jenny out of the store.

They conversed in general terms as they made their way to the Busy Bee Tearoom. Steamed-up windows semi obliterated the inside scene, but a decorative display of teapots ranged along the window ledge was still discernible.

Once inside, a waitress in a black and white uniform showed them to a table in the window, close to the row of vintage teapots. The tables and chairs were of dark wooden country style. The tablecloths were white and a brass ashtray sat in the centre of each table. It was a place trying to look countrified even though it was in the centre of the city.

Accompanied by the clattering of crockery, conversation between customers and waitresses calling out orders, they took their seats. A pot of tea sat between them. Thelma had ordered a piece of apple pie with custard. Jenny, still reeling from her encounter with a man she'd thought she loved, nibbled at a digestive biscuit. It was all she could stomach. She'd slipped the white card into her pocket.

'He's asked if we can meet up.'

'You're not going to are you?' Thelma sounded appalled.

Jenny shook her head. 'I don't think so. I mean, he shot off that night and never came back. No excuse. No further contact. I've often thought about meeting up with him again, but...'

Thelma couldn't keep her mouth shut any longer. Not once had Jenny said anything about Charlie's companion, supposedly the wife of a city councillor. She didn't believe a word of it.

'Jenny. I have a confession to make.'

Jenny blinked away the thoughts of Charlie, of going to the address he'd given her. 'I'm all ears.'

Thelma leaned forward and scrutinised her face and settled on Jenny's eyelashes. 'My, but your eyelashes are so long and thick. No need of mascara for you, Mrs Crawford. I use loads.'

Calling her by her married name was only meant in fun, but somehow jarred.

'And that's your confession? That you use far too much mascara?'

Thelma shook her head, eyes wide with intent. The truth had to be told. 'No. It's not. I know how you feel about Charlie, but he's not quite what you thought he was.' She said it with a toss of her head that gave the impression she knew lots of things Jenny wasn't privy to.

It rankled.

Jenny frowned. 'I was surprised that he didn't get in touch. I couldn't work out why and had no way of knowing where he was.' Her frown deepened. 'Come to think of it, we used to run into each other or arrange to go out for a drink – or to see Isaac and Ruth of course.'

'So you never knew where he lived.'

Jenny shook her head. 'Never.'

There'd been no need to. That's what she reminded herself. Especially when Roy was still around. In fact, he'd told her he lived away.

'I think he told me he lived in London. But that was a while ago when I first met him.'

With a flourish, Thelma took what was left of her cigarette and stubbed it out in the ashtray. 'Strikes me he's good at making up stories. Mention of distance is always guaranteed to camouflage the truth.'

'I don't think he was lying. Besides, he does seem to be a bit classy. I think he's been to a posh school.'

'He told you this?'

Jenny shook her head. 'But he was with a councillor's wife. He must know people.'

Thelma snorted. 'Poppycock! How do we know he's not just a hired man for the day.'

'You mean a chauffeur?'

'No. I do not mean a chauffeur! I mean that it's very likely that woman hired him.' She paused. 'For other reasons.'

Jenny shook her head. 'Why would she?'

Recognising it was time to tell the truth, Thelma sighed. 'He escorts wealthy women and they pay for his services. And don't look at me like that,' she said when Jenny looked so disbelieving. 'It's not the first woman I've seen him with.'

Jenny laughed. 'The other woman might have been a relative.' She shook her head.

There were times when it hit Thelma that she was too worldly wise for her own good. She'd lived a bit in her time. Jenny had not had nearly quite so exciting a life – especially where men were concerned.

Forehead creased in thought, she brushed a few stray crumbs from her lips. 'It's like this. The two women I've seen him with were older and very wealthy. The first one bought the kind of nightdress that a bride would wear on honeymoon. This second one – well – she was only buying silk handkerchiefs – or didn't as it turned out. Like a lot of her kind, she was difficult to please.'

Jenny's eyes were wide as saucers. Thelma bit her lip. How much information did she have to give? Surely Jenny knew what she was getting at.

'Charlie is a...' She paused, took a deep breath and then let it out. 'A gigolo!'

At first, she saw no response in those serene grey eyes – and then there was shock, followed by disbelief.

Jenny's shaking head released silky tresses of hair. 'That can't be true.'

'You do know what I mean, do you?'

'Of course I do,' Jenny replied hotly. 'I'm not stupid.'

Taken aback by the fiery expression and angry voice, Thelma retreated further back in her chair.

For her part, Jenny crumbled bits of biscuit between white-knuckled fingers and watched as the crumbs fell onto the plate.

After some thought, she frowned and asked, 'How do you know for sure? How do you know they weren't relatives? And, before you answer, it is feasible that this one was the wife of a friend – a councillor even.'

A sad smile preceded Thelma's answer. 'Would he have dashed out so quickly if she'd been his aunt or something? He would have introduced you to her. He dashed off on the night of the explosion when he saw me. He recognised me and knew the game was up.'

It was hard for Jenny to cope with the turmoil she was feeling inside. Best, she decided, to push it to one side, at least for the time being. She pasted a smile on her face and changed the subject.

'Never mind me. You told me you went along to see Bert's artwork. What was it like? Is he any good?'

Unknowingly, Jenny had veered onto the one subject that cheered Thelma's spirits up no end, so much so that she almost choked on a mouthful of pie.

'No wonder he was embarrassed about it. No wonder too that he kept it from his mother. He sculpts and paints nudes. Naked bodies.'

Jenny's jaw dropped. 'No!'

'Yes indeed. He can't get any models that late at night, so he uses photographs. Good they are too. His artwork, I mean, though he reckons they'd be better if he could get hold of real models.'

Jenny couldn't control her giggles. 'I can't believe it. Bert Throgmorton of the city council, a budding Leonardo da Vinci – or whatever.' She grinned, then paused as she spotted Thelma's secretive smile. The comment about using real naked models suddenly hit her. 'Thelma. You're not thinking of being one of his models.'

Thelma's smile widened. 'I don't see why not.'

Neither did Jenny. She'd seen paintings of naked women at the city museum. Like Thelma, they were curvaceous with creamy skin, wide hips and, seemingly, a total disregard for convention. That's if their smiles and glowing eyes were anything to go by, plus the fact that they were lounging around stark naked in sylvan groves beneath a perfectly blue sky.

'I think you'd make a very good model,' Jenny pronounced.

'Who knows where it might lead,' Thelma added with a

mischievous smile that made the ends of her eyes turn upwards, catlike at the corners. A glance at the teashop clock. 'Whoops. Time to go.'

Thelma swigged back the last of her tea and sprang to her feet.

She didn't enquire whether Jenny had got over seeing Charlie again. There was no outer sign of it so she presumed she was all right inside too.

A soft drizzle dampened the oncoming afternoon. Once she'd put up her umbrella, Jenny waved once, twice, three times before Thelma disappeared inside Bertrams.

She caught a glimpse of herself in the large expanse of glass to one side of the double doors. Behind the glass, the garish faces of mannequins looked out at her. One of them was wearing a fox fur, just like Charlie's companion. The glassy-eyed expression was not dissimilar to that of the woman handling the handkerchiefs, the one who'd so admired her outfit.

On another occasion, she might have laughed out loud. The fact was that anything like her outfit wouldn't be found in the store. Under Thelma's instruction, she had cut a large second-hand dress into two ample portions. One piece made a three-quarter-length coat, the other a skirt. Congratulating herself might have been enough, if it hadn't been for everything else.

A bus pulled up at the bus stop. Should she get on it and go home, or should she go to where she thought Charlie might be?

Though fearing what she might find, Jenny couldn't help herself. The bus pulled away. Jenny cut across the back of it through the cloud of smoke from its exhaust. A mix of anger and disbelief fuelled her footsteps from a steady walk into a determined march. She had to know for sure whether he was the lounge lizard Thelma reckoned he was. A man paid by women to be their companion, friend, perhaps even lover.

24

As Jenny walked, she fingered the white card nestling at the bottom of her pocket.

Back here. Back to where she'd used to live with Roy and the kids. Back in Blue Bowl Alley. The majority of memories she had of that place were best forgotten.

The open roads around the city centre were left behind. Her footsteps trod a familiar route, echoing over the uneven cobblestones. On leaving the busier thoroughfares of the city centre, she entered the familiar lanes and alleys. Nothing much had changed, except perhaps they were more derelict, more decaying, than they had been. Some had already been reduced to piles of rubble, but for the most part, people were clinging onto the only home they'd ever known.

When she'd lived here, the buildings had altered little since medieval times. Since her leaving, demolition had begun, buildings torn down. The gaps they'd left were like missing teeth. Daylight shone through holes in half-demolished walls. Plants, mostly weeds of course, sprouted defiantly from between broken brickwork.

Some still stood defiantly, though warped with time. In the beginning, they might have towered straight and strong above the narrow lanes. Nowadays, they looked like a gathering of old people, clinging together to stop themselves from collapsing. Time had claimed them.

Curious glances came her way. It wasn't often they saw someone so elegantly dressed. At one time, they might have known her and she might have passed the time of day with them. But not now. She didn't want to linger. She had a mission, one that made her feel sick to her stomach. But she would do it. She wanted to try to understand.

She took the card from her pocket, read it again, then put it away.

The address was not in one of the more ancient buildings of the Pithay but one dating from a later period. It was built of red brick with a bay window and a large front door. A brass knocker gleamed. Inside, to either side of the windows, Jenny could see wooden shutters folded back against the walls. There was no plaque on the door stating the business carried out inside the office. Just a notice saying, 'please knock'.

Three raps. That was all she gave it. The sound echoed around the narrow lane. She looked up and down. Anyone who hadn't heard must be deaf, she thought. As it was, no heads appeared behind the small square windows of the adjoining buildings. Nobody came out of a door to complain about the noise or enquire what she wanted.

From inside came whistling, plus the sound of footsteps tramping down bare wooden stairs.

It was a lover and his lass.

The door opened stubbornly, a bit at a time, until it finally slammed back against the wall.

The hallway was dark, but not dark enough to cloak the identity of Charlie Talbot. He didn't look that surprised to see her. It was as if he'd expected her. Keeping his gaze fixed on her, he stood against the door so she could enter. He accompanied the action with a casual wave.

She entered, aware of leaving the light outside. This hallway was like a burrow, narrow and straight between its walls, which meant she brushed slightly against him as she passed.

'Can I take your coat?'

'No thank you.' She shrugged herself more comfortably into the dark green jacket which helped hide her shivering, a probable result of the cool airs of the building. But mostly, if she was honest, because she was close to him.

'My office is upstairs. First floor. First left.'

Quelling the nervous tension she was feeling, she made her way up the stairs and turned left as he'd instructed.

He'd called this room his office, but it was more than that. At the far end was a gas stove, a small sink beneath a pair of pale green cupboards. A bed took up space in another corner. It unnerved her. Four armchairs formed a semicircle in the alcove of the bow window. Across the way, she could see beyond the gap between the houses to the main road. A policeman paced slowly along beneath her. On reaching the building she was in, he looked purposefully upwards.

What with the bed and the way the policeman scrutinised the building, a respectable woman would feel anxious.

Charlie was in his shirtsleeves. She couldn't remember seeing him like that before. There was something vulnerable about it, as though he'd removed an outer shell. He stood with his hands in his pockets.

'Would you like tea?'

She shook her head, clutched at the handle of her handbag

and cautiously looked around the room. 'This doesn't look much like an office.'

'That bit does,' he said, pointing at a sideboard set against the wall. Piles of papers were on it. A wooden chair in front of it. 'Please. Sit down.'

He pulled out an armchair from the four gathered in the bay window whilst he remained standing with his back to her. He surveyed the world beyond the window and began to talk.

'They've pulled down a lot, but not all of it. Not as much as I thought they would. Apparently the property owners objected to such a big scheme. Said that some of the buildings were perfectly useable.' He made a sound of disapproval, like a steam train that was running out of breath. 'What they're saying is they want more in compensation from the council. The council refuse, so many of these houses will be left standing. Stalemate, so for now it's stopped.' He pointed. 'Look. You can see the damp running down the outside of the wall. Heaven knows what it's like inside.' He turned round. 'I know why you're here. You want to know what I've been up to. To put it simply I'm making friends and influencing people. That's my intention anyway.'

'Thelma says you're a gigolo.'

He laughed uproariously. 'Does she indeed.'

His laughter made her feel self-conscious, so much so that she hesitated to ask the question she wanted to ask, but ultimately it came out.

'The woman. The councillor's wife. Is she one of those you want to influence?'

A slight smile. 'You're curious.'

'Of course I'm curious. Curious that you left me without saying goodbye on the night of the gas explosion. That hurt. And now, today, I see you with this woman...' Anger coloured her cheeks and her words were hot. 'And Thelma tells me she isn't the only one. She's seen you with other women.'

Other wasn't quite true. One other was closer to the truth. But she was angry. She wanted to hit out at him. Thelma had mentioned a Mrs Justin-Cooper who was married to a judge. She'd also stated that the one she'd seen him with was a different one.

'Ah yes.' He smiled when he nodded. 'Maisie.'

'Maisie?'

'Maisie Harcourt. She's married to a city councillor. I'm trying to keep everyone on side, Jenny. You saw what I did for Isaac and Ruth, got them out of that fleapit they were living in and into a new home. If I have to bend a few arms, call in a few favours...'

'And the women?'

He glanced at her and said, 'Women have more influence than you can possibly imagine. That's how I get things done. I get to know people and ask for their help.'

'Or blackmail them into it?'

'If I have to.'

'That still doesn't explain why you left me in the lurch that night.' Her eyes moistened when she narrowed them, but she would not cry.

He dug his hands deeper into his pockets and hung his head. 'I recognised your friend and she recognised me. I wasn't worried about what she thought about me... that I was...'

'A gigolo!'

He looked bemused. 'How very American. Very much a figure of speech from the silver screen.' He paused whilst she simmered before saying, 'I suppose in a way I am. If I can raise money for people who need it, then I'll be what they want me to be.'

Her eyebrows shot up. 'Seriously?'

He shrugged. 'I'm a spoilt little rich boy, Jenny, and enjoy being unconventional. I like kicking over the traces, behaving in a way that my parents disapprove of.'

'You don't really...'

'Free meals, cars, nice clothes – not that I didn't have nice clothes anyway. It's the power it gives me, using my influence to enhance the lives of those of meagre means.'

She tilted her head to one side and eyed him inquisitively. A small frown furrowed her brow. 'If you're rich, why are you living in this place?'

'My parents disowned me.' He took his hands from his pockets and ran them through his hair. His eyes strayed once more to the scene on the other side of the window and then back to her. 'I'm a member of the Communist Party. Do you know what that is?'

She nodded. 'Politics.'

'This is the local headquarters. Members meet here and some who live a fair distance away sometimes stay in the rooms downstairs. We believe in living as the working class live.'

His involvement with the Communist Party explained why the policeman looked up at the house so pointedly when he strolled past.

'Why would you want to do that?'

'Because it's what we believe in.'

He knelt so they were face to face, only inches apart, his hands resting on the arms of her chair.

'I've no need for riches. Money. Things.'

She looked at him appalled. 'But you don't know what it's like to have nothing.'

What did he know? What was she doing here? The Charlie she'd thought she loved was not what he'd seemed. He fell back as she got to her feet.

'I'm off.'

'I'm just trying to help.'

She tried to brush past him but he stopped her. He was so close, his lips just a shade from her hair. She kept her head down.

'You know, I thought the Great War would put an end to all this.' He shrugged and adopted a helpless stance. 'Families deserve better. The heroes coming back from the Great War were promised better housing, better wages, better everything. Didn't happen though, did it.'

She'd heard much the same from Roy, his remarks delivered with bitterness and ire. He'd been a lad when he'd joined up in the last year of the war, but he'd served with older men. Pre-war, those men had struggled to get a job. In a terrible way, the war had been their saviour. It got them three square meals a day and a lice-free bed. But it had also caused recurring nightmares. Men of like mind had exchanged views, determined that they and their families would never want again.

The sound of a door slamming reverberated through the house. Hurrying feet thudded up the stairs. Someone shouted: 'Charlie! Are you there?' A high-pitched, slightly melodic woman's voice floated up the staircase.

Charlie looked mortified and slightly embarrassed. He swore under his breath.

'A friend?'

He didn't get chance to answer.

A sombrely dressed figure, hair shorn close to her head, almost fell through the door. She looked from one to the other. 'Am I a bit early?'

'Yes.' He folded his arms and looked at her.

Brown eyes glowed from the girl's pixie face.

For a moment, their looks held, then she blinked.

'I'll just pop back out and get us some liver. I've got the onions. Won't be long.'

Whoever she was, she seemed to belong here – with him.

'That's Patience. She's a member.'

'I would suggest that she's more than that,' Jenny replied hotly, turned on her heel and made her way to the door. She felt an interloper in his world and half of it she didn't understand.

'Did your friend Thelma really say I was a gigolo?' He smirked as though it was the funniest thing in the world. 'These are tumultuous times, Jenny. We're all getting by as best we can.'

'Aren't we just,' she said, not without some animosity. 'I have to go.'

He followed her down the stairs to the front door.

'I need cigarettes,' he said to her when she reached the front door and turned to look at him.

He followed her outside. They stood uncomfortably, as though hesitant to say goodbye.

His gaze shifted around the narrow alley. 'I'm beginning to like it here – the place, that is. The people – or at last some of them,' he said a trifle ruefully. 'As for this time we're living in...' He shook his head disconsolately. 'Clouds are gathering. Both in this country and abroad.'

'Of war?'

His jaw tensed when he looked at her. 'I don't know. Troubles for certain. A war at home? I hope not. A war between factions of your own is always a tragedy.'

Listening to him speaking of a very serious subject did not frighten her. Perhaps because it was him speaking, the timbre of his voice as warming as a hug on a dark night. It made her feel safe. No one had ever made her feel like that before. But she was married and he inhabited a different world to hers. The talk of war brought a newsreel to mind, one she'd seen at Filwood Broadway Picture House. Men marching a leg-flinging goose step, arms flailing from side to side, flags flapping above their heads.

'I have to go.'

She had no business being here. Charlie wasn't for her. She knew that now – or thought she did.

'Thank you again for what you did in the past, but we're from different worlds and I'm a married woman. I've got kids to think about.'

His hands were back in his pockets. 'It was my pleasure.' He grinned. 'Knocking the breath out of that bloke who laid into old Isaac gave me great satisfaction.'

'He was my husband.'

His eyebrows arched in surprise. 'Oh really?'

Suddenly, she felt awkward, foolish at coming here.

'I think I should be going.'

Even before his long legs were striding out of the alley, he was whistling another song she recognised. *Early one morning, just as the sun was rising, I heard a maiden singing...*

She'd been reluctant to accept Robin's invitation to go for a drink, but only because she'd had a crush on Charlie. That was gone now, along with the need to have anyone. Just a bit of company. That's all she needed.

25

It was the next day when Jenny saw Robin and confirmed her plans.

'I will work for you in the shop, but only two days per week and then only to fit in with the girls going and coming home from school.'

The money would come in handy. That's what she told herself, though deep down she knew it wasn't the whole truth. Robin needed some help. She felt sorry for him and wanted to help and although she loved her house serving in the shop would bring her into contact with people. She could do with a little socialising.

'Great,' he said, looking like a man who'd won a few hundred on the football pools, not just found himself someone to help in the shop.

'I decided the money would come in handy.'

'Great,' he said again, tongue-tied almost.

She tucked her shopping bag more securely over her arm and laughed. 'Is that all you can say?'

'Um. No. What I mean is...' He threw back his head and laughed. 'I might get drunk tonight.'

'Why would that be?'

'Well. It's something of a celebration.'

Folding her arms across her chest, she frowned and feigned being cross, though a suppressed smile twitched at her lips. 'Robin Godwin, if you want to celebrate, you can take me out for a drink. How about tomorrow night?'

His jaw dropped. 'Do you really mean it?'

'I wouldn't have said it otherwise. It'll be nice to meet people.'

'Tomorrow night then.'

'In town. I'll get the bus in.'

He nodded. 'I'll drive the van. I won't be the source of any gossip – for your sake.'

'The Bunch of Grapes in King Street.'

'I'll be there.'

* * *

True to his promise, on the following night, Robin was there waiting for Jenny outside the Bunch of Grapes. At sight of her, he lifted his head, his smile lit by gaslight as he flicked his half-smoked cigarette into the gutter.

There was something pensive about the look he gave her. It was sheepish, a mix of wonder and disbelief.

'You look wonderful. You're a real looker, Jenny. Always have been.'

'Kind of you to say so.' She looked him up and down. 'You look very dapper,' she said to him, deftly smoothing his coat lapel where a speck of dust dared to exist.

He took a deep breath as though he was savouring the compliment prior to swallowing it.

'Shall we go for a drink?' he finally asked.

They toasted each other and their new working relationship with two halves of shandy.

'Is a half enough for you?' she asked him. Most men were pint drinkers.

He took a sip, swiped at his mouth and shook his head. 'I take things a bit at a time.'

Those dark eyes rose to meet hers as he smiled. She didn't need to be told that he was doing the same with her, taking things slowly and one step at a time.

'I'm only working for you, Robin. I must stress that. I've got my reputation to consider and what effect it might have on my girls.'

He raised his hands, palms forward in a gesture of surrender. 'I understand that, Jenny. Believe me, I wouldn't do anything to mess up yer reputation. Cross my heart and hope to die.' He made the requisite sign across his chest. It made her smile.

They both sipped more of their drinks, each wondering what next to say.

Jenny was enjoying the evening out. The girls had gone to the pictures with Thelma and her two. Cath and her two youngest had gone with them. Doubtless Cath would ask where she had gone. Jenny didn't want her to know that she was out with a man. Thelma had declared she would tell her she was going to meet up with her old friend Ruth – even though she was dead. Jenny smiled at the thought of it. Ruth would burst out laughing.

'So, how are your new neighbours in Mrs Russell's old place?'

Jenny frowned. 'I'm not sure yet. The mother is Spanish or Italian, I think, and can't speak much English. They have a lot of children and they seem to run a bit wild. They don't seem to wash much either.'

'Are they noisy?'

She nodded. 'They've been in next door and picked all the flowers from the garden too.'

'Ah. Tied them into bunches and sold them. I thought I saw them outside Arnos Vale Cemetery flogging them to people going in to put flowers on graves. I was there to visit me old mum's patch. Me dad too for that matter.'

'So that's what they did with them.'

'They've made a right mess of the garden at the back. I suppose all the roses in the front garden will go too.'

'Sound an enterprising lot – though a bit wild.' He frowned. 'I wonder what else they'll be getting up to.'

'That's my worry but at least they're not next door. I don't know who's moving in there yet. I can only hope that they'll be good neighbours.'

'Another half?'

Two more drinks sat on the small round table in front of them. The pub was relatively quiet. Cigarette smoke curled lazily around wall-mounted gas lights that made a fizzing sound. Conversation between customers was also low-key, interspersed only occasionally by tinkling laughter, a cough or a clearing of phlegm from a tar-coated throat.

'And how are your girls?'

She smiled as she always did when she thought of her girls. 'They're doing well at school. Miss Burton says that Tilly is very clever. She could go on to college. Gloria is a bit of a minx and is that bit younger. Anyway, I don't mind what they do as long as they're happy.'

'There's always the tobacco factory. It's good money.'

After talking about her children, their conversation naturally turned to his.

A worried look came to his eyes. 'I just hope to God that she don't move away. I don't know what I would do if I couldn't see my kids.'

Sympathy for his plight made Jenny do something she hadn't meant to do. She patted Robin's hand and told him not to worry. Touching him, even if in such a trivial manner, was such a personal thing.

There was pathos in his expression, a look that also hinted at hidden depths.

Swiftly withdrawing her hand, she turned her attention back to her drink, a sip to hide her discomfort. The feel of him had sent a spike of electricity up her arm.

The battered old wall clock, sited next to the dartboard, came to her rescue. 'Goodness. Look at the time. I'd best be going. Thanks for the drink.'

He raised his glass. 'This year is seeing quite a few celebrations. I could get used to it.'

The smoky atmosphere of the Bunch of Grapes dissipated in the clear night air as they headed outside. A faint drizzle misted gas lamps in copper frames. King Street was an old part of the city. The street lamps were very old the cobblestones even older.

As they neared the city centre, a double-decker bus went past that would have taken her all the way home. 'That's torn it. I'll have to get a tram to the London Inn and then a bus from there.'

He stood with her beneath a street lamp, the brim of his hat shading one side of his face. 'I could give you a lift in the van.' He said it hesitantly, unsure of how she might react. 'If you don't mind walking a bit first that is. I've parked it on the other side of Bristol Bridge. I can still get you home quicker than a bus or tram.'

She couldn't deny the truth of what he said. Hesitantly and not without apprehension, she agreed.

They walked away from the pub and towards Castle Street but

turned away from where brightly lit shops still attracted window-shoppers. Groups of girls tittered and flashed their eyes at groups of young men. Promenading up and down Castle Street and roundabout was how those without the money for anything else pursued young men who might end up as sweethearts. There were plenty of the opposite sex there too ready and willing to take advantage of the situation.

The flagstone pavements were uneven and the light rainfall had made them slippery.

Robin grabbed at her arm when she stumbled. 'These pavements are downright dangerous. Hold onto me.'

He kept a tight hold on her arm all the way to Bristol Bridge. *Almost as though he's afraid I might run away*, Jenny thought, her apprehension subdued.

On their way along, they looked down into the dank water of the River Avon.

'Mind if I stop for a smoke?' He fumbled in his pocket, brought out a fresh packet of cigarettes.

She declined. 'You have one. I won't.'

'Oh yeah. You don't smoke. I forgot.'

He put them away again.

His focus remained on the dark water of the river.

Her plan had been to get home as quickly as possible, but it felt as though her fingertips were burning after touching his hand. Something had changed that she hadn't meant to change. She'd been affected by touching him.

'Ships from all over the world come into Bristol.' He said it whilst continuing to regard the dark water. 'I did toy with the idea years ago of jumping aboard a ship and getting out of here. If it hadn't been for me mother, I might 'ave done. But once the old man was gone I couldn't leave 'er to run the business and whatever by 'erself, could I.'

'I suppose not.'

Mention of ships and travelling the world brought George to mind.

'You might have married a different girl if you had. Thelma's son has written to tell her that he's married an Italian girl who's taught him to play the mandolin. She's worried she might never see him again, though he has said he's bringing her home with him.'

Robin laughed. 'Imagine marrying someone because they've taught you to play the mandolin.'

Jenny laughed too. 'I didn't say he married her because of that.'

Before she could do anything about it, she was looking up into his face and he was looking down into hers. Would the inevitable happen? What's more, did she want it to happen?

The night was like a cloak around them, though essentially it had no strength to bring them together. That was purely down to them.

His arms were gentle around her. His kiss left her breathless.

Once his arms had let her go, she leaned away from him.

'You sucked the breath out of me.'

Even in the poor light, she saw the intensity in his eyes.

'I promised I wouldn't take things any further without your permission.'

It was as though a dam had burst inside her, a volcano had erupted.

'You have my permission.'

There it was. The emotion she'd held back broke through. She didn't want to be alone forever. The reason she had warned him off was in aid of keeping up appearances, mostly with regard to Roy, the man who'd gone off to join the army to be with other men. He'd wanted a man's world. With hindsight, their marriage had been an anchor to maintaining his own respectability, not hers. He had never really thought about her, nor about her children.

When Robin had dropped his hands from her arms, she had felt instantly colder. Now they were back on her shoulders and his lips were once again pressing on hers.

She took a step back both physically and mentally.

'I'm not sure I'm ready to get serious about anyone – especially under the circumstances.'

He looked disappointed but accepting. 'I'm prepared to wait. We both have problems to overcome.'

'Problems?'

She wondered whether he knew, what he'd heard. After all, Robin still had contacts in the heart of the city, not so far from where Roy had met up with his friends.

'He's abandoned you. He might have joined the army, but it's still like being abandoned. It must get lonely.'

She didn't contradict him. 'I do get lonely. You're the kindest man in my life. Give me time.' She'd surprised herself saying that.

Robin's smile was a little sad when he nodded and said that he understood.

The next kiss was long and lingering with a warmth that shot through her body. What had been asleep was close to waking and might have done.

At the same time as he kissed her, the door of the pub on the corner opened and a patch of amber light fell onto them, picking them out like actors on a stage or in a film. Figures came out. One of them froze and a shrill voice rang out.

'Robin Godwin. What are you up to?'

Robin turned to face the woman hurrying towards him. He turned from Jenny, though one arm remained protectively around her back.

'Ethel. I might ask you the same.'

He looked beyond her to the man she was with. He wore a pinstriped suit, boxy padding squaring his shoulders, almost as though the jacket was still on a hanger. He did not come any closer but just stood in the doorway, smoking and smirking but not getting directly involved.

'Don't get any ideas. That's just Brian, my brother-in-law.'

The man in the doorway grinned and flicked his cigarette into the darkness. For a while, it glowed in the gutter before going out.

The woman he'd named as Ethel looked Jenny up and down before saying sneeringly, 'I went to school with you and 'is wife. We've all gone our separate ways since then, but you surely know 'e's married, don't you?' She didn't give Jenny time to respond but went on, 'And 'e's got two kids. Ought to be with 'is wife, not kissing some floozy in the dark.'

'You always did 'ave a big mouth, Ethel Fox. No wonder you and Doreen get on so bloody well!'

Ethel turned over her shoulder and called out to the man in the doorway: 'Brian. Did you 'ear what 'e just said about me.'

The man shrugged, said nothing but maintained his smirk.

Robin took hold of Jenny's arm. 'Come on.'

'I will be telling 'er,' Ethel shouted after them. 'You just be sure I will.'

Maintaining a nervous silence, they hurried along to where he'd parked the van. Jenny should have regretted Robin kissing her, but she didn't. In fact, she felt sorry for him. He deserved some comfort and so did she.

From the passenger seat, she looked through the windscreen, watched his head bobbing up and down over the car bonnet as he turned the starting handle. On the fourth attempt, the engine chugged into life.

Once the starting handle was thrown into the back and he

was sitting beside her, she asked him, 'Is she really a friend of Doreen's?'

Out of the corner of her eye, she glimpsed the golden arrow that was the indicator light flick out just behind her head. They moved out onto Redcliffe Street, heading for home.

'She is.'

'Will she really tell her that she's seen you with me?'

'I've no doubt of it.'

He sat grim-faced, staring ahead at the road, his profile infrequently picked out each time they passed a street lamp.

'What will she do?'

Eyes still fixed on the road, greasy with wetness and light, he shook his head. 'You can never know with Doreen. She's a dog in a manger all right. Just because she doesn't want me, doesn't mean someone else can 'ave me.'

'I don't see what she can do. Can't you divorce her?'

He shook his head. 'She won't agree to it. And then there's the kids to consider. She'd do everything she could to stop me from seeing them. I only see them on the odd weekend and school holidays as it is. I reckon the only reason she'll leave things as they are is because she 'as them reporting back on what I'm up to.'

Jenny sighed. 'This is so unfair.' His arm tensed when she reached across and patted it.

She retrieved it quickly, folding her hands into her lap. No matter what happened, she would be his friend, and although they'd kissed and spoken sweetly, she promised herself things wouldn't go any further. Not if she could help it.

* * *

Jenny picked the girls up from Thelma's before going home to bed. Gloria left her cardigan behind and was in bed by the time Thelma brought it across.

Jenny offered her a cup of cocoa.

'You bet. I want to know everything that went on.'

The coal fire had reduced to ashes by the time the two women were sitting either side of the fireplace sipping at cups of cocoa.

Thelma looked amused, smiling above the rim of her cup.

Jenny felt her face colouring.

'Go on. I can see you enjoyed yourself.' Thelma settled herself further into the armchair and leaned forward, eyes bright with expectation. 'Tell me what happened.'

Jenny shook her head. 'I didn't mean for anything to happen, but it did anyway. I meant to keep everything just on a friendship level, but...' The look she gave Thelma was both bashful and guilty.

'You kissed.'

'We kissed.' Jenny nodded. 'I couldn't help myself, Thelma, and the truth is...' Jenny paused again before relating how it had been, how it had felt. 'I wanted more. I wanted it to go further.' Her eyes flashed wide open. 'Was it wicked of me? After all, I'm a respectably married woman...'

'With feelings!' she said vehemently. 'You're a woman with feelings. Goodness knows you've been by yourself long enough, though I for one wouldn't miss Roy if he was mine. Get on with your own life, Jenny.' She leaned forward. 'Never mind love, a woman has needs. If there's love as well, then that's a big bonus. But don't cut yourself off from the world, Jenny. Don't pretend to be something other than what you are. I certainly don't!' She smacked the arm of the chair with the palm of her hand, her face wreathed in smiles.

In response, Jenny felt as though the weight of the world had been lifted from her shoulders. Thelma's common sense and advice had helped her make her mind up. But there was something else she wanted to say. She told her about Ethel. 'Ethel Fox her name is. She's a friend of Doreen, Robin's wife.'

'She just saw you or she saw you in a clinch?'

'She saw us kissing. His arms were around me.'

Thelma frowned. 'Didn't you tell me that she's carrying on anyway?'

'According to Robin, she is. In all innocence, his daughter told him that she'd gone into her mother's bedroom and she was in bed with Uncle Simon. Robin can never forgive her for that, not just for her sin, but for not being more discreet.'

'That's shocking.' Thelma's face was a picture of disgust. She'd always been one for the men, but her kids and their feelings had always come first.

'I think if she finds out she'll cause trouble, Thelma.' Jenny shrugged. 'What kind of trouble, I don't know.'

Frowning was something Thelma tried to avoid doing. She'd read somewhere that the lines it left made you look old before your time. On this occasion, her frown was deep and prolonged.

At last, after thinking it through, she straightened. 'All you can do, my girl, is cross that bridge when you come to it.'

'I've agreed to work two half-days a week in the pawn shop. I'm wondering now whether I did the right thing.'

'Of course you did!' A hand, fingers tipped with bright red varnish, patted hers. 'Life's too short to let the likes of Doreen Godwin put a spike in it. Anyway, I'm sure a lot of people would like a woman behind the counter in a pawnshop. It's only a woman who can know how they're feeling, having to pawn their best bits and pieces. But the rent must be paid and the kids fed. That's all that really matters in this life.'

26

Thelma had one of her funny feelings about this evening. She hadn't had one for a long time, didn't believe in magic as such but did believe in female instinct.

'Well, whatever the collywobbles is about, I really don't care. All I care about is getting home.'

She was talking to herself. She'd always found it an effective way of coping with whatever life was throwing at her.

For now at least everything was good. Her life was running on a firm base and although she enjoyed her job, home was most definitely where the heart was.

She'd left Bertrams promptly and just for once the bus was on time. There was even room inside. She generally preferred going inside to up top where the air was thick with cigarette smoke. Downstairs was clearer although some did drift down from the stairs at the platform at the back.

She took one of the side seats positioned so that her back was against the window and she could scrutinise the passengers immediately opposite.

As was the habit, small smiles were exchanged. Most were women, their handbags and shopping bags piled on their laps.

Once the small smiles of relief subsided that another day at work was over, she settled down. Sometimes on the journey home, she nodded asleep; it very much depended on how busy she'd been.

Today had been preparing for stocktaking, which would take place on a Sunday two weeks hence. Although it was hard work and on one hand she did resent having to give up her Sunday, on the other it was better than a jumble sale.

Stocktaking meant sorting through the things that hadn't sold. Some would be destined for the January sales, but other items, already offered in previous sales and lingering in the store-room, would be available to staff at rock-bottom prices. Thelma relished the thought of that. She had her eye on a black coat, primarily for wearing to a funeral, but with the addition of a bit of leopard-skin trim around the collar and pockets, it would do nicely as a winter coat.

More people got on at the next bus stop than got off. Most of the seats downstairs were taken, except for one on the bench seat opposite the one she was sitting on.

The smell of strong tobacco came on board with working men dressed in overalls, others in khaki trench coats, caps on the heads of the former, trilby hats on the latter.

Like a queue of drab tortoises, they clomped their way up the stairs to the upper deck, cigarettes already hanging from the corner of their mouths.

The last one looked inside. On setting eyes on the spare seat, he took his cigarette from his mouth, pinched the end and slid it into his pocket.

He touched the brim of his hat briefly as he came inside.

'Excuse me, ladies,' he said, as he squeezed in between the two women sitting opposite her. 'Nice evening,' he added.

His smile was fixed on nicotine-stained lips. Flecks of used tobacco stuck to the corners. He didn't attempt to remove them. His smile widened, exposing yellow teeth.

There was distance between them, him on one side of the bus, her on the other. Yet Thelma knew how his breath smelled, knew even how it tasted.

Bile rose from her stomach. Suddenly, her lovely thoughts of Bertrams were replaced by a memory of a snowy night. She hadn't seen his face, but the strong smell of a seasoned smoker had stayed with her, the taste of his mouth covering hers, his hand stinking of nicotine.

'Get this bus every night, do you?'

The knowing smile on his face made her stomach curl. How dare he smile at her like that. It was as though he knew something about her, something she wouldn't want anyone else to know.

It wasn't entirely possible not to glance at him and when she did, he nodded at her as if to say, *Yes. It's me. It's me you were foolish enough to trust.*

It was him. The man who had almost ruined her life.

Fear swept through Thelma's body. She tossed her head and turned away. She would pretend she hadn't heard. Keep a fixed stare on her face, staring at anything rather than at him.

Even without glancing in his direction, she knew he was still looking at her, still smiling in that triumphant, all-knowing way.

All the joy of her day was gone. She felt sick inside.

It was dark outside but not snowing as it had been on that other bus journey that had changed into a nightmare. The bus was labouring up the hill, determined in its own mechanical way to get to the top.

Melvin Square and home were some way off. Was he going that far or would he get off before then? Should she get off and walk the rest of the way?

No. She would not. She wouldn't grin, but she would bear it.

'Hard work getting up this hill. Worse in the snow and ice though.'

He sat there, a self-satisfied smile on his face, his eyes boring into her.

There was now no room for doubt. He was taunting her. In her mind, she called him all the expletives under the sun. George would have been surprised at her even knowing the words. She bet that he did. Now, what would George do?

Brazen it out! That's what he would do.

Summoning up every ounce of courage she possessed, stony-faced she stared him out.

Not a word passed her lips. She needed to think first, but in the meantime...

The bus began to slow as it approached the next bus stop, the one immediately opposite the patch of grass where she'd been dragged and implanted with his seed on that terrible night.

'My stop,' he said, that sickening smile still on his face whilst her guts sickened and churned inside.

How dare he have the nerve to smile at her like that, to blatantly get off so close to the spot where he'd raped her and left her semi-conscious.

'Nice to 'ave met you. Might catch up with you again.'

His gloating and smug smile both sickened and angered her. Up until now, her courage had been a fragile, fluttery thing triggered by the memory. He'd made a grave mistake taunting her like that. The courage that had sunk to the bottom of her stomach now surged anew. She would get her own back on him. Somehow she would get her own back on him.

The smell of strong tobacco went with him, souring her nostrils until he'd stepped down from the platform and disappeared. She tried to see what direction he'd gone in, but it was too dark.

The bus moved on.

'Well, 'e was a cheeky sod,' said the woman next to her. 'Fancied 'is chances didn't 'e. His wife would be upset if she knew. Housebound she is.'

Thelma looked at her in amazement. 'You know him?'

The woman had a crumpled face, mainly since she had no teeth, her mouth constantly moving as she chewed her gums. A headscarf tied tightly beneath her chin. She smelled of glue so most likely worked in the paper bag factory.

'Yes,' she said, chewing her toothless gums between words. 'Sam Hudson. His wife's name is Beryl. They lives over thur...' She pointed back to the small crescent of houses set back from the more brightly lit Donegal Road.

'One of those houses?' Thelma asked. She kept her voice even, as though their conversation was commonplace. Her aim in this instance was to extricate more information, preferably to obtain a house number without having to ask outright.

'Can't miss where 'e lives. They've got a load of them 'orrible stone statues in the garden. Can't understand 'ow anyone would want them things in the garden. Flowers is all I want. Not them grinning devils.'

'Stone statues?' Thelma thought she knew what she meant but wanted confirmation.

The woman's hairy brows met over her purple-veined nose as she thought about what they were. 'Like ugly dwarves, but I don't think they're called that.'

'Do you mean gnomes. Garden gnomes?'

The woman's face brightened. 'Yeah. That's what they calls

'em. Gnomes. Garden gnomes. Ugly things they is. Would you 'ave them in your garden?'

'No,' said Thelma, shaking her head solemnly. 'No. I would not.'

27

Mrs Rees had brought in her husband's Sunday suit on Monday last and was now retrieving it.

'Here you go. Thanks for the business.' Jenny smiled as she handed over the bundle wrapped in brown paper. The half-crown was already in the cash drawer and pushed slightly to one side. By the end of the week, Mrs Rees, the telling yellow of a receding bruise beneath her eye, would no doubt be in again with the same suit to pledge. Her husband handed over his wages regularly half an hour after coming in from work. Not that Mrs Rees was a saint. Like her old man, she was known to like brown ale too much and the housekeeping went into the till of the off-licence rather than putting food on the table.

Taking the accounts ledger from the right-hand drawer, Jenny picked up a newly sharpened pencil. Robin wasn't a great one for keeping accounts, so she had some catching up to do.

She'd only just finished entering the latest pledge when the bell above the door jangled in its haphazard way. Someone else had entered the shop accompanied by a draught of fresh air from outside.

'Hello,' she said as she put the pen and accounts ledger aside. 'How can I help you?'

The smile vanished from her face when she saw who it was. She'd known Doreen, Robin's wife, from schooldays. Back then, she'd been relatively attractive and the boys had gathered around her like moths to the flame. Her looks had hardened and the selfishness she'd shown then was more pronounced now.

Her tongue was as sharp as ever. Hands gripping her handbag to her belly, she said what she'd come to say. 'You can keep away from Robin. We're still married and I ain't got any intention of letting 'im go.'

Doreen Godwin had once been a pretty girl. She was older now and the prettiness, if still there at all, was buried beneath liberally applied face powder, dark red lipstick, her lashes clogged with mascara.

Jenny took a deep breath and in a bid to better defend herself – if only from verbal abuse – got to her feet. 'Mrs Godwin, you're under a misapprehension. I only work here. I don't live here.'

'Misapprehension,' Doreen snarled. 'What kind of word is that, you posh little tart?'

Inside, Jenny was fuming. It took a good deal of effort to rein in what she really wanted to say, but she had every intention of standing up for herself.

'Robin is out delivering furniture. I'm only here part-time to serve in the shop and sort out the accounts. He has no one else.'

She emphasised the last words. Doreen could be here if she desired to do so.

Doreen sucked in her lips until they'd all but disappeared. Red spots appeared on her cheeks. The sucked-in lips suddenly pursed.

'Well, don't make yerself too comfortable. The way things are going 'e won't be able to afford to pay you. Not once 'e's paid me what 'e owes. We do 'ave two kids, you know.'

'Precisely. And those children need to be fed and provided for. That's why he needs to work and he works very hard. He pays me for what I do – which is purely helping out in the shop and doing the paperwork. Now, is there anything else I can help you with? If not, I am rather busy.'

'I wants some money. There's some in that cash drawer there.'

A cloud of powder left her chin as she jerked it towards the drawer just beside Jenny's hip.

Jenny placed her hand protectively over the battered wood of the cash drawer. 'I can't give you anything without his permission. The money doesn't belong to me.'

Doreen drew in her chin. Her eyes were blazing. 'I've a right to what's in there.'

'No you don't. You've only a right to what Robin gives you.'

'I'm his wife. Hand some over.'

Jenny shook her head. 'No. I can't. What's owing is between you and Robin. As I've just told you, I don't have the authority to give you anything. You have to discuss it with him.'

'You bitch! Give me my money.'

'No.' She was adamant. Nothing Doreen Godwin could do or say would make her budge.

A glove-covered finger pointed directly at her face. 'You'll be sorry. I'm warning you. You'll be bloody sorry.'

'I already am. Today started so well. Good day, Doreen. You know where the door is. Now, please leave.'

Doreen sucked in her breath. Perhaps she might have stayed longer, but Cath chose that moment to come in, her face cheery and a bag of shopping swinging in each and.

'Thought I'd come in to keep you company. Any chance of a cuppa?'

Not at all aware what she'd interrupted, Cath was all smiles. A venomous look from Doreen wiped it from her face.

'Is summut wrong? Am I interruptin' somethin'?'

Cath glanced nervously from Jenny to Doreen.

Jenny set her face firm. 'No, Cath, you're not. This lady is just going.'

Doreen's jawline waxed and waned as though she was chewing over the words. Her eyes glittered like chips of black jet.

Finally, she snarled, 'I'll be back.'

With a toss of her head and in a fume of loose face powder, she headed for the door. The bell clanged wildly above it as she tugged it open and sent it crashing against the wall.

Cath tucked in her chin and pronounced, 'Well, she don't seem very ladylike.'

'You're right about that.'

Cath cocked an eyebrow. 'She didn't seem to like you much. What 'ave you done to deserve that?'

Jenny sighed. 'Took pity on Robin.'

Cath gasped, eyes round as gobstoppers. 'Is that 'is wife?'

She stepped a fair pace as she followed Jenny through to the small kitchen at the back of the shop.

Jenny threw the fact that she was over her shoulder. In her estimation, Doreen Godwin didn't deserve her attention, but goodness knew where things might have gone if Cath hadn't come barging in.

The kettle went on the gas and the cups and saucers sat waiting on the draining board. The steam from the kettle misted the windows. Chair legs squealed across the cracked linoleum when Cath dragged it out.

'I'm all ears,' she said, waiting there, hands clasped tightly together on the table, leaning slightly and patiently, waiting for Jenny to tell her more.

Jenny clenched her jaw, determined to keep anything she said to the minimum.

'She doesn't like the fact that I'm working for Robin but doesn't want to do anything to help him herself.'

'But he's her husband?' Cath gasped. Devoted to her husband Bill, she sounded shocked to the core. Jenny had no doubt she would work her fingers to the bone if Bill required it of her.

'She doesn't quite see it that way,' said Jenny as she placed the teapot next to the cups, covering it with a knitted tea cosy.

Whilst pouring milk into the cups, she listened to Cath hold forth about how she couldn't believe that any woman could refuse to support her husband in whatever he did.

When Jenny told her they were separated, Cath's jaw dropped. 'No!'

Like most people, Cath was of the opinion that marriage lasted forever. Grin and bear it was the predominant attitude.

'Is she gone 'ome to 'er mother?'

Jenny shook her head and sipped her tea. Should she tell her some semblance of the truth, or the whole truth. She decided to keep it short and simple, though truthful.

'I don't know for sure, but I think she's got another man in her life. Perhaps more than one.'

If Cath was shocked before, she was doubly so now. 'Well I never!'

She sat back in the chair, face cupped in both hands, metal curlers rattling as she shook her head from side to side in disbelief

'She wanted money,' said Jenny. 'According to Robin, she only turns up when the alimony is due – housekeeping,' she explained, on seeing Cath's questioning frown. 'He has to give her so much a week to keep her and the two children.'

'Does he ever see them?'

'Yes. But mostly he must visit them. She only occasionally allows them to come here and then only for the day. She insists they stay for just a couple of hours and then come home. He must stop work and take them back to her in the van. As if it's not hard enough on him...' Her voice petered out and she realised how it must sound. 'I feel sorry for him. That's why I agreed to help him out.'

Cath shook her head dolefully.

'She wants him but doesn't want anyone else to have him. Not that it's anything like that,' Jenny said quickly. 'As I said, I just feel sorry for him. Oh well,' she sighed. 'There's nothing I can do. I'll tell him when he gets back, but I really should get back to work.'

'Then I'll leave you to it. I'm off to Rigby's now,' said Cath. 'I want a couple of skeins of double knit to make Bill a new jumper.'

After she'd gone, Jenny stood with her back leaning against the draining board musing about her feelings. Did she feel genuinely sorry for Robin or was it more than that?

Whatever her feelings, one thing was for sure. In her heart of hearts, she knew this would not be the last visit of Doreen Godwin. Doreen would keep Robin dangling on a hook, demanding money whilst taunting him with access to the two children. What would the next visit be like? Jenny didn't know. All she could do was cross that bridge when it came.

On Robin's return from a delivery, she told him all about it.

His look soured, eyed fixed on the floor. On raising them, he looked directly at her. 'I should never have married her. If I hadn't been on the rebound, I never would have.'

'You were on the rebound?'

A new softness came to his eyes. 'Yeah, Jenny. But I don't think the girl noticed.'

His smile was sad and his eyes held hers.

Feeling her face warming, she turned away, knowing she was the girl he was referring to.

* * *

Doreen was livid. She remained livid all the way home on the bus and her temper hadn't improved by the time she got back to the rooms she rented in Dover Place, Stokes Croft. It was further exasperated when her son, Simon, asked when he could next visit his father.

Her first reaction was to clip him around the ear and threaten to send him to bed with no supper. Her second was to rub at his reddening ear, kiss the top of his head and tell him that she would think about it.

A plan was forming. The presence of an attractive woman running the shop in her husband's absence had unsettled her. To put it mildly, she was jealous. The fact that she played the field – and was paying no rent to the landlord in lieu of services rendered – was beside the point. Gerald was her uncle, but even when she was younger, he'd always had a soft spot for her. She could play him like a piano, knowing the right keys to press in a man with a big ego and money in the bank. The kids had known other uncles, but this one really was related by blood, though Doreen chose to overlook the fact. He had money, treated her like a queen and that was all that mattered.

This wasn't the only property he owned, though was probably the one in the best condition. Some of the others were rank tenements where residents put up with crumbling plaster, draughty window frames and vermin of every description.

Gerald doted on her and she'd liked their arrangement, the children with her and her husband at a distance. However, she hadn't allowed for jealousy. She'd told herself that she had no affection for Robin and didn't want him anywhere near her. However, she had not counted on Jenny Crawford helping him run the shop. She remembered her when they were younger, the strings she'd pulled to get Robin away from Jenny – not that the silly girl had seemed to notice. She'd been besotted with Roy Crawford.

Choosing the right moment, she'd tuned into Robin's desire for Jenny. She'd manipulated him at the right time. In the throes of strenuous lovemaking, she knew that, in his heart of hearts, he hadn't been making love to her, but Jenny. Not that she cared. Claiming to be pregnant, she'd got him to marry her. The fact that their daughter hadn't been born until much later than nine months was neither here nor there. She had a ring on her finger and was married to the man she'd thought she'd loved.

Over time, both her tastes and her aims in life had changed. She wanted everything that money could buy and didn't want the humdrum existence of a wife and mother. She wanted glamour, nights out and a steady stream of money. She didn't really want Robin, but when Ethel, who'd also been at school with them, had mentioned seeing him and Jenny together, her blood had boiled.

Gerald took care of her, provided a roof over her head and a small amount of housekeeping. Robin supplied the rest.

Whilst Gerald was shaving, getting ready to take her out to the pub, she contemplated the plan that had so visibly formed in her mind.

Having made the decision, she told her children to sit down and, with great deliberation, divided a Fry's Five Boys between them.

'I've got something to ask you,' she said, smiling and feeling pleased with herself. 'How would you like to stay with yer dad for a few days. He's got two spare beds. How would that be, do you think?'

She already knew what their answer would be and couldn't help congratulating herself at the deviousness of her plan.

Their response was ecstatic, their faces bright with enthusiasm. Their voices rose in unison. 'Yeah! Yeah!'

The smile on her face was as lean as the one in her eyes. She had purpose in what she was doing.

'I'll get in touch with yer dad and tell 'im you'll be staying for a few nights. Are you very excited?'

They nodded their heads vigorously, the dear mites seemingly unable to believe their luck.

'Just one thing,' she said, her tongue gliding over the thick lipstick she had only latterly applied. 'I want you to tell me all about how it was when you get back.'

'Yeah, yeah!'

'Is that a promise?'

The same response.

* * *

'Cheers,' Doreen said later when she was in the saloon bar of the Black Cat with Gerald.

'You look like the cat that got the cream,' he said to her. 'What's to celebrate?'

'A few days to ourselves,' she replied, cosying up to him, her smile full of promises.

Yes, they would have some time to themselves, but most of all if she played her children right, she would know all that she needed to know about Robin and Jenny Crawford.

28

The woman peered at her from beneath a pile of unruly hair as fine as thistledown, as ragged as a bird's nest. A scruffy hat, long past its best, crowned the whole lot. Around her neck, she wore a knitted scarf, its ends tucked into the pockets of a hand-knitted cardigan of the same sludge-brown colour.

'Are you looking for someone?'

'Just walking,' Thelma replied and continued walking rather than get into a conversation about her purpose being there.

She had circled the same small crescent a few times. Until now, she'd not noticed that she was being watched.

The layout was like old villages surrounding a green. The council much favoured the concept. The front doors of each house were painted corporation green. To the side of the door was the living-room window. Up above were a large and a small window of the front bedroom.

Most of the front gardens boasted nothing more than a patch of overgrown grass and the ragged growth of privet hedges tumbling between tidier hedges. Some showed signs of being tended by a confirmed gardener, flower beds full of summer blooms. Only one had a selection of stone garden gnomes. Whatever colour they had once been was long gone.

Three times her steps had faltered outside the house she believed was the home of the man who had attacked her back in January.

She'd determined to accost the man's wife and tell her what he had done. But to what end? Would she tell the woman what had happened? Confronting her would not be easy. In her mind, she concocted the words she thought she might say – 'Excuse me, but your husband raped me. Did you know he did things like that?'

She gasped when a cat suddenly ran across her path.

To her great relief, the raggedy woman who'd been watching her had disappeared.

Whilst catching her breath, she fixed her gaze on a profusion of red roses squeezing through the evergreen leaves of the customary privet hedge. This hedge was one of the neater ones – clipped into straight lines and box like. It was his garden. Or was it? Was he the keen gardener or was the neat hedge, the explosion of red roses, the wife's particular interest?

'Pretty ain't it.'

Thinking herself alone, the voice took Thelma by surprise. She hadn't thought there was anyone around.

The speaker suddenly appeared in the gap allowing for the gateway between the tall boxy hedges. The woman was barely tall enough to look over the gate. Her face and form were fragile and birdlike. Her eyes too reminded Thelma of a bird, brightly darting around like a robin or blackbird in search of a grub or a snail.

'Yes,' said Thelma with breathless enthusiasm. 'They caught my attention. I do love red. Red roses, red berries, red dresses, red hair.'

The woman beamed. 'I like colour all the year round. I'd let them take over the whole hedge if I could, but Sam, my husband, won't hear of it. He likes privets, says it keeps our place private. Spends all his weekend keeping it in shape. Even in winter.' She laughed a strange nervous sound. 'He do like us to be private.'

'Everyone likes their own privacy,' said Thelma.

Suddenly she felt guilty about intruding. Not for its own sake, but because she was now getting a good look at the woman, Beryl Hudson. The urge to tell his wife all had been strong but that was before Thelma had seen her. At sight of her, at surmising her affliction, the anger she'd felt was somewhat subdued.

Thelma could now see that her first impression of the woman being small of stature had been wrong. The woman might once have been a little short, but nothing like she was now. Her spine was curved, the most severe form of dowager's hump that meant she was bent almost double. Twisted fingers, like twigs laid on their side, gripped the top bar of the garden gate.

'It sounds as though he keeps it all neat and tidy for you. You're very lucky.'

An unreadable response flickered in the woman's eyes and was gone.

'Yes. He knows I don't like people staring. They can't see me behind tall hedges. He does most of the garden, though I do tend my flowers – seeing as I'm almost level with them.' She laughed in a way that tugged at the heart, as if gazing at flowers was recompense for a curved spine.

'You don't get many visitors?' Thelma forced herself to sound cheerful.

Beryl tried to shake her head but settled instead for saying that, no, she didn't get visitors. 'Besides my husband, you're the first person I've spoken to in weeks. Except for the milkman and the baker.'

'You don't go shopping locally?'

Again, an attempt to nod. Thelma worked out that Beryl's curved spine prevented her from nodding or shaking her head, but the habit of trying to do so remained.

'No. He gets his sister to shop for us. She gets what we need and delivers it.'

'Well, that must be a big help.'

'I spend my time knitting. My fingers are all thumbs most of the time, but I still manage to do a bit of knitting. Only small items nowadays, like potholders, but it keeps me occupied.'

'It must do.'

'Are you married?'

'Widowed.' Thelma managed a woeful smile, determined it would be the only information she would divulge. To give more would be dangerous. 'And your husband. Sam. Where does he work?'

'The tobacco bonds down on the Cumberland Basin.'

The moment the words were out Thelma was overcome with the memory of his smell: raw tobacco and tobacco dust as much as chain-smoked cigarettes.

Her breath caught in her throat but was expelled with surprise when Beryl said, 'Fancy coming in for a cuppa?'

The bird bright eyes were full of pleading and Thelma immediately felt sorry for her. Loneliness deserved her pity. Though common sense urged her to refuse, curiosity won the day.

'I'd love to – if it's no trouble.'

'None at all, though my hands...' She held them up. 'I haven't got a good bone in my body. You might have to put the kettle on and make the tea yourself.'

The garden gate opened silently on well-oiled hinges. The garden was immaculate, everything in order and growing where it was meant to be.

The house turned out to be the same. Not a thing out of place. The brass fire irons glowing like gold in front of an empty grate, the cushions plump and set squarely in the armchairs and settee, the walls the same dull cream as every other house on the estate bare of pictures. The clock sitting on the mantelpiece above the fireplace was square, the coalscuttle was square. Even the patterns on the cushions, in the hearth-rug and on the curtains, were square, oblong or triangular motifs. There were no circles, no soft edges; everything included angles. Nothing was out of place and the precision with considered placement would have made her shiver if she hadn't been wearing a coat. The house held little warmth even in mild weather.

'You have a lovely home,' Thelma finally said though she was sitting on the edge of her chair, scared to touch anything in case she put it out of place.

The praise that Thelma didn't feel was met with appreciation.

'Sam does it all. I can't, you see...' She again drew attention to her disfigured hands and fingers.

'He sounds like a saint.'

'He's taken care of everything since I became like this.'

For a moment, she held her hands in front of her face, staring at them as though only now discovering how very disfigured they were.

What had she been like beforehand? Thelma wondered.

'It came as quite a shock. Altered our lives it did.'

Thelma swallowed the home truths she'd planned. The poor woman didn't deserve it. Instead she followed her out into the kitchen, which was as pristine and unencumbered by clutter as the living room. A green checked wipe-clean tablecloth matched the curtain hanging beneath the draining board. The curtains hanging at the kitchen window were plain yellow. The two colours should have lifted the atmosphere, but Thelma couldn't help feeling they were fighting a losing battle. Not that the rooms weren't bright enough, it was the sombre thought that something about this house and the people in it were quite wrong. No amount of colour could hide the darkness lurking just beneath the surface.

Twisted fingers lost their grip on the kettle. It dropped from her hand, the lid flew out and clattered across the floor.

'Let me,' said Thelma, her heart full of pity but being careful not to reveal such a feeling in her voice.

She ably filled the kettle from beneath the tap, set the lid back on and placed it on the gas.

After finding the matches, Thelma did the honours, lit the gas ring and got the kettle boiling.

His wife pointed to where the cups, saucers, milk and sugar rested in pristine order on the lower shelves. Thelma put everything needed onto a tray along with the teapot. Beryl handed her a red and yellow striped tea cosy topped with a knitted robin.

'That's pretty.'

Beryl beamed. 'I made it myself.'

'It's pretty.' Thelma turned it this way and that. 'Especially the robin. He makes me smile.'

'Me too.' Her smile vanished. 'I can't knit like that now. Too fiddly for my fingers.'

All the shouting and indignation Thelma had thought would constitute this meeting had been part of a false vision. Beryl hungered for company and for all her desire for revenge, Thelma couldn't begrudge her moment of happiness. But despite wanting to be kind, her nerves were on edge. Even though she knew he was at work, her heart was beating like a hammer. What if he came home unexpectedly?

'Do you usually buy your wool in Mrs Rigby's?'

'I want to, but it takes me such a long time to get there and besides...' Fear flashed in her eyes but quickly vanished. 'The fact is that Sam doesn't like me going out. He says I should keep out of sight, that people only make fun of me.' Her eyes glistened with tears.

The anger Thelma had nursed for herself she now shared with someone who was also a victim of the same man. His wife.

'How about I fetch you a skein or ball of wool? How would that be?'

Clutching a screwed-up handkerchief, crooked fingers swiped at the wetness in her eyes, Beryl's look visibly brightened. 'So kind.'

'Double-, three-ply or four-ply?'

'I like four-ply, but my fingers cope better with double nowadays.'

'I'll get you some. I presume you'd prefer red?'

The strained sorrow became a smile. 'Oh yes. So kind.'

Gripping the cup with both hands, she sipped at her tea. Thelma observed her over the rim of her cup. How could he treat a woman like this? The anger she'd had for him had doubled. What sort of life did the poor woman have? Caged like an animal, dissuaded from going out or having discourse with any other human being. The man was a monster.

A little more conversation, mostly about knitting and the garden, before Thelma declared her intention to leave.

Beryl looked disappointed. 'Do you have to go now? Can you stay for another half an hour?'

'Just a few minutes more. My girls are due home from school. They'll want their tea.'

Getting home in time for the girls was an acceptable excuse but not the truth. She couldn't risk running into him. The very thought of it made her shiver from head to toe.

'I see.'

That sad imploring look again, full of pathos, of deep-rooted despair.

Thelma determinedly buttoned up her coat. Despite being sympathetic to this woman's plight, she couldn't risk hanging around too long.

Thinking her host might also be cold, she turned her attention to the coal fire which presently burnt only insipidly. She picked up the poker. 'I'll stoke the fire up a bit for you before I go.'

As she did so, her eyes alighted on a shoe hanging by its heel over the brass fender. The coals glowed. Her hands gripped the poker and nausea rose from her stomach. She froze.

Beryl saw her interest in the shoe. 'That's my Cinderella slipper,' she said laughingly. 'That's what Sam calls it. He found it lying all alone in the snow and brought it home.'

'In January. When it snowed?'

'That's right. We sat down with warm soup on either side of the fire and he told me a story about how Cinderella had run away from her prince out here on the green.' She laughed again. 'Sam's very good at telling stories. We had a fine time that night. He was in a good mood.'

'Cinderella's slipper.'

'That's the story he wove around it. He's always telling me stories to lift my spirits. Better than telling me about what happened at work each day.'

There was joy in her eyes, but inside Thelma there was only a sick feeling. On the one hand, she wanted to grab her missing shoe and run. On the other, it was far past redemption; soaked through, it had dried out and shrunk in front of the fire. Time had taken its softness.

Just as it's taken mine, thought Thelma, though she knew it wasn't true. She would go to the wool shop. She would see Beryl again.

She headed for the door. 'Don't bother to get up. I can see my own way out.'

'Wait.'

Thelma paused, hand on the doorknob.

'You didn't tell me your name.'

Should she tell the truth? No.

'Eunice. My name's Eunice.'

An imploring voice called after her. 'Call again. Please. With or without the wool.'

Thelma hurried away; her face aflame, though all over she felt as though she'd been doused in ice.

* * *

'Hello. Prince Charming here. Is Cinderella at home?'

Sam bent down and kissed her cheek. Beryl turned her head in the hope that he would also kiss her lips. As usual, it pained her when he didn't.

'Have you had a good day?' he asked.

'Yes.'

The excitement in her voice made him turn his head. 'You sound happy.'

She'd been unsure as to whether she should tell him. After all, he discouraged her having visitors. He discouraged her going out. She decided that on this occasion it would do no harm.

'I've had a visitor.'

She saw the slight crinkling of a frown, but told herself all would be well.

'A woman was looking for someone. She was a bit lost, so I invited her in for a cup of tea. We had a lovely chat. Her name was Eunice. See?' She pointed at the cups still sitting on the tray, not trusting herself to take them out to the kitchen without dropping the tray and smashing the lot.

Sam picked up one of the cups. His frown deepened when he saw the imprint of female lips in a bright red lipstick. The deep red colour was familiar.

'Who was she looking for?'

His wife looked confused. 'I don't know. I forgot to ask.'

'You let a complete stranger into the house?' He shook his head. The corners of his mouth curled with contempt. 'You really are bloody stupid at times.'

'But she was nice. And I told her about you finding the shoe and telling me that Cinderella had dropped it, and everything...'

He stooped down, snatched the shoe and passed it from one hand to the other. His look darkened, though inside he felt a surge of excitement. He'd not kept the shoe for his wife's sake but for his own. It aided his memory of that night – the excitement, the soft yielding flesh of a woman and his own aggressive hardness. He'd determined to have her the moment he'd seen her. Given the chance, he would have her again. Unwittingly, his wife had aroused his desire, the need to replay his pleasure all over again. The shoe had done that to some extent, but now...

There was no guarantee that it was the same woman he'd had on the snowy ground who had dared visit his house. He'd recently seen her on the bus for the first time since that blizzard. He'd recognised her instantly, but nonetheless had alighted at his usual stop. Was it coincidence that she had inveigled herself into his house so shortly after that?

'What else did you notice about this woman you invited into *my* house? This Eunice? Describe her to me.'

His wife's smile faltered. He'd designated the house as his – not shared between the two of them. He took that tone on those occasions she'd displeased him – like now.

'How old was she?'

Beryl trembled. 'I'm not sure.'

A sharp slap landed on her cheek, jarring the stiffness of her neck so much so that it almost moved.

'Um... late thirties, forty perhaps.'

'Eyes?'

'Dark. I think.'

His face was level with hers, menacing, intense.

'Hair?'

'Dark. Glossy. And she was smartly dressed,' she added, desperate to escape another slap. 'A green suit and a black coat. She wore black shoes, a bit like the Cinderella shoe.'

'Do you know where she lives?'

'No.'

He turned his back on her as he murmured, 'Only tarts wear bright red lipstick.'

'But she wasn't a tart. Not a woman of the night. She has two children.'

'As if that makes a difference,' he growled from the hallway as he hung up his hat and coat.

For the rest of that evening, things went on as they normally did. He cooked a meal for both of them, then carried her up to bed whether she wanted to go or not. Before closing the bedroom door, he wished her goodnight. She heard the key turn in the lock.

Back downstairs, he sat nursing a glass of stout as he listened to the radio. He wasn't giving it his full concentration. Other thoughts dominated his mind, drowning out anything else. Firstly, there was the excitement of that snowy night last January. Secondly, his stupidity on this last occasion he'd seen her. Why go and sit right opposite her? Worse still, he'd spoken to her, perhaps too glibly, too gloating. She hadn't seen much of his face on their first meeting, but she had heard his voice. Apart from that, he thought she hadn't a clue as to his identity. But now he recalled the woman sitting next to her, a familiar face he was sure had once been a friend of his wife. *I'm a bloody fool*, he thought to himself, *I should have been more careful.*

29

Jenny was dealing with pledges left in the pawnshop that Monday morning, entering them in the accounts book. Some of the items weren't worth the amount of money lent against them. A Sunday suit, a fox fur long ravaged by time, and a cruet set the owner had assured her had solid silver shakers. The letters EPNS – electroplated nickel silver – said otherwise and some of that had changed colour to a coppery sheen.

The same items came in every Monday, the owner short of cash until their husband's next pay day. Most of the customers were women, wives of husbands who drank away a good portion of their wages over the weekend.

Robin's children, Simon and Susan, had arrived that morning before Jenny. Robin had left her to get on with things whilst he went along to Connaught Road School to arrange for them to attend for the rest of the week.

'Will you be able to manage?' he asked her before he'd left. 'A clip around the ear should be enough if they cause trouble.' He laughed.

She did not foresee any problems, though they were bound to

be a little confused to be passed like parcels from one parent to another.

From upstairs came the sound of doors and drawers being opened and closed. She guessed the two of them were nosing around. Perhaps Robin had given them permission to do so or perhaps not. Either way, it was none of her business. Even when she heard the clumping of footsteps down the stairs, she kept her head down – that was until a tousled head of hair appeared through the wire screen in front of her. It looked as though it hadn't seen a comb for a week. There followed his face, deep-set eyes and an upper lip crusted with dried snot.

'I'm Simon. Who are you?' he said, pressing his dirty nose and face against the wire screen.

Jenny slammed the accounts book shut. 'I'm the woman who's about to wash your dirty face!'

'I washed it yesterday.' His protest was loud and adamant.

'Well, today is another day.'

'I don't want it washed.'

She grabbed him before he could dart away. 'Whether you do or not, you're having it washed.'

Keeping a firm grip on his shoulder, she marched him up the stairs to the first-floor bathroom, wetted a face flannel under the tap and rubbed away at his face.

'That's cold,' he shouted.

She kept hold despite him wriggling like a rat in a trap.

'Tonight you can wash in warm water from the kettle, but for now let's get the worst of this off.'

'I ain't washing me face again tonight. I bloody well ain't. Ouch,' he added when she very lightly clipped his ear.

'No swearing. Your father won't like it.'

'Me mum don't mind. I can swear all I like.'

'That might be all right with your mother, but your father won't like it.'

The turn in events had surprised Jenny. Up until now, Doreen had taken a devilish delight in using their children as a weapon. Robin had been devastated by her behaviour and had jumped at the opportunity to have them with him. When he'd told her, Jenny had questioned Doreen's sudden change of heart.

Robin had shrugged. 'I never was able to read Doreen's mind.' A worried frown had darkened his expression. 'It's something to think about though. I never know what she's up to.'

They'd agreed there must be a reason but had no idea what it was.

'But I am glad they're coming here,' he'd added, happiness dancing in his eyes.

Jenny had felt happy for him. At the same time, she'd agreed to increase her hours from two half-days a week to three. Although Robin was like a dog with two tails since they'd arrived, looking after two children and running a business was hard. He'd appreciated her agreeing to work slightly more hours.

Holding Simon with one hand, Jenny ran her fingers through the boy's hair and grimaced.

'I'll get your father to wash your hair tonight with vinegar. And comb it through with a Derbac comb. You've got nits.'

'Let me go.'

The thin arms flailed at her, fists tightly clenched, legs kicking. Unable to restrain him, she let him go. He flew into the arms of his scowling sister who had appeared in the doorway.

'You leave my brother alone. I'll tell my mum. I'll tell her you hurt him.'

Jenny rolled down the sleeves she'd pulled up to wash Simon's face. 'I washed his face. That's all I did, young lady. I'm astounded your mother didn't wash him before he came.'

She rinsed off the face flannel, folded it and placed it on the edge of the sink.

'Don't matter if 'e ain't 'ad a wash. None of your business to make 'im wash.'

Jenny sighed. Perhaps she had been a bit impetuous with the clip around the ear, but washing the little tyke was of benefit to him more so than to her.

'How about you? When was the last time you washed?'

'None of yer bleedin' business.'

Jenny had to admit that the girl's face looked clean enough. All the same, she was taken aback at such appallingly rude behaviour.

'How about your hair. Have you got nits too?'

Susan's scowl deepened. 'No, I ain't. Me mum would 'ave said so. Mucking us about like that.'

'I am not mucking you about. Being clean will keep you healthy.'

The girl poked out her tongue. 'Sod off. Come on,' she said, tugging at her brother's shoulder. 'We ain't 'anging around where we ain't wanted.'

Before leaving, she threw Jenny a surly look and a parting threat.

'I'm gonna tell my mum that you made my brother cry. You just see if I don't.'

Jenny sighed. Robin's offspring showed no sign of being grateful for their visit. Did they care for their father at all? She didn't know.

The moment Robin came back through the door, the kids got to him first.

He looked surprised when they threw their arms around him. Judging by his reaction, Jenny surmised that it didn't happen that often. This was all put on, designed to denigrate her and get their father on their side.

'She scrubbed my face,' Simon wailed, pointing an accusing finger in her direction.

'And she said we had nits,' his sister added, triumph already beginning to gloat in her eyes.

Robin looked at Jenny enquiringly. 'Do they?'

She nodded. 'Simon certainly does. I haven't checked Susan's hair, but it's likely that if one has them so does the other. As for scrubbing his face, the crust beneath his nose was disgusting.' In an attempt to build bridges, she pointed out that they wouldn't want their classmates at the new school to make fun of them.

Robin's eyes met hers and a slight smile curved his lips.

'Well, ain't that the truth.' He gave both son and daughter a quick hug. 'I had a talk with the headmistress. She looks forward to you joining the school, if only for a few days a week. You'll meet her tomorrow. So I want you to make me proud of you. Got that?'

He looked to each of them in turn. Jenny appreciated him backing her up, but the two children exchanged looks that hinted at conspiration, as though they were keeping a secret that only they knew.

'We love you, Dad,' said Susan, looking up adoringly into her father's face, a gloating look thrown in Jenny's direction when he patted her shoulder and kissed the top of her head.

Jenny folded her arms and kept a straight face, though it hurt her jaw to do it. Unseen by her father, the girl's piercing blue eyes were throwing daggers in her direction. It was clear to her that Robin's daughter had sworn instant enmity towards her, the boy too, though to a lesser extent.

'Right, you two. You don't have to go to school until tomorrow so you can go out to play for now. How would that be?' He leaned slightly away from them as he smiled down into their faces. Susan's face was all smiles, as though butter wouldn't melt in her mouth. Simon's expression was amiable enough, though Jenny had no doubt that wherever his sister led him he would meekly follow.

Once Robin had come back from seeing them to the door, the kettle was already boiling.

He was standing at the end of the table cap in hand as he ran his fingers through his hair.

Jenny asked him what was wrong.

The look he threw her was troubled. 'Susan asked me if we were sleeping together.'

Jenny's eyebrows arched. 'She's only eleven, isn't she?'

Looking as though his body had turned into a sack of rags, he sagged into a chair. Work-hardened hands rested on the table, fingers gripping so hard that his knuckles turned white.

'Either they're growing up faster than I thought, or...' He looked down at his hands, his frown intensifying as he did so. At one point, he clutched at the teapot, as though he might strangle it into smithereens. Only it wasn't the teapot he wanted to throttle.

Jenny placed the cup and saucer in front of him. 'Here. Get that down you.'

She sat at the table to one side of him and sipped her tea, watching him over the rim of her teacup. She knew he was thinking that his children were seeing things they shouldn't see. Doreen was blatant in her behaviour.

'So how did the meeting at the school go?'

He nodded. 'Fine. That Miss Burton is a very good woman. Must be getting on a bit though.'

'She's very dedicated.'

'And very nice. I'm surprised she's not married.'

Jenny shook her head sadly. 'Teaching is a vocation. There's a choice, marry or teach. The authorities don't allow both.'

'That's stupid.'

'Of course it is. If Miss Burton had married, a good teacher would have been lost.'

'Was there ever a chance that she would?'

Jenny nodded. 'Oh yes. Her fiancé was killed during the war – in the fields of Flanders, I believe. The teaching profession gained from a very heartfelt loss.'

Their tea finished, they sat there in silence until interrupted by the sound of the bell above the shop door.

'For me I think,' said Jenny, getting to her feet.

Before she had chance to go, Robin grabbed her hand. His eyes looked up at her pleadingly. 'I'm sorry to burden you with the kids.'

'You're not burdening me, plus they have every right to be here. You're their father.'

He nodded. 'I know that, but they're no angels. They take after their mother in that respect.'

'Robin,' she whispered. 'They're just children.'

She smiled, let go his hand and headed for the shop door.

Her smile melted as she headed out into the shop. When she saw who was standing there, she stopped dead.

'Roy!'

He was as rugged as ever, perhaps more so given his army training. Thanks to a tropical sun, his skin was the colour of polished teak, his eyes the blue water of a deep well.

'You weren't 'ome. A neighbour told me you were working.'

Her stomach churned as she remembered how he'd stopped her from getting a job in the past even though they'd needed the money.

'Only part-time. Two or three half-days a week. That's all.'

She tried not to tremble and told herself she had nothing to feel guilty about.

In the past, he would have dragged her out of the shop by her hair. Today he just looked her up and down. 'You're looking well.'

'Thank you. So are you.'

'Roy.' The sound of Robin's voice came from the back of the shop. 'Home from the wars, eh,' he said, extending his hand to be shaken.

To Jenny's surprise and relief, Roy shook the proffered hand. There was no sign of the old aggression, the need to be dominant and surly towards those he felt in competition with.

'I've come to check on things, to see Jenny and the girls before I ship out again.'

Robin jerked his chin in understanding. 'Off again? Where to this time?'

'The Far East. Singapore in fact.'

'Ah! The fortress of the Far East. That's what they call it, don't they?'

'So I understand.' Roy looked from Robin to Jenny before saying, 'I'm going to be away a long time. It could be two years or more before I see them again. I've got a few days off before I report for duty.'

'Such is the way of the soldier,' said Robin, somewhat conciliatory.

Roy turned to Jenny. 'When will you be coming home?'

Jenny looked from him to Robin. 'I usually leave here by two o'clock...'

'Go now,' said Robin. 'It's getting on for midday.'

Roy appearing had come as something of a shock. Staying in the shop was preferable to spending the afternoon with him. But for the sake of appearances...

'Right. I'll get my coat.'

They said little as they made their way across the broad expanse of grass in the centre of Filwood Broadway. A rank of shops ran along each side. At one end was the Broadway Picture House. A garish poster advertised that week's film. Jenny couldn't read the title. No doubt Thelma would tell her what was on this week. She usually knew because an old friend worked there. Thelma had a lot of friends, both old and new. Jenny was glad to be one of the latter.

'How are the girls?' Roy asked.

'They're fine. Both doing well at school.'

As she said it, she thought of Robin's two going to the same school – although on a part-time basis. A few days with one parent and one school, a few with the other and a different school.

'You ain't seeing nobody then?'

The question caught her off guard. 'No,' she replied quite honestly. 'I have the odd night out now and again but mostly with Thelma and my other friends.'

She counted Robin as being one of those friends but had no intention of saying so. She enjoyed her evenings with him, but only on the proviso that he didn't take advantage of the situation. Not that she felt that it wouldn't happen. In fact, she was sure it would. But not yet. Not until she was ready. In the meantime, she was still married to Roy.

'And you,' she asked hesitantly. 'Are you still enjoying the army?'

'Yes.'

She fancied he straightened as he replied, shoulders back, head held high as though he was marching in formation on the parade ground.

Two chevrons on his shoulder caught her eye.

'You've been promoted.'

'Corporal,' he said proudly, then went on to say, 'I'm not intending it stop there. In no time at all, I'll be a sergeant. That's what I'm aiming for. It's all about proving yerself, not being afraid to get in there and do your bit.'

Jenny heard the determination in his voice and didn't doubt he would do his 'bit', as he called it. She wondered what he'd done so far.

'It wasn't clear, but it looked as though you'd been in Palestine. Is that right?'

'Yes. Heat, sand and Jews and Arabs fighting each other. Cracked a few heads, I can tell you.'

The thin moustache he'd nourished in his Mosley days was still there, stretching as he smiled triumphantly. Knowing him as she did, his descriptions made Jenny feel queasy.

'I thought you might have been posted closer to home, what with the rumours of war with Germany.'

'That won't happen,' he stated abruptly. 'Adolf Hitler is all bluster.'

Jenny wasn't so sure but kept her opinion to herself.

Once inside the house, she put on the kettle, asked if he wanted something to eat and whether he'd like the hot water for a cup of tea or for washing.

'I'll use the cold water in the bathroom. I'm used to cold water. Not that it stayed that cold for long, not out in the desert and suchlike. The sun heats it up in no time. Do you know we could fry an egg just by putting a pan out in the sun on a flat stone?'

She shook her head. 'That's amazing.'

'A different world,' he said, his words accompanied by a far-away look in his eyes. He wanted to be back there. She could see that. The world he'd chosen suited him very well.

He'd brought a razor, shaving soap and other things with him. Once he'd shaved and washed, he opened his kitbag a little further.

'I've brought a few presents for you and the girls – seeing as I won't be here for a long time.'

She voiced her astonishment. He'd never bought a present for any of them before. She was further astonished when he handed her a prettily wrapped parcel.

'This is for you.'

Jenny couldn't help but show her astonishment. Roy had never bought her anything in her life – except for her wedding ring.

Wrapped carefully in tissue paper was the finest piece of material she'd ever seen. The colour reminded her of an aqua sea, the area where gentle waves lapped at the land. Fine silver threads ran through it, and holding it up to the light, it was so sheer she could see her fingers through it.

'It's beautiful,' she whispered. She was grateful but more thankful that he hadn't objected to her working. He'd said nothing to Robin either. She surmised he preferred the world he'd chosen for himself.

She was very aware that he was watching her intently, eyes narrowed and a slight smear of sweat on his upper lip along with that narrow, black moustache.

'Why don't you put it on?'

At first, she was surprised, but then said, all right, and wound it around her head turban fashion.

'Take your clothes off.'

She started. The old Roy had suddenly returned.

She shook her head as she removed the turban.

'No.'

'I would have liked to see you in it. Girls in the bars used to wear little except a piece of that around their privates.' He shrugged. 'The sight of them dancing in just a veil didn't do much for me, but I thought seeing you wearing just that might be different.'

Face flushed, she shook her head and tossed the lovely item aside.

'I think it's too late for that, Roy, for me naked in front of you. You've chosen what and who you really want. I'll keep your secret, but please show me some respect.'

It had come as something of a shock when he'd told her he preferred the company of men and would therefore be joining the army. Even though they'd had two children together, she could see that this other side of Roy had been there a long time ago. Truth was they were happier apart; in fact that was the way she preferred it.

At first, the old dark look was there, like a thundercloud behind his eyes. Then it was gone, shrugged away as though it didn't really matter much anyway.

He sat down in one of the armchairs. 'I fancy a sandwich.'

Relieved at his reaction, Jenny offered him what she had. 'Cheese and pickle?'

'That'll do.'

After that and a cup of tea, he went upstairs to lie down. She wondered whether he would look for any sign that she'd had a man to stay. She hadn't, but that didn't mean to say he wouldn't look. They were still married. She was still his, though for how much longer she couldn't be sure.

Household chores kept her occupied whilst he slept. There was shepherd's pie for the evening meal and by adding a few vegetables she could stretch it to include him. A roly-poly pudding with jam for afters.

She went and dug up a few potatoes from the garden. Digging her spade into the hard earth gave her the opportunity to think. Roy hadn't warned her he was coming home. So far he'd not criticised her for getting a job – for Robin of all people. No matter how uncharacteristically amenable he seemed, she couldn't help the old fear clutching at her stomach. What might come next?

'Your man. He is a soldier?'

The voice came from next door, number one. Mrs Arkle who lived in Mrs Russell's old place was stealing veg from the garden.

'Yes. He's in the army.'

Mrs Arkle sometimes pretended that she didn't understand or speak much English at all. Today her voice was clear enough. Short in stature, only her head and shoulders showed above the hedge.

'Ah!' Maria Arkle nodded in understanding. 'My brothers were soldiers. All dead now.'

'I'm sorry.'

Maria shrugged. 'They chose the wrong side and wrong place. Your man don't come 'ome very often.'

'No. He was stationed abroad.'

'Ah! Now he stay 'ome?'

'No. He's been posted to the Far East. To Singapore.'

'Ah! Long way.'

Jenny felt Maria's dark eyes on her, but rather than meet the enquiring gaze, she bent to her task, digging up a few more potatoes – a few carrots too.

'If you not going to use all those, I have them. I pay.'

Jenny straightened and looked at the crop she'd dug up. 'Why not,' she murmured to herself.

Once she had the potatoes plus what else she'd lifted from number one, the plundering Mrs Arkle disappeared.

A wintry white mist stole what light was left of the afternoon. After scraping the dirt from the spade and her boots, Jenny went back inside, put the kettle on and slid her chilled feet into a pair of warm slippers.

By the time the kettle was boiled, Roy had appeared and she'd begun making pastry.

'Jam tarts for when the girls get in – by way of a celebration, your homecoming,' she explained, though he hadn't asked her what she was making. 'The girls will be pleased.'

Or at least Gloria would. Tilly had never been close to her father.

With a cup of tea in hand, Roy left her in the kitchen. There was a strange silence about him. She was curious but knew better than to challenge him. If he remained silent, she could cope.

Though I should make some kind of effort, she told herself. *After all I'm not likely to see him for a very long time.*

Taking her tea with her, she went into the living room. He was standing at the window, his back facing her.

Jenny sat in a chair. Staring at his broad back reminded her of times past. She'd fallen for his air of confidence, his masculine features. Only later, once they were married, did she get to know the man inside the virile frame.

She asked a question she hadn't planned to ask. 'Do you miss Blue Bowl Alley at all – and the Pithay?'

She thought she saw him stiffen. 'It was 'ome to me. I was born there. This ain't,' he said, nodding at the front garden and beyond it the oval of green grass and trees.

She knew his real reasons for taking this house – not for her but to ingratiate himself with his Blackshirt superior.

'How long will you be in Singapore?'

'Forever I hope.' He turned round and looked at her. His eyes were bright, full of excitement. 'Adventure. That's what the army gives me. And pals. All blokes together. You might as well know I got no intention of coming back. That's what I want to tell the girls.'

He wasn't coming back. A more obvious question arose.

'Two years separation and we can divorce.' Now it was her eyes that flashed. 'If you're not coming back, there's no need to for pretence.'

No need to speak the truth, she thought. His pleasure in the company of other men was neither here nor there – not if he was never coming back.'

'I'll think about it,' he said.

There was no time for protest. The girls had come home from school.

Gloria threw herself into his arms. Tilly held back but thanked him for the present he'd brought her – a doll made of soft black velvet that jingled with bells. He didn't seem to realise that she'd grown and was no longer interested in dolls. Tilly loved books.

He gave Gloria a stuffed grey camel with a yellow saddle and harness.

'Are you staying home with us now,' Gloria asked with undisguised enthusiasm.

He shook his head. Over the top of his daughter's flaxen hair, his eyes focused on Jenny. 'I'm going away and I won't be back. The king needs me to guard a place in the Far East called Singapore.'

'No,' Gloria cried and burst into tears. 'You can't go. You've only just come back.'

Whilst Roy hugged Gloria with both arms, Tilly held back. Just as Jenny thought there was no change, Roy held out his arm and beckoned Tilly into it.

'Come on, chick. Let me give you one last hug. And remember, your dad's opted to serve the king. It's what I want to do. That's what I came back to explain and to tell you to be yourselves and do whatever you want to do. Including reading all them books you read.' The last remark was accompanied by a tighter hug for Tilly. It was the first time Jenny had seen Roy give her extra attention.

The girls were allowed to stay up until their eyelids closed and their parents took them to bed.

Jenny fully expected Roy to share her bed and it filled her with trepidation. She'd got used to sleeping alone. However, there was still the question about divorce.

Back in the living room, she brought the subject up again.

'I want to know your intentions, Roy. As you've said, live the life you want. That's what you're doing, but what about me? I'm trapped.'

He pursed his lips as he thought about it, his brows furrowed almost hiding his eyes. 'Wait until the girls are grown.'

Jenny bit down her fury. She wasn't accepting this. 'I want a divorce. If you don't then I'll—'

'So you can marry Robin bloody Hubert!'

The outburst was loud and unexpected.

She didn't see it coming when he gripped her around the throat and shook her head like a dog would a rat.

An odd calmness came to him, almost as though he'd been unsure of where he was and had suddenly returned to reality.

He let her go and turned to his kitbag, piling the things in that he'd taken out. 'We'll see about it when the girls are grown up. I'm off. There's a train back to camp at eleven. I'm getting on it.'

He said no more, not looking at her before exiting the room, the house and Coronation Close, she suspected forever.

It was the last time she'd ever see him or even hear from him. Jenny didn't quite know why, but a dark shadow remained where he had once been. As time went on, it would hopefully diminish and finally disappear.

30

The months were flying by and things were changing, most inconvenient rather than earthshattering.

'If you could take on doing the Saturday shift, I'm willing to give you the whole of Wednesday off – though every two weeks, mind you. I couldn't see my way to doing it every week.'

Thelma had always thought herself lucky to have both Wednesday half-day closing and Saturday afternoon off. The reason for this was that Mr Bertram was very family-orientated. A widow needed a job but she also needed that bit of extra time at home. The single girls usually worked Saturday afternoons from eight in the morning until nine at night. Saturday was shopping day for those who did have the time off and the single girls were given extra incentives like a discount off any item of clothing they fancied.

The change had come because not one but three of the single shop assistants had got married. Although not admitted as such, speculation was rife that at least two of them was in the family way. The third had been ordered by her bridegroom to quit the job the week before they married. Hence Thelma and everyone else was commandeered to fill the gap.

It amazed Thelma that regular customers used to her not being there after midday on a Saturday still sought her out.

'My husband loved that cocktail dress you sold me. He suggested it made me look ten years younger.'

The woman concerned was well into her fifties but still had a twinkle in her eye.

Thelma whispered into her ear that the expensive corset she'd bought had also been a very wise investment.

'Keep young and beautiful.' The words were stolen from a popular song. It was obvious from the sudden flush on the customer's face that she was familiar with the rest of the chorus.

'Keep young and beautiful if you want to be loved.'

Was it too much to suppose that this ageing coquette had reaped the delights of keeping herself trim and lovely? Thelma was in no doubt of it.

Mr Bertram thanked her for putting in the effort.

'I'm sure we'll get fresh staff before very long, though I must say none of these young girls are keen to work Saturday afternoons. I can't help thinking it won't be too long before they're demanding a five-day week. And where will the retail trade be if that happens?'

Thelma replied that she couldn't possibly say.

Miss Apsley stopped her on the way out.

'Your stepping into the breach is very much appreciated, Thelma. Hopefully it won't be for long.'

'Wednesday should make up for it,' Thelma replied. 'A full day! Wonders will never cease. I'll tell you here and now that I'll make the most of it.'

'You make sure you do.'

Display lights in the store windows dipped as she made her way out, calling goodnight to the others.

Frost glittered when hit by moonbeams. A sickle moon peered from behind a bank of ragged clouds.

Thelma pulled her coat collar up around her neck and headed for the bus stop, her footsteps crunching as she picked her way over the icy pavements.

Shielded from passers-by and the darkening shop fronts by the broad brim of her hat made her unaware of the passing crowds. People were walking in all directions, steamy breath dampening the collar she clutched around her face.

Thelma groaned on seeing that the queue at the bus stop was longer than usual. She'd be hard pushed to get aboard, let alone find a seat.

Behind her were the steps down from the new road onto the old. If she remembered rightly, it cut back up some way along to the previous bus stop. If luck was on her side, she could get on the bus there before it came to this bus stop.

With that in mind, she turned and headed for the steps. They were dark and slippery but needs must. She wanted to get home for her girls. Although her shoes were pinching, she marched on, forcing herself to think of other things besides her aching feet. Bert figured, of course. She'd promised to model for him once he'd finished the work he was presently doing. Some might think it a bit saucy, but she didn't feel that way at all. Bert's hobby intrigued her and there was no doubt in her mind that he was very good at what he did. She was looking forward to it.

Perhaps it was the effect of the encroaching darkness that made her think of Beryl. Stricken by a cruel illness was bad enough but being married to *that man* was doubly so. On one hand, Thelma still wanted to expose him as what he was. On the other, she was unwilling to add another heavy load to the one Beryl already had. The poor woman didn't deserve it.

'I will get her the wool,' she said under her breath.

Dense shadows fell across the road and up the walls in the darkest part of what was little more than an alley. Some distance ahead, an old-fashioned gas lantern provided the only light. Echoes of footsteps sounded from the walls, a double echo, one sound of footfall lighter – her own – the other heavier and sounding from some way behind her.

Gripped by fear, she quickened her step. The darkness ahead was intimidating, yet she steeled herself to go through it.

The clattering of footsteps intensified to an army of footsteps. For a moment, she envisaged a host of devils were on her trail. Human or otherwise.

'Get a grip,' she muttered to herself and dared to stop, dared to look round.

'Oi. What are you up to?'

Like the footsteps, the voice echoed around the old city walls and past the rear entrance of Averys', wine merchants who had been here for centuries.

Assuming the loud shout was for her, Thelma ran. It didn't matter that she was running into darkness. All that mattered was that she had to get away.

A loud scuffling sounded, but still she ran. Even when she heard running footsteps following her, she kept running.

'Stop. Stop. I need to speak to you. There,' he said, grabbing hold of her arm. 'I need to speak to you.'

'Let me go.'

'Thelma isn't it? Jenny's friend.'

The voice was only vaguely familiar. As he spun round and caught the light from the lantern on his face, she knew who he was.

Alternate shades of dark and light picked out the contours of his face.

'Charlie,' he said. 'Charlie Talbot. Remember me?'

She patted her heaving chest, her heart still thudding with fear. 'What do you want? Why are you following me?'

'I'm not,' he said, letting go of her arm and raising his hands palms outwards. 'Not exactly anyway. You're being followed, but not by me. Every time you stopped, he dived into a doorway. Nobody up to any good would do that. He made me suspicious so I followed him. I thought I should warn you.'

'Who was he? Did you know him?'

Charlie shook his head. A shock of dark blond hair fell onto his forehead as he pushed back his hat. 'Never seen the bloke before. I might recognise him again, though it was a bit dark. Oh, and he smelled of tobacco dust, as though he worked with it. A lot of blokes who do, come out with it in the turn-ups of their trousers. Part of the job. Some of them make roll-ups from that alone.'

It was hard to breathe, not just from the running but because of his description. It could only be one person.

Charlie frowned. 'You all right?'

Thelma nodded.

'Where are you going?'

'To the bus stop.'

'I'll walk you there. Come on. Give me your arm.'

Before he'd described Sam Hudson, she would have refused his arm. Now, knowing who'd been following her, she hung onto it for grim death.

'You're trembling.'

'Yes,' she said. 'I am.'

Charlie waited with her until the bus came. Just as she'd guessed, it was only half full. She'd get a seat inside downstairs;

right at the front, she decided, so Sam Hudson wouldn't see her if he did get on.

Charlie asked her how Jenny was.

'Fine. Her husband came a few days ago. He didn't stop.'

She sensed he wanted to ask more, but her brusque response had put him off.

Charlie saw her onto the bus and stayed watching until it had pulled away. His feelings about Jenny were complex. She wouldn't know that, of course. He'd purposely not been in touch and wasn't sure whether he should be. It was something he needed to think about.

* * *

Wednesday. Thanks to her stepping into the breach when three salesgirls were off, she'd been given the entire day off and, with Beryl Hudson in mind, Thelma set her sights on a trip to the wool shop that morning. It had to be morning. Like everyone else, Rigby's subscribed to Wednesday afternoon closing.

Jenny eyed her suspiciously when she made the suggestion. 'You sew. You don't knit.'

Thelma grimaced. 'You're right. I drop more stitches than I keep on the needles.'

Jenny perched her head sideways, an inquisitive pose like a sparrow thinking it was missing a bug. 'So?'

'I'm getting some wool for a friend. She's housebound. She can't get out much.'

Cath's sudden arrival through the back door meant there would be three of them. 'I do like a bit of knitting. I knitted bootees, hats, matinee jackets and everything when my kids were babies.'

Cath also asked what Thelma was doing buying wool when

her knitting was abysmal and got the same answer. She was totally accepting of it, which suited Thelma. She wasn't ready to go into details about Beryl Hudson. The time would come, the story preferably kept between her and Jenny. Jenny would respect her wish to keep things private. The whole street would know if Cath got to hear of it.

Jenny too wanted a chat with Thelma, not that Roy's brief visit was a secret. Curtains had twitched at several houses in Coronation Close. Cath had already asked and been told that it was prior to him being posted to the Far East. She wanted to talk with Thelma how to go about getting a divorce.

'I'll go and fetch me knitting bag,' said Cath.

With just the two of them left, Jenny said, 'I didn't know you had an invalid friend. Would I know her?'

Thelma shook her head, looked a bit undecisive until finally admitting it was a new acquaintance. 'I'll tell you when we've got a bit more time.'

She'd been turning over what she would say, not only about Sam and Beryl but also about bumping into Charlie. To her mind, Charlie spelled trouble for her friend. Not that Jenny would take any notice if she gave her opinion. When a woman cared for a bloke that was it. Nothing anyone else could say would make one 'apporth of difference. Best to not say anything and protect her from herself.

Jenny sighed. 'I've something to tell you. Roy won't be coming back. Not ever.'

Thelma raised her eyebrows. 'Well, that's not a terrible thing – is it? You know, seeing as it's been between you.'

'No. It's not. I asked him for a divorce. I feel cheap doing it, but—'

'You are far from cheap, Jennifer Crawford! And why should you put your life on hold, seeing as he's not coming back?' She cocked her head in the same inquisitive manner Jenny had adopted. 'What did he say?'

'That we should wait for two years or so until the girls were older.'

'That's not fair.'

Jenny shrugged. 'We have to agree on a legal separation. When that will happen, I don't know, what with him being overseas.'

Their conversation was necessarily short. Cath came back within twenty minutes, her slippers exchanged for a pair of lace-up stout shoes and a bigger scarf covering her metal-covered head.

'Looks like rain,' said Jenny as she put on her coat. She eyed the thick bank of cloud that looked to be only a few feet above the rooftops and reached for her umbrella.

'Let's get going before it buckets down.'

* * *

Rigby's wool shop had an old-fashioned exterior. Sinuous wood nymphs were carved into the dark green window frames. Tulips, their stems as sinuous as the wood nymphs, bordered the glass of the door.

Inside was just as ancient. A single light bulb hung from the centre of the ceiling. The counters fronted a range of shelving stretching from floor to ceiling. Stuffed into each shelf were balls and skeins of four-ply, three-ply, double knit and treble; white, lemon, pink, blue, light blue, dark blue, light green and dark green; enough variety to make anything from baby clothes to men's chunky jumpers.

Norah Rigby, a pleasant-looking woman, wore wire-rimmed spectacles, hanging on her chest from twisted strands of wool that served as a necklace. Only when somebody requested the details of a pattern explained or she needed to use the till did she resort to placing them on her nose.

Two middle-aged customers, one wearing a hairnet, the other a battered hat, were already perched on the two stools. Work-worn fingers squeezed a skein of rust-coloured wool placed in front of her, then did the same to another.

'This 'as got a bit more give,' the woman wearing the hairnet pronounced, pointing to the skein on the right-hand side. 'I think that's the one, don't you, Mary?'

'Up to you, Mavis,' said the other. 'Will your Wilfrid like the colour though?'

The other woman laughed. 'Wilf will wear what I says 'e's goin' to wear. Anyway, 'e don't notice colour. Colour blind 'e is.'

Thelma tried to remember what wool Beryl had asked for. When it came to her turn, she opted for four-ply in crimson.

'That's the only one we've got left,' said Norah. 'If you run out, there won't be any more.'

'If that happens it'll have to be striped,' returned Thelma. 'It'll do for now.'

She took the brown paper bag containing the skein of wool and dropped it into her shopping bag.

Cath perused balls of dark green wool she intended knitting into a jumper for one of her boys.

'I'd like twenty balls of that colour. I'll pay for three to take with me now – if you can keep the rest back for me until I need them.'

It was Norah's practice to keep back enough for the whole job, the wool paid for when required.

Jenny rummaged through the box of remnants but couldn't find anything to take her fancy.

It had been Jenny's intention to go straight home with her

friends, but across the green Robin was waving to her as they left Rigby's wool shop.

'Lover boy,' said Cath in a manner that Jenny regarded as immature.

'He's an old friend,' she countered. 'And I work for him. You go on without me. I'll catch up.'

She walked briskly across the grass and smiled at him. But when she got there, he didn't give her the welcome she'd been expecting.

'Is something wrong?'

'Something's gone missing.' He stood aside, signalling that she should come inside. 'A woman came in to retrieve a valuable item. I don't know what she's on about but thought you could tell me.'

'What woman was that?'

'A Violet Osbourne. She came in on Monday with a silver rattle. Do you remember her?'

Jenny nodded. She'd worked on Monday until three o'clock. Nothing out of the ordinary had happened. Mrs Peacock had brought in her customary pledge – a pair of willow pattern plates that she said had belonged to her grandmother. A few other regulars had come in bringing the same items they'd pledged the week before. The only other customer had been one she'd never seen before; this Mrs Osbourne.

Jenny cast her mind back. The main thing she'd noticed about the woman was that she'd smelled of mothballs, but that wasn't what Robin wanted to know.

'I remember. She wanted five pounds against a silver baby's rattle. She said it had once belonged to her great-grandmother. If that was indeed true, it dated back to the early nineteenth century.'

'Worth five pounds.'

'At least. Far more valuable than most pledges that come in and out from one week to the next.'

'And you put it in the cupboard?'

The locked cupboard acted as a safe for valuable things and doubly protected behind the chicken-wire screening.

Jenny nodded and felt the colour draining from her face because she knew what he was about to say.

'It's not in there.'

Jenny frowned. 'But it must be. We're the only ones with a key.'

She tried not to stare at the muscles that erupted against his shirtsleeves when he folded his arms.

'Someone must have borrowed your keys.'

'There was no one else 'ere, except for the kids.'

'The kids. You've asked them?'

He looked awkward, defensive even. She understood his reluctance to challenge his children, but not to do so only served to enhance her anger – and what he might be suggesting.

'I didn't take it.' She shook her head resolutely.

'I didn't say that you did, but...' His voice trailed away. It was then that she realised what he was insinuating.

'Roy barely stepped across the threshold. So it wasn't him either.'

'I didn't say...' He didn't look entirely convinced.

She batted away the hand that sought to reassure her. 'Don't touch me!'

She backed away. Roy had done many things in his time, but she couldn't believe that he'd even had the time to steal anything.

'Can you give me a good reason for thinking that he stole it? Bearing in mind that we were both here when he came in.'

'The back window was smashed.'

'And the cupboard forced open? I can't say I'm surprised. You could do with buying a proper safe.'

A sheepish look came to his face.

Jenny frowned. 'What?'

'I forgot to lock it. The kids were playing up. I 'ad a job getting them settled.' He shook his head. 'They're tiring me out. I went to bed. I forgot to lock it.'

He rubbed at his forehead. There were dark circles beneath his eyes. He did indeed look tired out.

Jenny sighed. 'Oh, Robin.'

Up until now she'd felt sorry for him, what with Doreen being a cow and the kids playing up. But not locking the cupboard was downright careless. And what was she going to say to the woman when she came in to settle what was owed and have her possession returned to her?

'Was that the only item taken?'

'The takings were upstairs with me. Can you remember what else was in there?'

Jenny thought about it, then shook her head. 'The other stuff wasn't worth putting in there. It was ordinary.'

'I'm sorry I accused Roy, but I know he had a bit of a reputation down at the docks.'

Jenny had to admit that he was right. Roy had sometimes brought home stuff that had 'fallen from a lorry'. But to actually break in?

She shook her head. 'No. He wouldn't break in.'

Robin dragged his feet as he made his way into the pawn-broking side of the business, through the chairs, tables and potted plant stands filling the front of the shop.

Jenny followed him. The cupboard where valuables were stored was still hanging ajar and two glass panes were missing. 'There's no glass on the floor.'

Robin peered over her shoulder. 'I didn't notice that.'

'You're really done in, aren't you?'

He threw back his head and groaned.

'When do the kids go back to Doreen?'

'End of the week.'

'Well, I would suggest that you sort them out before then or you're the one to explain the loss of the rattle to your customer. They're obviously the ones responsible, put up to it by Doreen.'

'Just wait till they get 'ome from school.'

Jenny smiled. If her girls had done something similar, Roy might have taken his belt off and given them a good beating. But Robin wasn't at all like that.

'I'll see you tomorrow then.'

Though distracted with angry thoughts, he accompanied her to the door.

'I feel such a bloody idiot.'

Jenny's attitude to him softened. 'You're a caring father. Give them a good talking-to and they'll own up.'

The smile she wore as she walked away didn't last long. The kids were hostile both to her and to their father – except when it suited them. But how was this suiting Doreen? She had a sneaking suspicion that Robin's offspring had been primed to make trouble.

31

It was on the Wednesday two weeks hence that, with the wool in a carrier bag, Thelma made her way to visit Beryl.

The weather in July and August was far better than it had been for the coronation. Thelma was as resolutely royal as ever and had been outraged on hearing of the attempt on the new king's life in Belfast. He'd survived, but it still sent shivers down her spine.

The semicircle of houses looked as though they were sleeping in the unaccustomed sunshine. Nobody was around.

Hand resting on the garden gate, Thelma stopped and took a deep breath. At the back of her mind was the fear that Sam Hudson might not be at work. The fear was unsubstantiated – after all, most men who were employed around the docks and in the tobacco bonds were at work.

'Don't be daft,' she muttered to herself. Taking a firm grip of the top rung of the metal gate, she pushed it open and headed for the front door. Taking her courage in both hands, Thelma jerked at the knocker, three short raps in a row.

Nobody came.

Rather than repeat the action, she took a few steps backwards. Halfway along the garden path, she surveyed the upper windows of what must be the front bedroom.

A small hand from up there gave a weak wave.

Thelma waved back then pointed at the front door.

Unable to shake her head, Beryl waved her hand in a telling gesture. No.

Thelma interpreted the gesture as a refusal to answer the door. Had her husband ordered her not to answer? She wouldn't put it past him. He'd been bound to see the cups and perhaps, bubbling with excitement, Beryl had told him she'd had a visitor. Thank goodness she hadn't given her real name.

In an effort to induce her to come down, Thelma took a skein of wool from the carrier bag and held it high enough for Beryl to see it.

'Wool,' she mouthed.

Again, Beryl waved her hand and with what was obviously heroic effort she made a locked gesture with her hand, her deformed fingers crunching into a telling clasp.

Thelma readily understood. 'You're telling me the front door's locked?'

Again, a wave signifying no. Not the front door. Her lips formed a single word. 'Bedroom.'

Though she could not hear the word, Thelma could read Beryl's emphatic lip movements. The bedroom door was locked. Beryl was locked in.

When Thelma looked up again at the window, Beryl's crooked fingers were desperately trying to open a window catch; first one, then the other. Neither gave. Crittall windows were metal and unless the catches were oiled regularly tended to stick.

The pale, small face disappeared, only to reappear at the smaller window of the front bedroom. Tremendous effort went into opening this window. Beryl's face was warped with pain. Determination won through. The smaller window burst open.

'You're locked in?'

'Yes.'

Her voice was tiny and trembling.

'I'll go for the police,' Thelma exclaimed angrily.

'No. No. Please don't. You'll only make him angry. Anyway, I've got these.' She held up a pair of knitting needles. 'So kind of you to get me some wool.'

Thelma considered how best to get the wool up to her. 'Can you open the window wider?'

'Yes.'

Both hands pushed at the window, and on its stiff hinges, it jerked open.

'Right. Stand back. I'm going to throw the bag up to you.'

Beryl stepped back but did not entirely disappear.

Setting her handbag down between her feet, Thelma took the carrier bag in her right hand and began to swing it. Finally, putting all the effort she could into the throw, she sent it flying upwards and into the opening.

There was silence and the same empty space before Beryl reappeared, her expression one of joy.

'Thank you. Thank you so much.'

'Can you close...?'

Before Thelma had finished the sentence, the window was eased shut.

Feeling satisfied but sad, Thelma waved one last time and turned for home. The girls would be home from school soon. Normality and the means of burying her simmering anger – at least for now.

* * *

It was late on a Friday afternoon when Sam Hudson stood yet again opposite Bertrams Ladies Modes. Pure coincidence had led him here on that first occasion, on his way home. If he hadn't gone to the pub with his mates, he wouldn't have seen and followed her. His aim had been to strike up conversation. Her sour look on the bus had cut no ice with him. He'd convinced himself that deep down she'd enjoyed the romp in the snow and, though she might not admit it outright, was hungry for a repeat performance.

The telephone box was occupied when he got there, the woman inside seeming to be fiddling around with the phone without making a call.

'Timewaster,' he growled. He followed it up with a sharp rap on the glass. 'Are you goin' to keep me waitin' all bloody night?'

The woman pushed open the door without warning, its edge hitting him in the chest.

'Tart,' he snapped, rubbing at his chest.

'Ran out of pennies,' she said artlessly.

'And need to earn some more,' he sneered.

She didn't refute that she'd been placing a business card just above the phone – hence the lingering.

'Give me a try,' she quipped in a lofty manner.

'Sod off.'

He didn't bother to watch her saunter off. He knew her sort of old. Took the money but didn't give satisfaction – at least not the sort that he enjoyed.

Inside the phone box was warmer than outside but only slightly welcome. The smell of old sweat, and worse, permeated the air.

The phone number of Bertrams was emblazoned beside the business name so he had no need to look it up in the telephone directory. All he had to do was to word his enquiry just right. He already had an idea of what to say, though would have to adjust his accent to suit.

The phone rang three times before somebody answered.

A plummy female voice stated, 'Bertrams Ladies Modes.'

'Ah. I wonder if you can help me.'

'If I can, sir.'

'I want to buy a birthday present for my wife, but I want it to be a surprise. She's very insistent that one of your salesgirls always sells her something that suits. The trouble is I can't remember her name. I think her name might be Eunice, though I'm not quite sure.'

'I'm sorry. We don't have a Eunice. Can you describe her perhaps?'

His storytelling skills came into play as he described the woman who'd smelled of gardenias, wore satin blouses and had a voluptuous and firm figure.

'Well...' The voice was hesitant. 'I think you've described Mrs Dawson.'

'That might be her. She lives on the Knowle West Estate near Melvin Square. Would that be her?' He knew this because of the bus she travelled on. That was its destination.

'Yes. I believe she does live there.' The woman who'd answered was unbelievably helpful.

'Ah, that is such a relief. I'm sure my wife will be pleased with whatever I buy her if Eunice...'

'Thelma. Thelma Dawson.'

'Precisely. If Thelma Dawson has anything to do with it. Can you give me her address?'

Suddenly the voice turned hesitant. 'I'm sorry. We're not allowed to give out private details of our staff. Can you tell me your name again?'

He slammed the phone into its cradle.

'Well,' he said, smiling to himself. 'I know who you are Thelma Dawson.'

* * *

Miss Apsley frowned as she put down the phone. She'd been happy enough to answer the man's questions at first, but eventually he'd overstepped the mark. A male caller for Mrs Dawson. Bertrams did not approve of men asking after its female employees unless in a professional capacity. She'd thought that the reason at first, but as the call had gone on... 'No, no, no.' She shook her head. Bertrams had a reputation to maintain. She decided to have a word so waylaid Thelma on her way out.

In the confines of the small cubicle that served as her office, she told Thelma in no uncertain terms that gentlemen callers were not welcome.

Thelma frowned. 'Bert never phones. I've told him not to.'

'Oh dear,' said Miss Apsley, the rigid set of her shoulders sagging as realisation hit her. 'I think I've made a terrible faux pas.'

Thelma eyed her with growing alarm. 'A man phoned, but not Bert?'

Miss Apsley nodded, licked her lips and related the content of the phone call.

Thelma's face drained of colour. 'You told him my name?'

'I thought... Oh my goodness. I'm so sorry, Mrs Dawson. I really am. I shouldn't have told him. At least I didn't give him your address.'

'I suppose that's something.'

'Have you any idea who might request it?'

Thelma didn't reply. She was thinking of the journey home, of the crowded bus, of the dark and the shadows thrown by the leaf-less trees in Coronation Close.

* * *

On the bus home, she sat nervously, eyeing the other passengers, averting her eyes from any man that smiled at her.

Sam Hudson wasn't on there. She tried telling herself that the call had been genuine. At least it helped calm her fears.

Once off the bus, she hurried along the main street and then into Coronation Close. At one point, she did think she heard foot-steps but didn't look round. All she wanted was to get inside her house where a fire glowed in the grate and her girls had a stew on the stove.

'There's a letter,' said Mary.

With glowing eyes, the two girls took her hat and coat and waited for her to open it.

'It's from our George,' said Alice.

Thelma patted her chest as though that could calm the excitement she was feeling.

With a cup of tea set beside her, she tore open the flimsy envelope and began to read.

Dear Mum,

Me and Gina will be with you in the New Year. We'll stay with you at first and decide what we're going to do about a place to live. We've started a family. Didn't mean to just yet, but it just happened.

Love George

Suddenly everything in the world was wonderful. It no longer mattered that her dearly beloved son had met a girl she'd never met and the fact that she was foreign. What did any of that matter compared with the fact that she might be having a grandchild. She was over the moon.

The whole family were still bubbling when Bert came knocking. Thelma handed him the letter.

'Cuthbert Throgmorton, you're courting a soon-to-be grandmother.'

He looked surprised when he took off his hat. 'Am I? Well, there's a thing.'

So taken with the wonderful news, Thelma forgot to ask him if he was the man who had phoned. It no longer seemed important. She was going to be a grandmother and would tell everyone in the close once she got the chance.

* * *

Sam Hudson had been careful. He'd stolen a bicycle and followed the bus as it chugged through Queen Square, through Bedminster and up the hill into Knowle West. The bus was so slow that at times he could easily have overtaken it.

Once she was off the bus, he slowed right down, then ditched the bike, leaving it leaning against a round red post box just before the bus stop on the corner of Melvin Square.

From there, he followed her on foot, keeping to the shadows and at times walking on tiptoe.

At one point, she'd stepped up her speed but thankfully never looked round.

He was glad to see the trees on the centre island of green around which all the houses were built. Coronation Close was very much like the place where he lived, though larger and having more houses.

He saw her go into one. He couldn't see the number from

where he was hidden, but it didn't matter because it was on the end and adjacent to the main road.

When a set of car headlights came into the close, he melted into the trees where the darkness was intense and he was hidden unseen.

A man got out and went into the house – her house. Was it her husband? He had no idea. Not that it mattered. He was sure that he was the man she really wanted. Why else had she entered his house and had tea with his wife? He was convinced it was her red lipstick that had stained the teacup. Anyway, the woman on the phone had more or less confirmed his description of her. And then he'd followed her and here she was.

Anyway, he would make good his case, make friends with her, with her husband, her neighbours, her friends and her children. At present, she might not be entirely convinced that they were made for each other. But in time she would. He would see to it.

32

Bert took Thelma to the pub for a drink to celebrate George's news and invited Jenny to go with them. Cath promised to keep an eye on all four girls, who had voted to play snakes and ladders at Thelma's house until both she and Jenny got home.

Nothing that had happened or would happen could stop Thelma from bubbling with laughter, downing drink after drink until she decided she'd had enough.

Whilst Bert was in the gents, Thelma turned to Jenny. 'I want this baby to be born.'

Knowing what was going through her mind – the loss of the child at the beginning of the year – Jenny patted her hand and said reassuringly, 'They're young. They'll be fine.'

'How about you and Robin,' Thelma asked cheerfully.

'We're good friends. Whether it goes further is anyone's guess. Remember, I am still married. And so's Robin.' The corners of her lips turned downwards. 'His kids have been a nightmare. They staged a break-in and stole a piece of silver.'

Thelma looked at her astounded. 'His children did that?'

Jenny nodded. 'He found the stolen item in one of their bags.

At first, Robin thought Roy had broken in, but the glass lay outside the window not inside.'

'Little horrors!'

'He thinks Doreen put them up to it. She wants to cause trouble between me and Robin – and she has done. I'm not sure I can forgive him for blaming Roy. There was no reason for it except... Robin being biased against him.'

Bert was talking to someone up at the bar, giving Thelma time to decide about telling Jenny that she'd seen Charlie. She decided that she would, it might raise her spirits.

'I saw Charlie the other night.'

Jenny's drink had been halfway to her mouth. It remained there, untouched as her mouth hung open. 'Charlie? Where?'

'I was heading for the bus.' She decided not to mention that he'd thought she was being followed. 'He asked after you.'

Jenny shook her head, though could not hide her small smile of triumph. 'I think I made the right decision there. Perhaps Roy is right. It's best to wait until the girls are older.'

'You'll be too old for men then,' Thelma laughed.

'Perhaps. Then I'll buy a rocking chair and take up knitting.'

Thelma laughed along with her at the prospect of both of them knitting for grandchildren. In Thelma's case it was a certainty. In Jenny's place merely a possibility.

Jenny sipped at her drink before asking if Thelma had passed on the wool she'd bought to her friend.

Thelma nodded. 'Yes.' Divulging anything would ultimately lead to questions about Sam Hudson. Only George and the expected grandchild mattered. To that end, she said, 'I think I should take up knitting in earnest for my grandchild. Can't wait,' she squealed. 'I just can't wait. Here's to new life – and Coronation Close.'

'Coronation Close,' said Jenny. 'The best thing that ever happened to me.'

33

It was around eleven o'clock in the morning in early October when the new tenants began moving into Mrs Partridge's old house.

Like all the others in the close, Mrs Partridge's old place had just three bedrooms. It hardly seemed large enough for the family who were to move in. Jenny counted five children.

Their belongings formed a pyramid shape on the horse-drawn cart. On top of it sat a small boy, his face half hidden thanks to the overlarge woollen hat he was wearing.

Behind the horse-drawn vehicle, a man and woman bent their backs into pushing a handcart loaded with more of their belongings. So, seven people in the house. It wasn't that unusual but did make her wonder how they would all fit in. She surmised that some of the children would be top to tail, just as her girls had been back in the days when they'd lived in Blue Bowl Alley.

The neighbours watched, some tutting in disapproval at the sight of the newcomers and the noise they brought with them. Raucous voices and choice words rang out as the new arrivals tramped in and out of the house carrying bits of furniture and household items.

Cath came knocking on the pretext of borrowing a cup of sugar. From the front doorstep, they both scrutinised the new arrivals, Cath whispering under her breath that they looked like gypsies, Jenny shushing her and telling her not to be rude. In response, Cath snorted indignantly and went home.

Their clothes looked as though they'd seen better days, their hair was matted and wild. The man had a shiny head and wore a red muffler around his neck. The wife wore a battered hat perched on top of a mass of untidy curls, hair clips hanging from wispy strands around her face.

To be neighbourly, Jenny decided to pop round and offer a cup of tea.

'You two can come with me,' she said to the girls.

'Why?' asked Tilly, wrinkling her nose in disgust.

'You always question,' said Jenny as she put the kettle on.

'I don't think I want to,' said Gloria. Her nose wrinkled in the same disapproving manner as her sister. 'They're scruffy. They'll smell.'

Jenny rolled her eyes. It seemed both needed a good talking-to about being kind and the advantages of charity.

'They're just poor. Now come on. Let's take out a tray. I'm sure they'll appreciate it.'

Balancing a tray of cups and saucers, she headed out of the house feeling she would be doing her new neighbours a great service.

Reluctantly, the girls trailed behind her, Gloria carrying a sugar bowl and Tilly a plate of biscuits.

The woman saw them coming, stopped what she was doing and stared as though they were wielding a machine gun not a tray of tea and biscuits.

Jenny fixed a smile on her face. 'I thought you might like a cup of tea.'

Frowning, the man came to stand beside his wife, looking as though he was ready for a fight. The children gathered round, their faces wary until they spotted the plate of biscuits. Grubby hands dived fiercely onto the plate, grabbing what they could and sending Tilly backwards into the hedge.

'Mind yer manners,' shouted their father, arms whirling like a windmill and accompanied by a thwacking sound as his heavy hands landed clouts around heads and they fell back to avoid more blows.

To Jenny's surprise, he didn't turn to her to apologise but snatched the plate from Tilly, who looked as terrified as his own children.

'Bloody 'ell, Ada. They ain't left a crumb.'

Ada, the woman in the battered hat with straggly hair, looked down at the plate and shook her head. 'You ain't left us a bleedin' crumb. You little beggars,' she shouted, lashed out and landed a few whacks herself.

'There's plenty of tea,' said Jenny.

They glugged the tea in one gulp. The kids did the same, though only once they were sure of avoiding their father's heavy smacks.

Once the tea was gone, they went back to ferrying the last of their possessions from carts to house. Jenny's tea plate went with them but she did manage to retain her cups, saucers and three teaspoons.

'Let's go indoors.'

All three sighed with relief once they were back inside.

'Told you so,' said Gloria, wrinkling her nose in the same fashion as before. 'They smell.'

Tilly had nothing to say, absorbed as she was in making a

sugar sandwich whilst the basin was within sight.

On Thelma's return from work, Jenny mentioned what had happened. Together they observed the scene from Jenny's living-room window.

'I don't think the Arkle family like our new neighbours in Dorothy Partridge's old place.'

Thelma grunted her agreement. Beneath the muted glow of the street lights they watched as the scruffy Arkle children were facing off the new arrivals from number one.

'The Arkle kids have been out there most of the day and so have the new lot,' said Jenny.

'They should be in school,' declared Thelma.

'The school inspector is going to have his work cut out. Two families now instead of one. He's always coming round to see why the Arkle kids aren't in school. Not that he gets anywhere. Mr Arkle shouts at him to shove off and Mrs Arkle, if she's there by herself, shakes her head and tells him she doesn't speak English. Though she does.'

She went on to tell Thelma about Robin seeing Mrs Arkle and the kids selling bunches of flowers at Arnos Vale Cemetery.

'So that's where all the flowers have gone from Mrs Partridge's garden!' Thelma sighed.

'And the vegetables from the back garden. I didn't have the heart to say anything. Mrs Arkle cooking them up is better than seeing them rot.'

'I never thought I would say this, but come back Mother Partridge. All is forgiven.'

'Is it?'

'Everything changes. People move on. Or die.'

They fell silent. Dorothy Partridge had been standoffish and difficult, but for good reason and all thanks to a terrible war. As for her husband Harry, they both spoke of him, wondering where he was and hoping he was all right. Living as a woman for all those years in order to avoid prison must have been difficult. But at least they'd been respectable and kept a tidy garden. The new family that had taken over her house were of the same ilk as the Arkles. In time, they might get used to them, though might was a very big word.

Jenny said it out loud. 'We'll get to know them in time and they'll get to know us.'

'Right,' said Thelma. 'And we do have Bert to hand.'

Jenny smiled. 'When he's not sculpting and painting nude women.'

Thelma laughed. 'Just one woman. Nude or otherwise.' She looked at Jenny, her eyes shining. 'He's asked me, Jenny. He's asked me. For his next project.'

'Will you?' Jenny asked.

Thelma folded her arms and took a deep breath. 'It could lead to me being Mrs Bert Throgmorton? He don't mind that I'm going to be a grandmother.'

They stood for a while watching the horse and cart move away from the kerb, the empty handcart now tossed in the back, rumbling off into the darkness.

'I feel sorry for them,' said Jenny.

Thelma nodded. 'The family name is Warren according to Bert. They were living in a caravan in Leigh Woods but somebody set it on fire. He wasn't sure if they'd done it themselves. There but for the grace of God and all that.' She sighed. 'They could do with our help – a few bits and pieces.'

'Just as you did me.'

'There's a jumble sale down in St Stephen's church hall in town. We've got three new salesgirls at Bertrams to take on the Saturday afternoon shift so I've got this Saturday afternoon off. Fancy going?'

34

Autumn was golden and hung on into late October even at Filwood Broadway.

Robin's business was going very well and Jenny was enjoying working there, though after the incident with the silver baby's rattle she kept a close eye on his children.

They did seem more subdued after Robin had paid Doreen a visit and told her there would be no more maintenance if she put them up to stealing again.

'You should be ashamed of yourself, encouraging our kids to be thieves. Who knows where they could end up?'

Doreen had been her usual belligerent self, shouting and swearing, but on seeing he was adamant and terrified at the thought of losing part of her income, she backed down.

At least for now, thought Jenny. She'd support him all she could after all he was the main man in her life nowadays. It was rumoured that Charlie Talbot had left the area, off up north to stir things on behalf of the working man, though in all honesty the working class didn't seem that aware of it.

It was a long way off but Thelma was already planning a welcome home for her son and new daughter-in-law.

'I've been asking about council houses. George hasn't said he wants to settle down in Bristol, but it is his hometown isn't it? Stands to reason doesn't it?'

Jenny didn't contradict her but did ask if she was already knitting things for the forthcoming birth.

Thelma shook her head. 'No.'

'You've been going to the wool shop a lot.'

'For a friend,' said Thelma in a muted tone. She went on to tell Jenny how she'd been visiting Beryl Hudson, the incapacitated woman who had the misfortune to be married to Sam Hudson, the man she hated most in the world.

Jenny looked at Thelma with astonishment.

'You're still visiting her?'

'Yes. When I can. Thing is I can't be nasty to the poor woman. I've been there a couple of times now with bundles of wool. Sometimes he's locked her in the bedroom and sometimes I get to take tea with her. Mind you I'm quick to wash the cups up afterwards.' She shuddered. 'I certainly don't want that rotten sod finding me there or know that I visited. We'd both be for it.'

They both agreed they lived full lives and thoroughly enjoyed helping people who needed it – even the two new families who'd moved into the close.

Both Thelma and Jenny managed to go to a few jumble sales where they bought some things for themselves and some for the new lot at number five. At first, the Warren family had been wary and sometimes downright surly. In time, they'd swallowed their pride and even invited them into the house.

The interiors of their house had been as untidy and dirty as they'd expected, but they were poor, they told themselves. They couldn't help it.

Thelma and Jenny had declined having a cup of tea after seeing Mrs Warren wiping out a teacup with a dirty dishcloth. But at least the ice was broken.

What remained was a festering feud with the Arkle family. Nobody could quite understand why. Both families were as poor as church mice, but they'd taken an instant dislike to each other. Surely poverty should have been the levelling factor between them?

Thelma wisely pronounced that as long the feud didn't affect them, there was nothing they need do about it.

'Besides, I've got my own family to think about.'

'You mean George and his bride, plus a new arrival!'

'I can't wait.'

'It's a while yet.'

'I can't help it,' Thelma retorted. 'A new baby. Who would have thought it.'

Jenny didn't remind her best friend that there had been the prospect of another baby earlier in the year. The thought saddened and angered her. She knew the same was true for Thelma. The attack shouldn't have happened, but the baby was not to blame. A baby never was.

On their way to the bus stop and home, Thelma and Jenny walked arm and arm saying nothing but mutually cosy with warm thoughts.

A flock of mallards, male with green necks, quacked voraciously and took off as a barge on the river blew its horn.

Thelma's attention was diverted to the boat and the water. She was thinking about George and the year to come when he would be home and introduce her to his new wife.

'George and getting married,' she said suddenly. 'It wasn't anything to do with her being Italian, Jenny. I knew you thought that, but it isn't true.'

Her lips spread in a wide smile, Jenny tossed her head. 'I know. It's because you love him and worry about him.'

'Hmm. That's what Bert said.'

'Bert's a wise man.'

'And you're a wise woman, Jennifer Crawford.'

'Jennifer! It's been a long time since anyone called me that.' She laughed at the very thought of it. Roy had never called her Jennifer. Her mother had only called her by her full name when she'd done something wrong. It always sounded as though she was shouting it out in capital letters.

They fell into the easy comfort of two friends. Sometimes they talked a lot. Sometimes they didn't need to, their silences as meaningful as their words. There was understanding between them.

Thelma was first to break the silence. 'Seems a long time since you moved into the close.'

'It was quite a year when I first came here and got to know you. The old king died and the new one, who now calls himself Duke of Windsor, let you down.'

'All turned out for the best though didn't it.'

Jenny agreed with her. 'Oh yes. Everything turned out for the best. I lived a lonely life until I moved into Coronation Close. Except for having my kids, it was the best thing that ever happened to me. It's good to have friends.'

Thelma nodded and gave the arm she held tight to her side an affectionate squeeze. 'You can say that again. Plus we got a new king and whole family who look to be worth their salt.'

'I think you're right.'

They both had obstacles to face and overcome in the coming year, but living in Coronation Close was something to celebrate whatever fate might throw at them.

MORE FROM LIZZIE LANE

We hope you enjoyed reading *Shameful Secrets on Coronation Close*. If you did, please leave a review.

If you'd like to gift a copy, this book is also available as an ebook, hardback, large print, digital audio download and audiobook CD.

Sign up to Lizzie Lane's mailing list for news, competitions and updates on future books:

http://bit.ly/LizzieLaneNewsletter

Why not discover *The Tobacco Girls*, the first in the best-selling Tobacco Girls series from Lizzie Lane.

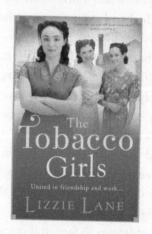

ABOUT THE AUTHOR

Lizzie Lane is the author of over 50 books, a number of which have been bestsellers. She was born and bred in Bristol where many of her family worked in the cigarette and cigar factories. This has inspired her new saga series for Boldwood *The Tobacco Girls*.

Follow Lizzie on social media:

f facebook.com/jean.goodhind
y twitter.com/baywriterallat1
⊙ instagram.com/baywriterallatsea
BB bookbub.com/authors/lizzie-lane

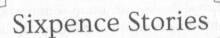

Sixpence Stories

Introducing Sixpence Stories!

Discover page-turning historical novels from your favourite authors, meet new friends and be transported back in time.

Join our book club Facebook group

https://bit.ly/SixpenceGroup

Sign up to our newsletter

https://bit.ly/SixpenceNews

Boldwood

Boldwood Books is an award-winning fiction publishing company seeking out the best stories from around the world.

Find out more at www.boldwoodbooks.com

Join our reader community for brilliant books, competitions and offers!

Follow us
@BoldwoodBooks
@BookandTonic

Sign up to our weekly deals newsletter

https://bit.ly/BoldwoodBNewsletter